Mimosas,
Mischief,
And Murder

THE ELLIE AVERY MYSTERIES
By Sara Rosett

MOVING IS MURDER

STAYING HOME IS A KILLER

GETTING AWAY IS DEADLY

MAGNOLIAS, MOONLIGHT, AND MURDER

MINT JULEPS, MAYHEM, AND MURDER

MIMOSAS, MISCHIEF, AND MURDER

Mimosas, Mischief, And Murder

Sara Rosett

KENSINGTON BOOKS
http://www.kensingtonbooks.com

KENSINGTON BOOKS are published by

Kensington Publishing Corp.
119 West 40th Street
New York, NY 10018

Library of Congress Control Number: 2010942791

ISBN-13: 978-0-7582-2685-3
ISBN-10: 0-7582-2685-3

First Hardcover Printing: April 2011

10   9   8   7   6   5   4   3   2   1

Printed in the United States of America

Mimosas, Mischief, And Murder

Chapter
One

"I shot you."

Normally, that's not a sentence I want to hear, but since it came from Nathan, our four-year-old, who was buckled into his car seat in the back row of the minivan, and since he had brought nothing more lethal than toy cars, books, and Legos for this road trip, I decided to ignore it.

"No, you didn't," Livvy replied with the certainty of an older sibling. "I had my shield up." She casually turned a page in her middle-grade reader. She was working her way through a series of mystery books and I hoped her stack would last her at least until lunch. Her second-grade class was in the middle of a fierce competition to see who could read the most books. Livvy was currently in second place.

"My laser gun shoots through shields," Nathan countered, waving his gun of plastic building blocks at Livvy as he added shooting sound effects.

Livvy put down her book. "My shield is laser-proof."

Nathan stretched his pudgy arm into the air. "I'm shooting over it."

"You can't hit me. I'm invisible."

I glanced at Mitch. His expression was impassive as he focused his attention on the double yellow stripe of the two-lane Georgia highway. I could tell he'd blocked out the escalating war of words behind us. He was shut away again with his thoughts. He'd been like that a lot lately and I was trying to give him some space and not pester him.

"My lasers are invisible, too, and they can find you," Nathan said, peppering his words with more firing noises.

"Not if I fly away."

I knew from experience this game of one-upmanship could go on for hours. I gave up on ignoring the kids. "Look, kids, there are the peach orchards," I said, tapping my window as we passed the squatty rows of barren trees. "They prune the trees so they'll stay low to the ground and it will be easier to pick the peaches," I said.

"My lasers can chase you," Nathan said.

"Not if I fly supersonic."

"They go super—, super—," Nathan stumbled over the big word, caught his breath, and said, "They go real fast. They can catch you."

I put down my knitting and picked up a small tote bag I'd stashed at my feet. I hated to break it out so early in the trip, but we'd played the License Plate Game, which had fizzled after a few minutes because of the paltry number of cars on the road this Tuesday morning, and we'd already spied trees, billboards, cars, fences, and signs in our short-lived game of I Spy.

"That's it for the imaginary shooting game. No more of that," I said as I twisted around and handed the bag to Livvy. "See what you can find in there."

Livvy strained, grabbed the bag, and plopped it down on the seat between them. "Oh, I want—"

"Share!" I commanded. "Or it goes right back here with me. Besides, there are two of those."

Livvy released her death grip on the Etch-A-Sketch and burrowed through the bag for the second one.

I turned back to my knitting, glad that in our rush out the door this morning for our drive from Georgia to Mitch's hometown of Smarr, Alabama, I'd remembered to pick up the scarf I'd been working on for eons. I called it my never-ending scarf. I'd started it over a year ago, thinking I'd give it to my friend Abby for her birthday. It seems I was a tad overoptimistic when it came to estimating how long a knitting project would take.

I worked steadily, my needles clicking away as the miles slipped past. The usually lush green countryside was dominated with the muted colors of a southern winter—pale yellow grass, leafless dark brown trees and bushes, and the faded taupe and beige of the tangled undergrowth.

We stopped for lunch in Columbus, the only large city on the drive. By the time we'd crossed the state line, clouds covered the February sky, veiling the landscape with a gray sheen of mist. The view was still treed with loblobby pines and it didn't look that different from Georgia, but I knew if we continued to drive south and west across Alabama, the land would flatten as it sloped toward the Gulf. We'd made that drive once, when it was just Mitch and me, down to Mobile, then over to New Orleans. We'd been newlyweds. I glanced at Mitch's silent form out of the corner of my eye. We'd talked the whole drive during that trip.

The kids were chattering away in the backseat. They were angling and stacking books to make a house for the action figures that came with their kids' meals at lunch. I finished a row of knitting as I said quietly, "So you really think we should stay at your parents' house for over a week?"

Mitch pulled himself out of his reverie and said, "Yeah, why not?"

"Don't you think it might be a little too long? Livvy's going to miss so much school . . ."

"It'll be fine," Mitch said as he looked away from the road to me. "Livvy's teachers said she can make up the work, right?" I nodded and he said, "You worry too much. Have I ever told you that?"

"No, never," I countered and saw a half smile appear on his face. "It's just that your mom is busy as it is and she'll feel like she needs to cook for us."

"She likes to cook."

"I know, but . . ."

"Ellie, we stayed with your family for a week last summer."

"But we were at a beach house and everyone pitched in and cooked. Livvy was out of school. That was different."

"Was it?"

Oh boy. Here we go. I'd never realized until we had kids how touchy an issue visits with our families could be. Mitch's job as an air force pilot meant that his schedule was always in flux, which made planning holiday visits difficult, to say the least. It was hard to keep visits evenly divided and make sure everyone got to see the kids. We ended up having visits on the fly, dropping in as we drove across the country during our moves or snatching a few days when one of Mitch's training classes happened to be in the same state as one of our families. Add in the tug-of-war between us wanting a yearly family vacation and our families wanting us to visit for special occasions, and I almost wished we all lived in the same town. But friends assured me that situation didn't solve the problem, either. "It only makes it worse," one friend had told me ominously. Of course, the chances of us ever living close to either of our families was so slim I didn't need to put that on my list of things to worry about.

I dropped my hands and the scarf puddled in my lap. "I'm glad we're going to be there to see your mom get her award. I'm just saying I don't want to impose."

During a phone call last week, Caroline, Mitch's mom, had told us she would receive the Realtor of the Year Award this week at an awards banquet. She'd won plenty of sales awards, but this was a prestigious award, given to a single Realtor each year, which recognized community involvement. Caroline was a volunteer with Habitat for Humanity and regularly organized fundraisers for a local women's shelter.

"We're not imposing. We're family," Mitch said. "Besides, I'm down to 'use it or lose it,' so we might as well use it since Book Daze starts next week."

Mitch had a certain amount of time off that he couldn't carry from one year to the next. If he didn't use it, he lost it, so when we got the news about his mom's award, we decided to take a few days and drive over. I still wasn't convinced that we wouldn't be overstaying our welcome, but we were on the road and the plans had been made.

Livvy asked, "Book what?" She might have trouble hearing us when we told her to do her chores, but she had excellent hearing when anyone mentioned a book, library, or bookstore.

"It's a book festival," Mitch explained. We'd already passed a few signs for the festival, placed along the highway, that read, SMARR BOOK DAZE—ALABAMA'S FINEST LITERARY FESTIVAL.

I could tell the signs had been used year after year because most of the paint was slightly faded, except for a bright white square that had been repainted so this year's dates could be added. The length of our stay had mushroomed when Mitch's aunt Nanette called and insisted we stay until the festival began. She'd been inviting us for years and since we were going to be there anyway . . .

I asked, "Aunt Nanette volunteers at the festival every year?"

" 'Volunteer' is too mild a word for it. She runs it."

"Is a book festival like a book fair?" Livvy asked, straining against her seat belt from the backseat.

"Sort of, but it's probably bigger than the book fairs you have at school," I said.

"That's an understatement," Mitch added. "It draws authors from across the country. There will be all sorts of books, discussion panels, guest speakers, and door prizes. The Friends of the Library have a huge used book sale, too. Aunt Nanette is president of the Friends."

Livvy's eyes widened. Mitch and I both knew what was coming next as she said, "Can we go? Please? Please?"

"Of course," Mitch said. "That's one of the reasons we're staying for a whole week."   ·

"Good. I can look for the new book in the Infinity Mystery series," Livvy said with a nod.

Nathan said, "I want a book, too,"

Livvy continued, talking over him, "The next one is called *The Spiral Secrets* and it's so new that the school library doesn't even *have* it yet."

"Can I get a book, too?" Nathan asked again. "I want one about trucks."

"Yes, Nathan, you can get a book, too," Mitch said. "Now, I know a game we can play."

The kids tensed in anticipation.

Mitch winked at me. "The Quiet Game."

The kids slumped back against their seats, groaning.

"I have a dollar bill for the winner," Mitch said.

"That's bribery," I murmured.

"An essential parenting skill. Although, I like to think of it as an incentive."

"Look, we're here," I said a few minutes later as we pulled into the circular drive in front of Mitch's parents' house.

"Mom's out!" Livvy said, delighted. "You said something."

"You're out, too, Livvy," Mitch said. "So that means Nathan is the winner,"

Nathan smiled and sat up a little straighter. I shot Mitch a warning glance as Livvy's face fell. She wasn't used to losing.

"Don't worry," he said as he pulled his wallet out of his pocket, "we'll play again."

The house was a low-slung rancher with crisp white-painted brick accented with black shutters. It sat far back from the road under a massive white oak, its leaves a bare tracery against the low, gray clouds. Two twisty, miniature evergreen trees in pots flanked the red front door. It was exactly the sort of house you'd expect a Realtor to own, a house with spacious rooms, including a huge kitchen, in an established neighborhood that would never go out of style. The circular drive was crowded with cars. "Why is everyone here?" I asked.

"I don't know. Maybe they wanted to see us," Mitch said, but I could hear the puzzlement in his voice.

Livvy bounced in her car seat, her disappointment over losing the game gone. "We can swim! I want to swim first!" The kids loved the pool in the backyard.

Nathan, never one to be left out of anything, caught her excitement and bopped in his car seat. "Let's swim. I can swim."

Swimsuits. I'd forgotten to pack the swimsuits, which would be the first thing on a long list of items I was sure I'd overlooked. I glanced at Mitch, but he was busy edging the minivan into the only slot left in the driveway, a tiny space behind Aunt Nanette's Mini Cooper, emblazoned with the British flag.

"We don't even know if the pool water is warm," I said, glancing at the late February sky. The mist had tapered off, but the clouds still hung low. Somehow, our visits usually coincided with the sticky humidity of midsummer.

We unloaded everyone from the van, a sharp breeze nipping at our jackets. As we hurried up the driveway, I saw a Lexus with a Crimson Tide license plate frame, and said, "Looks like Uncle Kenny and Aunt Gwen are here. In fact, it looks like everyone is here."

"I know. Weird. They're usually at their office until late." Uncle Kenny and Aunt Gwen had an extensive business empire that was a hodgepodge of different companies. They owned many of the roadside boiled peanut stands that dotted the South and had several shops that sold sports merchandise. Mitch didn't ring the doorbell. Instead, he opened the door and walked inside the hardwood entry with magnolia-tinted wainscoting. The scent of coffee and a hint of wood smoke filled the air. Before we'd taken a few steps, we were caught up in a whirlwind of hugs, kisses, and exclamations.

Mitch's aunt Gwen reached us first, her arms stretched wide to hug as many of us as she could at once. "What a fine-looking family y'all are. So sad that it happened last night. Funny how things work out—that y'all were coming over already."

Aunt Gwen released us and I caught Mitch's eye. He gave a small shrug. He didn't know what she was talking about, either.

"How are y'all doin'?" asked Uncle Kenny as he shook Mitch's hand. His voice was quieter than usual and had an especially solicitous tone that I'd never heard from him. He was usually about as subdued as a cavalry charge.

The *y'alls* continued to fly thick and fast through the air as we worked our way through the crowd, hugging and greeting everyone. I didn't see Mitch's dad, Bill, but his mom had both Livvy and

Nathan in her arms, her silvery pageboy fluttering around her face as she squeezed them close. I wasn't sure how she'd managed to get them both on her hips, since she was so trim and delicate.

After she put the kids down, I gave her a hug as I said, "It's so good to see y'all." Now I was saying "y'all," too. It was hard to resist the pull of the southern speech patterns. They were so warm and friendly.

Caroline left her hands on my arms as she pulled away to look into my face. She lowered her voice. "So how are the kids taking it?"

"Umm . . ." I glanced at Mitch as he came to stand beside me. "How are they taking what?" I asked.

Caroline's gaze ping-ponged between our faces. "You don't know? Didn't you get our voice mail? We figured you were already on the road by the time we started calling everyone and we just assumed you'd gotten it. I meant to call you back, but things have been topsy-turvy around here. I should have remembered that there's hardly any reception on that road." She released me, then reached over to tuck her arm through Mitch's and pull us a few steps away from the kids. I noticed the room had grown quiet and Aunt Gwen was on her knees asking Nathan about the Lego tower he clutched in his hands.

Looking like she hated to say the words, she said, "Grandpa Franklin passed away early this morning."

"What?" Mitch had pulled out his phone and was scrolling through his calls, looking for the missed call, but he stopped and his gaze shot to Caroline's face.

"I'm afraid it's true, honey." She rested one hand on her collarbone. "We're all in shock. Your dad is over there now with Aunt Christine, straightening things out. I'm so sorry to hit you with this right after you walked in the door. Aunt Christine found him last night. They rushed him to the hospital, but he died there."

The doorbell rang and Caroline ushered a dark-headed woman, bearing a foil-covered casserole in a glass dish, to the kitchen.

"Mitch, I'm sorry," I said.

Mitch said quietly, "I guess it wasn't unexpected. He was eighty-two."

"I know." I put my arm around his waist.

"You know what I just realized?" he said. "I don't have any grand-parents now."

Mitch's maternal grandparents had died in a car wreck when he was a teenager and Grandpa Franklin's wife, Millie, had passed away nearly twenty years earlier after a struggle with cancer. I snuggled closer to him. "Technically, that's true, but my grandmother thinks of you as one of her own. In fact, I think she likes you even better than me. She always makes fudge when you come to visit and she only does that for her very most favorite people." The irony of the situation was that Mitch usually made healthy food choices and didn't eat many sweets, but he always ate a small piece, which left the rest of the fudge for me—not that I'm complaining. I love chocolate in all its forms.

When he didn't reply, I looked up at his face. He was fingering the buttons on the phone, staring at it but not seeing it.

"Mitch?"

He blinked, then said, "Come on. We'd better tell the kids."

We explained the death to the kids in terms as simple as possible and watched both of them carefully to see how they took the news. They hadn't spent a lot of time with their great-grandfather, so I wasn't sure how they'd react. Livvy frowned and looked thoughtful. I knew it would take her questions awhile to emerge. I wasn't even sure what *I* thought. I felt as if our world had been picked up and shaken, like we were in a giant snow globe. Everything felt off and odd. Looking at Mitch's face made my heart hurt. To lose someone so suddenly was jarring and I knew that since I felt a little off-kilter, he had to be feeling twice as unsettled. He'd spent many afternoons at his grandfather's house when he was growing up.

I drew both of the kids into a double-armed hug and was enveloped in the scents of baby lotion and freshly laundered clothes. Livvy pulled away quickly, but Nathan stayed snuggled on my shoulder. With his head tucked under mine, he asked, "What happened to Great-grandpa Franklin?" He had picked up on our sadness and his eyes were shiny.

"His body stopped working. That happens when you get old. He was eighty-two," I said.

He pulled away and asked suspiciously, "How old are you and Dad?"

"Not that old," I said with a smile. "Great-grandpa Franklin was *really* old and his body just wore out, but Dad and I are fine. Our bodies are going to last a long, long time."

"So that means no swimming," Livvy said flatly and I nodded.

"No swimming?" Caroline said. She'd just escorted the casserole lady to the door and was walking back through the corner of the formal living room where we'd gathered the kids to break the news. She reeled back in mock shock. "Of course you can swim. The pool's heated. Bill and I swim laps every day and I have plenty of spare suits, even those with the floaty inserts." Caroline leaned down and said to Livvy and Nathan, "Let's go look and see what we can find." Nathan put his hand in hers and they went off to one of the spare bedrooms with Livvy hurrying to catch Caroline's other hand.

Mitch and I moved through the kitchen into the den at the back of the house. I nearly sighed with relief when I recognized some of the relatives. Mitch's family tree is as massive and involved as an ancient live oak intertwined with kudzu and it's hard for me to keep all the relatives straight, but I did know Aunt Nanette. She was sitting on the sofa near the fireplace with her Afghan hound, Queen, at her feet. They both had long noses and feathered gray hair. Besides her love of books, Aunt Nanette was a fan of anything British. She owned the Mini Cooper painted with the Union Jack. She had a regal air about her and looked like she should be presiding over the tea tray in a country estate. "Ellie, dear, how are you? Exhausted after the drive, I imagine."

"Well, it certainly felt like more than three hundred miles," I said as I dropped onto the cream sofa and felt the warmth of the popping fire even from several feet away from the fireplace.

"You should help yourself to some food. It's been arriving all day. Mostly green bean casserole, the kind with the canned French fried onion topping, for some reason."

"No thanks." I didn't think I could eat, which says a lot about how stunned I felt. I could usually always eat, but right now food didn't sound good. I stretched my legs out under the glass coffee table topped with a flower arrangement and two fragile figurines. I made a mental note to remind Livvy and Nathan that there was no throwing or running in the house. "We had to stop quite a bit. The kids can only stay strapped in the seats for so long and then we have to give them a break." I glanced around the room and saw Mitch talking to Uncle Bud, who was a real estate broker and always had at least a day's worth of stubble. The sleeves of his flannel shirt were rolled up and revealed the phoenix tattoo on his forearm. Jeans, flip-flops, and a baseball cap with the logo "Love's Travel Stop" embroidered on it completed the look.

Uncle Kenny and Aunt Gwen had returned to playing gin rummy at the dining room table. I saw several other relatives who looked vaguely familiar, but if I was playing a round of Jeopardy and had to name them, I'd lose, no question about it.

"The neighbor brought over some pickahn pie, too," Aunt Nanette said.

I looked uncertainly toward the kitchen. *Pickahn* pie? "Um . . . oh, pecan pie," I said as I spotted the nut pies on the counter. "I'm sure we'll have some later."

I didn't see Mitch's favorite cousin, Dan, or his wife. "Is Felicity here?" I asked, because I'd learned at the family reunion we'd hosted that it was smart to find out what kind of mood Felicity was in. That way I'd know whether or not to avoid her. You'd think that she'd be able to rein in her temper on a day with such bad news, but with Felicity you never knew if common sense would win out over her temper.

"No. More than likely, she's over at Father's house. So distressing, really. Probably already rearranging the furniture. She could at least have the common courtesy to wait until the will is read. Or, until after the funeral," Aunt Nanette said with a sniff of disapproval.

"I don't understand." Queen had moved to my side and I ran my hand down her silky coat. Petting Queen made me miss our dog,

Rex. We'd dropped him off at the kennel this morning where he'd be cosseted and pampered. Aunt Nanette's hand flicked the air impatiently. "The silly girl thinks Dan is going to inherit Father's house."

I stopped petting Queen. "Why would she think that?" I'd barely been able to take in the idea that Grandpa Franklin was gone, so talking about inheritance seemed crass, but I would have thought Grandpa Franklin's children, including Mitch's dad and his brothers and sisters, including Aunt Nanette, would be the logical recipients.

"You knew Dan lost his job?" Aunt Nanette said and I nodded. He was an information technology specialist and had been laid off several months ago.

With a small shake of her head that indicated disapproval, Aunt Nanette said, "It was right about that time that it started. Looking back, it's easy to see now, but at the time . . . well, I suppose none of us wanted to admit that Father's age was finally catching up with him. Felicity recognized it right away—she's a grasping little thing—and she made a point to visit him several times a week, always dropping broad hints about how tight things were for them financially and what a relief it would be for them if they didn't have to pay rent."

One thing I'd learned about Aunt Nanette was that she didn't suffer fools gladly. She'd managed the business office of Gardner's Concrete for thirty-five years, never tolerating slacking off, swearing, or anything else she deemed unseemly for the organization. Apparently the owners, the Gardner brothers, had lived in fear of her and spent an inordinate amount of time on job sites, but their books always balanced, their invoices were always paid, and they didn't have a lot of delinquent accounts after Aunt Nanette got after "the lates," as she called them. I thought her assessment of Felicity might be a little on the harsh side, but it did match up with the rather pouty girl I remembered from our brief encounters.

"I thought Dan found another job," I said.

"Yes, but it's with a smaller company and he had to take a significant pay cut."

"I didn't realize." Nanette nodded and I went back to the other thing she'd said that puzzled me. "You said Grandpa Franklin was beginning to show his age. We hadn't heard anything about that."

"It was nothing alarming or I'm sure Bill and Caroline would have called you. Just normal aging . . . forgetting things, names of people, misplacing his checkbook, things like that. He couldn't manage arithmetic in his head anymore. The doctors said it was all perfectly normal, considering his age, but a few weeks ago, Christine said she heard him carrying on a conversation with Mother. We didn't think too much about it. It was only one incident. Then one morning last week, he came in from the backyard and told Christine to make some tea because Millie and George were thirsty."

"Oh," I said, faintly. George was Franklin's brother and he'd been dead longer than Grandpa Franklin's wife, Millie.

Aunt Nanette smoothed down the fabric of her floral dress. "Just goes to show . . . you never know when your time will come. It was his time to go. It was quicker than we thought it would be, is all. Wish Christine could get that through her head instead of blaming herself."

"Why in the world would she do that?" Queen shifted her head and I scratched her ears.

"Oh, she stays over some nights in the spare bedroom." That did sound like Aunt Christine. I'd never have thought Aunt Nanette and Aunt Christine were sisters. Besides being complete physical opposites—Aunt Nanette was thin as a toothpick and Aunt Christine had a roly-poly figure—their personalities were like yin and yang. Aunt Christine was a retired kindergarten teacher and had taken on the role of primary caregiver for her father. She lived in the same area and had a nurturing, gentle spirit. "Of course, last night wasn't one of the nights she stayed." Aunt Nanette raised an eyebrow and said, "I think she had a hot date."

I'd heard about the budding romance. "The pharmacist?"

Aunt Nanette nodded. "You wouldn't believe how many things Christine needs from Walgreen's now. She's in that store constantly. At least she has one of those fancy store cards and gets points, so I suppose it's not a total loss." Her smiled faded as she said, "I'm sure that's what all this break-in nonsense is about. She feels guilty because she wasn't there. She'd mentioned getting a home-care nurse to give her more time to date Roy, but some people," Nanette's gaze lit on Uncle Bud as she said, "weren't happy with the idea of paying for something that Christine had been doing for free." When she realized I'd noticed the direction of her glance, she looked almost guilty and said quickly, "But we won't have to worry about that now."

Queen was slowly sinking to the floor in dog heaven as I rubbed her ears. "There was a break-in? At Grandpa Franklin's house?"

"So Christine says, but, well, Christine always was as flighty as the fluff off a dandelion. Summer is just like her, you know. Capricious ways tend to run in our family," Aunt Nanette said, referring to Mitch's younger sister. I'd met Summer during a trip to Washington, D.C., a few years ago and gotten to know her quite well. It sounded, to me at least, as if Summer had settled down now. She was working for a state representative in Florida now, but it's hard to live down your reputation, especially with your family.

As Queen collapsed, she bumped the coffee table and set a figurine rocking. Aunt Nanette called Queen back to her side as she returned to the subject of Aunt Christine. "She thinks someone broke into the house last night and they've got the police out there now. Christine didn't notice it until she got back from the hospital. We had a storm last night and the power went out at her house. She's a light sleeper—takes after Father in that—so she went over to check on him after the worst of the storm blew over. The power was still working at his house, so she expected him to be awake, watching The Weather Channel or reading a biography, but he was still in bed, which isn't like him. Any kind of storm disturbs him. She checked on him and couldn't wake him. He only had a faint pulse, so she called nine-one-one. They took him to the hospital, but by early morning . . . he'd passed." Aunt Nanette, who had been speaking so matter-of-factly, stopped abruptly. It was as if someone switched off a newscast. I reached out a tentative hand. Aunt Nanette was not a person who hugged or even touched. She noticed my hand and gripped it. "So silly to give in to emotions. We all knew his time would come." She squeezed my hand and then released it.

She sat up even straighter, which I hadn't thought was possible. "There. I'm fine now. Of course, Christine left to go with him to the hospital and didn't look around the house. She was busy calling us."

Talking about the death obviously distressed her, so I asked, "She didn't notice the break-in until later?"

Aunt Nanette's tone shifted to slightly scoffing. "More than likely she's imagined the whole thing." Back on the comfortable ground of discussing Aunt Christine's peculiarities, Aunt Nanette visibly relaxed, her shoulders slipping from their stiff posture. "Fool's errand," she summarized. "She went back there this afternoon to pick out a suit for the funeral home and that's when she noticed the back bedroom window was open."

Caroline returned to the living room with Livvy and Nathan, who were both outfitted in swimsuits and carrying colorful beach towels. Caroline stopped to talk to Mitch. The kids began hopping around like popcorn in hot oil.

"Looks like I'll be at the pool," I said to Aunt Nanette, although I really wanted to stay and find out more about the break-in.

When I reached Mitch and Caroline, I heard her say, "Why don't you go check on him? He's been over there for an hour." Caroline's soft drawl transformed the word "hour" to "hower." She continued, "He said something about fixing a window lock, but he should be done by now. We'll have to start making decisions about the funeral soon."

"Sure," Mitch said and looked at me. "Want to go with me to Grandpa Franklin's house? Dad's there because there was a break-in."

"I heard, but looks like I'm on lifeguard duty."

"Oh, go on," Caroline said. "I'll watch the kids. There's nothing else I can do here until Bill gets back." I opened my mouth to protest, but she said, "I'd like to . . . to get out of the house for a bit."

I realized that outwardly she looked just the same—impeccably groomed from her hair to her perfectly polished toenails—and she gave off that air of quiet capability that she always had, but when I looked at her eyes I saw they were pink and swollen. I also noticed that she didn't have on any jewelry at all and that was like me not having any chocolate kisses with me—one of my favorite vices. Caroline had an extensive collection of jewelry from simple gold hoops to chunky necklaces and always wore pieces that coordinated perfectly with her clothes. Seeing that she'd even forgotten to put on her wedding ring told me that, in her own understated way, she was having a tough time. "Go on." She shooed us toward the door. "I'd like the time with the kids. Take my mind off things."

"Okay," I said and leaned in to whisper, "Nathan is a great swimmer. Livvy's more tentative."

Caroline nodded and led the kids to the pool while Mitch and I went to the van. One glance at Mitch's face told me he was lost in his thoughts. I didn't know if it was his grandfather's death or the other thing that was bothering him. I had no idea what "the other thing" was, but for weeks we'd had these stretches of silence. I knew Mitch well enough to know he was working through something and I'd learned the hard way that if I poked and prodded him about it, he closed up more tightly, like a turtle retracting into its shell.

I stifled a sigh and dug in my purse for chocolate. I offered some to Mitch, but he shook his head. As we drove, I focused on the trees that flicked by the window. The undergrowth and screen of vines that usually made the road a corridor had died away for the winter and I could see the carpet of fallen leaves interspersed with the bare, brown tree trunks for several feet before the trees thickened, blocking the view deeper into the woods.

When Mitch grew up in Smarr, it was just a small town on the road to and from Montgomery. But over the years it had grown, first into a bedroom community for Montgomery and, later, its suburbs had spawned businesses like restaurants and shopping centers. Eventually, several corporations moved to the community. Caroline and Uncle Bud had ridden the wave of development, boosting their careers.

Mitch's parents' house was on the outskirts of suburban Smarr. Grandpa Franklin's house was farther beyond theirs in a more rural area. Even though the change of scene was dramatic, the two houses weren't that far apart. The drive only took about ten minutes. Out here, big box stores and fast-food chains seemed a million miles away. In fact, the area was fairly populated, but most of the houses were set back at the end of long drives, deep in the trees and hidden from the main road.

"Doesn't Aunt Christine live out here, too?" I asked. It seemed a waste to drive in complete silence now that we were actually alone. We so rarely had the opportunity to carry on an uninterrupted conversation.

"Down that road, over to the left," Mitch said as we flew past a mailbox. "It's the first turn after the historical marker about Addison McClure's birthplace."

"Sally Addison McClure was born here? Does she still live here?" I asked. I knew from my high school English class that McClure, one of America's most famous authors, was from Alabama—it was the setting for her single renowned novel, *Deep Down Things*—but I had no idea her birthplace was so close to where Mitch grew up.

"No. She moved before I was born. To Atlanta, I think. But she was instrumental in getting Book Daze going. Grandpa Franklin knew her. They played together when they were kids."

"Wow," I said. "He always had good stories. What did he say about her?"

"Not much," Mitch said and silence descended again.

I wasn't sure if it was the mention of Grandpa Franklin that caused the abrupt shutdown in our conversation or if it was something else. I squirmed, then said, "Mitch, you know if you need to talk, I'll listen."

He glanced at me quickly, surprised. "I know that," he said without hesitation. He had one hand on top of the steering wheel and pointed to the road. "It's been years, but I think I could find my way to Grandpa Franklin's house blindfolded. We were always going here when I was a kid. He let me and Dan ride a dirt bike he had in the garage." Mitch glanced at me quickly with a small smile that turned up the corners of his mouth. "Mom didn't know. It was a secret. Still doesn't know, even today, I don't think. Grandpa Franklin had a lot of secrets," he said softly, almost to himself, as he focused on the road again and made a right-hand turn onto a long gravel driveway.

He frowned as we neared the end of the drive. "What are all these cars doing here?"

"I thought it was only your dad, Aunt Christine, and maybe Felicity," I said as we neared the first car. It was a four-door sedan with a light bar on top and the words CULVERTON COUNTY SHERIFF on the side. I felt a terrible sinking sensation in the pit of my stomach.

Mitch rounded the slight curve and a strip of yellow tape barred the drive. He threw the minivan into park and we both jumped out. Before we could even get to the line of tape, which I saw was printed with the bold words DO NOT CROSS, a uniformed officer, a young man with closely cropped brown hair and a smattering of freckles, stepped in our path.

"No one beyond this point. You'll have to back up."

Mitch wasn't listening to him. He was scanning the scene behind the tape barrier. Several official cars and SUVs were parked around the front of the Arts and Crafts–style bungalow with faded blue trim and a porch swing. The front door was propped open and a group of people in uniforms stood on the wide front porch, between the hefty porch pillars that had a base of smooth river rocks set in concrete. Wooden pillars extended upward to meet the sloping roofline. A dormer window in the half story upstairs broke up the roofline. Off to the side of the house, a tire swing, which hung from a large mimosa tree, spun slowly in the breeze. I didn't see Mitch's dad or Aunt Christine anywhere.

The young officer in front of us said, "I need you to turn that minivan around."

An engine rumbled to a stop behind us and I saw it was another minivan, this one black. I stared at the small, almost delicate lettering on the side. CRIME SCENE UNIT. I whipped around to the young officer. "What's going on?"

"Murder investigation."

Ellie Avery's Tips for Preserving Family Treasures

As with any organizing project, it's important to take time to survey the task before you begin. Decide how you can break the project down into manageable tasks. For instance, instead of thinking, "I want to organize all the memory boxes in the garage," you could set a goal of organizing photos first, school papers and projects next, and historical/genealogical items last. Not only does dividing one large job into several more manageable tasks provide you with a game plan, it also keeps you from feeling overwhelmed.

Chapter
Two

"Murder investigation?" Mitch and I chorused as a woman in her midthirties slipped under the tape line beside us, causing her shoulder-length black hair, which was pulled back in a clip, to slide over her shoulder and reveal the word "Sheriff" across the back of her bulky black jacket. She gave the officer a disapproving look and said, "I believe what Officer—" she paused to read his nameplate and add a measure of reproof as she stared at him, "—Taggart *meant* to say was that this is an investigation of a possible crime scene." The woman's words were clipped and there was no trace of the soft, unhurried rhythms of Officer Taggart's southern accent.

The young officer blinked and I could see him fighting down a flash of anger. He nodded curtly and said, "Of course, Detective Kalra. Sorry."

Mitch assumed his dealing-with-bureaucracy tone. "Look, I see you're busy, but we need to know what's going on here. I'm Mitch Avery. That's my grandfather's house. My dad and aunt are supposed to be here. Can we go inside?" Mitch's years in the air force had given him plenty of experience untangling red tape. He had much more patience in that area than I did. Dealing with the minutia of official procedures drives me crazy, but Mitch had learned how to work the system: be understanding and courteous. And sometimes he brought out the big guns—his smile, which somehow brought people around to his side.

Mitch wasn't smiling at Detective Kalra, which I thought was probably good. She looked like the type of person who cut straight to the point. I doubted Mitch's special please-help-me-we're-both-on-the-same-side smile would have any impact on her. Detective Kalra pressed her full lips together as she looked us both over. "Wait here," she instructed before she crossed the gravel drive and went up the steps to the house.

Mitch and I exchanged glances while Officer Taggart ignored us and checked the knots that held the tape line up. We stepped back and I said, "At least she seems to be the right person to talk to here."

"Yeah, she's definitely checked out on peanut butter and jelly," Mitch said in a low voice. Officer Taggart shot us a puzzled look, but I knew exactly what Mitch meant. A few years ago, Mitch had requested his flight meal, asking for a peanut butter and jelly sandwich. The airman making the meals had said, "I can only make you a peanut butter sandwich. I've been checked out on peanut better, but not on jelly." The situation was typical of the absurd rules and regulations that are layered throughout government bureaucracy. Since the peanut butter and jelly incident, if we found someone who could cut through all the red tape and get things done, we'd say that the person was "checked out on peanut better and jelly." Detective Kalra certainly seemed like the person who was in charge here and could get us into the house.

We shared a grin and the creases at the corners of Mitch's eyes crinkled together. The knot of tension and worry that had been with me since Mitch retreated into his withdrawn, thoughtful mood eased a bit. It was so nice to have this shorthand language of references that we understood perfectly, but would be utter nonsense to anyone else.

Detective Kalra emerged from the house and crossed back to us. "Only one of you," she said as she lifted the tape line. Mitch glanced at me and I nodded for him to go. It was his grandfather. He ducked under the yellow strip and followed her to the house.

"So where do you want me to move the van?" I called to Officer Taggart, who'd moved to the other side of the yard. I figured I'd be as cooperative as possible. We didn't want to annoy anyone in law enforcement.

"Put it over there beside the garage." I found my extra set of keys in my purse and climbed in the van. There wasn't much space to maneuver because the crime scene van had parked so close behind us, but Officer Taggart waved me back and forth until I'd inched out of the confined space. I parked in the small clearing beside the detached garage and blew out a puff of breath, relieved that I hadn't dented the bumper on the crime scene van.

I hopped out of the van and made my way carefully down the tiny path that ran beside the detached garage, which was in the shade and smelled earthy and slightly damp. Set at a right angle to the house, the garage was as old as the house and built in the same Arts and Crafts bungalow style. Grandpa Franklin had given up driving. During our last visit, Caroline told us that Bill and Aunt Christine had convinced him to sell his car after he'd nearly run down the mailman on a foggy morning. He hadn't wanted to give it up, but they'd persuaded him. Grandpa Franklin managed to sell his immaculately maintained Town Car for more than Blue Book value and that had made him happy. He'd then used the garage for storage, and I doubted anyone had been inside for weeks, if not months, but it was included in the yellow tape enclosure that circled the house.

There was no sign of Mitch or any other relatives in the yard. The air felt sharp and cold against my face and when I breathed out, I could see a trace of vapor in the air. I shoved my hands in my pockets and settled in to wait. The sun was sliding lower behind the clouds, seeming to hurry along the evening darkness. It felt as if it was closer to six, when it would be fully dark, rather than four.

Officer Taggart had moved the tape so that the crime scene van was able to park in front of the house. He'd secured the tape back in place and was now swiveled to face the house, with his back to me as he talked to another officer. The crowd on the porch was gone and the front door was closed. I couldn't see anything through the windows, but I did spot Bill's Saab parked around the far side of the house by the kitchen door. The other officer went into the house and Officer Taggart spotted me. He walked over and I expected him to tell me to step away from the yellow tape, but he nodded to me and said, "I doubt it'll be much longer, ma'am."

"Really? They're almost done?"

"Yes, ma'am. There's hardly anything to process. Just a window."

I wanted to ask him about the window, but a woman jogged up the drive and gripped the tape line with her gloved hands. "What's going on, Officer?" She was dressed for exercise in a long-sleeved pink T-shirt and had an orange Windbreaker tied around her waist over black running pants. Her short hair was caught up in a tiny ponytail that extended only half an inch. The rest of her dry blond hair stuck out around her flushed face in a crackly halo. Red earmuffs accented her flushed cheeks. She was breathing hard, sending out white puffs of air as she exhaled. She looked familiar to me, but I couldn't place her. Was she one of Mitch's distant relatives?

Officer Taggart dropped back into his official capacity and said, "Step back, please."

She released the tape and said, "Please tell me nothing has happened to that sweet Mr. Avery. He's alright, isn't he?" Her voice had a definite nasal quality and there was no southern drawl in her quick speech pattern, so she wasn't related to Mitch. All his relatives had grown up in the South and had the accent to prove it.

The earlier reprimand from the detective must have made an impression because Officer Taggart only said, "I can't really say, ma'am."

"Well, who can tell me?" she persisted. "I want to make sure he's okay."

"I can't say anything else. It's Mrs. Key, isn't it? Would you like to sit down on the porch swing?"

"No. I mean, yes, I'm *Ms.* Key—actually, call me Maggie. But no, I can't sit. I have to cool down," she said as she paced in a circle with her hands on her hips. Her breathing was slowing now, returning to normal.

Her gloved hands fluttered up to her forehead, then down to her throat. "Something's happened to him, hasn't it? You'd be able to tell me, if he was okay. Since you're not saying anything . . . then . . . something *has* happened to him. " She ripped off the gloves and I saw she had tiny, delicate hands. She pressed her fingers to her lips.

Maggie Key, I repeated in my mind. That name sounded familiar, too.

Officer Taggart glanced around, looking as if he wished the detective would show up and dispatch the jogger. She was blinking her large brown eyes rapidly and was on the verge of tears. Clearly, dealing with weepy women was not his forte. "Don't you live up the road?" he asked. "Would you like an escort home? We can give you a ride."

She removed her fingers from her lips. "Yes, I live up the road, up on that rise," she said with a vague gesture over her left shoulder. "I knew something was wrong last night. There was so much activity down here. I can see it from my office."

I glanced behind her at the low hill on the other side of the road. I could only see a roofline and the dull gleam of two windows.

She switched her balled up gloves from hand to hand and I wondered if I didn't know her, if it was just that she reminded me of someone . . . my crazy aunt Donna—that was it. She had the same fussy, dithering aura of my aunt Donna, as if there were a million thoughts and ideas buzzing in the air around her and she flitted from one to another with dizzying randomness.

Maggie continued, "It was so unusual—that's why it caught my attention. I couldn't get back to sleep after the storm, so I decided I might as well get some work done. I was in my office. It's always so quiet around here, but after the storm I saw a car—a little red one, I think. It drove in here. I saw the color when it pulled up near the porch light—it was either red or burgundy, it's hard to tell in the dark—and I thought it was odd. I hoped he wasn't sick. I just assumed it was his daughter coming to check on him, but I remembered this morning that she drives a white car, so it couldn't have been her, could it?"

She clinched the gloves and Officer Taggart said, "Wait here, ma'am. I'll see if the detective can talk to you."

Before he reached the front door, it opened and Mitch came outside with his hand under Aunt Christine's elbow. At least, I thought it was Aunt Christine. I looked closer. Yes, I recognized her plump figure and round face, but everything else about her looked different. Her hair, which had been short and gray, was longer and fell in soft brown waves around her face. And instead of the functional pastel cotton sweatshirts and stretchy pants with elastic waistbands she usually wore, she had on a smart black and white jacket with a geometric pattern. And were those boot-cut jeans? I blinked. Aunt Christine looked good. She'd had quite a makeover. But when she was closer to me, I could see her shell-shocked face. She was unsteady on her feet and I don't know if she would have made it across the yard without Mitch. He helped her under the tape line and I immediately took her other arm. She didn't look as if she could stand up on her own. "Aunt Christine, are you feeling alright?" She didn't answer me and I realized she was repeating something in a low murmur. Concerned, I looked at Mitch. "Is she sick?" I asked quietly.

Mitch gave me a half nod, a warning, I realized. "She's exhausted. She's been up all night. We need to get her home. Detective Kalra cleared her to leave." We helped Aunt Christine into the van and as we pulled away from the house, I saw Detective Kalra speaking to the jogger. Maggie Key. I chewed on my lip, still not quite able to place her.

It only took a few moments to reach Aunt Christine's small white frame house with the ornamental wishing well and porch glider. We parked in the carport, which was empty, and I wondered where her car was—still at the hospital, or maybe at Grandpa Franklin's house? The side of the carport facing away from the house was covered with a trellis interwoven with coral honeysuckle.

I helped Aunt Christine out of the van and we inched our way along the wall of fragrant vines. The bright red trumpets stood out sharply against the dark leaves, the only spot of color in the landscape of dark green pines, brown tree trunks, and fallen leaves. I was surprised at how wobbly she was. She stumbled on the steps and I steadied her. Mitch hurried to catch up with us. He found her keys and unlocked the front door.

Her gaze was focused on the welcome mat as she repeated the phrase, "I didn't mean to. I didn't mean to."

I scrunched my eyebrows together and said, "Didn't mean what, Aunt Christine?" but I couldn't break into her abstraction. "Aunt Christine, what did you—" I began, but Mitch shoved the door open and guided her inside.

"Here we go. You need to get some rest."

Being back in her own house must have penetrated her reverie because Aunt Christine pulled herself away from both of us and moved slowly to the snack bar that divided the living room from the kitchen. She put her purse on the counter and stepped out of her low-heeled boots, another change in her wardrobe. A yellow and green bird was squawking at her from its cage in the living room. "Hello, Einstein," she said as she filled a small cup with water, then went to the cage and topped off the water bottle. She checked the food, all the while talking to the bird, apologizing for leaving him alone. I supposed she was moving on autopilot, going through her usual just-arrived-home routine.

The small living area was furnished in a shabby chic style with a pink upholstered couch, white wicker chairs with cabbage rose cushions, and delicate tables painted in a distressed white finish. I thought the art on the walls was modern art, which didn't quite go with the rest of the room, but then I looked closer at one of the pictures near me and realized it was a child's painting of a flower, proudly signed, "Elizabeth, age 5," and I realized that the artwork was probably from her kindergarten students.

She shuffled back to the kitchen to place the cup in the sink and then stopped abruptly as she looked across the counter at us, as if she was noticing us for the first time.

Her eyes watered and she began to sob. I hurried over to her and put one arm around her shaking shoulders.

"He's gone. He's gone and I shouldn't have . . . I wish . . ." Her words became incoherent. Mitch was fingering his cell phone and said quietly, "Think I should call Aunt Nanette?"

I shrugged. I didn't know what to do to comfort Aunt Christine.

"No! Not her!" She sniffled and wiped under her eyes. "Not

her," she repeated, but in a calmer tone. "I'm just so tired. It's hitting me all at once. That he's gone."

I squeezed her shoulders and said, "Of course. You've been up all night and need to get some sleep." I steered her through the living room to the small hallway, which led to the bedrooms. She went in one of the bedrooms and I followed her, uncertainly. "Do you want any help? Would you like to change clothes?"

"Yes, I'll change," she said, opening a closet and removing a leopard print track suit, "but I can manage." She crossed the room to the master bathroom and closed the door. This room continued the shabby chic theme. A peach-and-cream comforter covered the white wrought-iron bedframe. The walls were painted the same peach shade. A stenciled border of ivy leaves ran around the top of the walls and satiny, cream-colored curtains pooled on the hardwood floor. The room felt cozy and extremely feminine. A dressing table with a peach satin skirt was scattered with lotions and makeup.

The door opened and Aunt Christine came out wearing the track suit. She had the clothes she'd been wearing draped over her arm. She looked like she was ready to drop. "Let me take those for you." I hurried over. "I'll hang them up. Do you want me to get you anything? Call anyone for you?"

"No, I don't need anyone. I just need to lie down." She curled up on the bed and closed her eyes.

I hung the clothes on her peach padded hangers, then covered her with a throw that was folded over a bench at the end of the bed. She was already breathing heavily and she reminded me of my kids, who, after an exhausting day, were able to drop off to sleep as soon as their heads touched the pillow. She twitched in her sleep and began murmuring again. I leaned down to readjust the throw and heard her say, "I'm so sorry, Dad . . . I didn't mean to hurt you."

Chapter
Three

A hand came down on my shoulder and I jumped.
"Ellie," Mitch said, nodding to the door.

"Did you hear that?" I asked, not budging. I listened for more, but Aunt Christine's breathing was slow and even. Her face looked peaceful and relaxed. With her full, slightly flushed cheeks, she reminded me of the saccharine-sweet Rococo paintings of matrons, all delicate white skin with an excess of flowers and ruffles and cupids.

Mitch hissed, "Come on. Let her sleep."

I reluctantly followed him out of the room and closed the door gently. "What was she talking about? She's sorry she hurt Grandpa Franklin?"

"Nothing. She doesn't know what she's saying."

Mitch's phone buzzed and he reached to answer it. We'd had a little competition going for a while, with each of us setting the ringtones on the other's cell phone with the cheesiest, most embarrassing songs we could find, but when "MMMBop" by Hanson rang out at full blast during Mitch's staff meeting, well, that was the end of that game. His phone has been set to vibrate ever since.

Mitch answered and mouthed to me, "It's Dad."

I nodded and moved around the room, absentmindedly looking at pictures and giving the bird a wide berth. I stopped to examine several small, round metal objects with ornate crests, mounted in a shadow box hanging on the wall near the bird cage. Most were a coppery color and had ornate engravings. Several had an eagle with its wings spread and a crest in the middle. Another, smaller one had a banner with writing entwined with three pillars. A slip of paper under each coin had a date from the 1850s and a location written in calligraphy. They were Civil War buttons, I realized. The shadow box was part of a grouping of framed black-and-white photos, some even faded to brown. The clothes, dark suits for men and Gibson Girl sleeves and long skirts for the women, indicated the photos were from the early 1900s. I wondered if they were Avery relatives.

Mitch joined me as he put his phone away. "They're finished at the house. Dad's going to board up the window and then head back home."

"Look at these buttons. They're from the Civil War," I said.

"Mom did say that Aunt Christine was treasure hunting with her new boyfriend. I called Aunt Gwen and asked her to come stay with Aunt Christine. As soon as she gets here, we'll go back to Grandpa Franklin's house, pick up Aunt Christine's car, and drive it back over here."

I turned to Mitch, who'd shifted to stand in front of the bird cage, and asked, "So what happened inside Grandpa Franklin's house?" The drive to Aunt Christine's house had been so short that I hadn't had time to ask him about it.

The bird made whistling noises as Mitch said, "They said it's routine. Because Aunt Christine called nine-one-one about the break-in, they had to come out and investigate. But there's nothing to worry about. It's all cleared up now, I'm sure."

I tilted my head and studied him. "But there must have been some reason to call in the detectives and the crime scene unit. They must have found something . . ." I paced over to the wide front window that looked out over the wishing well, the drive, and the bank of spruce and pine trees that sheltered the house from the road. "Why did she say she didn't mean to?" I asked, turning back to him. "And she said she hurt him. Why would she say that?"

The bird hopped onto a perch and twisted its head in a move that, if a human attempted it it would have resulted in a trip to the emergency room. "I don't know," Mitch said. "Let her get some rest and she'll be fine." Mitch leaned down and said in a soft voice, "You're a nice bird. Can you talk, little fellow?"

The bird screwed its neck in the other direction, shifted around on the perch, and squawked at Mitch.

I raised my eyebrows and braced my hands on my hips. "Mitch, what is going on?"

"Nothing. Nothing's going on." Mitch murmured something to the bird and it danced along the perch. "Aunt Christine has been up for too long and doesn't know what she's saying. She was so worn out, she could hardly stand up."

We'd been married long enough that I could tell Mitch was . . . well, not exactly hiding something . . . more like avoiding the topic.

"Mitch, tell me what's going on. I know you're not that interested in birds. Talk to me. Tell me what happened at Grandpa Franklin's."

Mitch straightened up and gazed at me intently for a moment, his brown eyes serious. "I'll tell you what happened, but you have to promise you won't blow it out of proportion and overreact."

I frowned as his words stung. "Me? Overreact?"

"Yes, you."

"I don't overreact—"

"There was the time we realized that we'd both given Nathan a dose of Tylenol before bed. And what about when you found out the little girl in Livvy's class had been teasing her about her hair?"

"Mitch! You were worried about those things, too. You're the one who called poison control," I shot back, but I could see a hint of a smile in his expression.

"And you're the one who wanted to confront the mom at Back to School Night." He was smiling now as he said, "That would have been bad, you have to admit."

"Yeah, she probably would have punched me." That mom—I later learned the teachers referred to her as The Mom From Hell—had quite a reputation at school. She'd intentionally run into the other person's car when she got cut off in the carpool line, and she'd thrown a stapler at a student teacher. "Or at least taken a swing at me with that suitcase of a purse she carries."

This was just like Mitch, using humor to diffuse my irritation. I shook my head at him. "Okay, you've made your point. I do over-react, *occasionally*," I allowed, "but I won't now." I perched on the flowery seat cushion of a wicker chair beside the couch, where Mitch had dropped down. I noticed the bird was gnawing at a string of blocks hanging inside the cage. There was a bell on the end of the toy that jangled in the silence as Mitch gathered his thoughts.

"Aunt Christine was talking like that at Grandpa Franklin's house, wasn't she?" I said slowly. "All that about being sorry and she didn't mean to . . . do something. And you—and your dad, I bet—bundled her out of there as fast as you could before that really sharp detective could pick up on it."

Mitch shifted forward to the edge of the soft couch, which seemed to be swallowing him. He rearranged a few of the frothy lace throw pillows behind his back, then said, "When I went in the house, Dad and Aunt Christine were at the table in the kitchen. The detective was with them, taking notes, asking questions. Aunt Christine seemed okay. A little shell-shocked, maybe, but she was answering the questions. Anyway, I went over and sat down. The detective—what was her name?—Kal-something?" Mitch pulled a business card out of his back pocket. "Kalra. Detective Kalra. She was taking Aunt Christine through what happened."

Mitch paused and I raised my eyebrows. "What did she say? I still haven't heard all the details."

"Aunt Christine said she went to check on Grandpa Franklin after the storm died down, sometime after midnight. When she got there, he was unresponsive and she called nine-one-one. She didn't look around the house, so she doesn't know if the window in the back bedroom was broken before they went to the hospital, or after."

"The window was broken?" I asked. "Aunt Nanette said it was open."

Mitch adjusted a lace pillow under his elbow as he said, "Well, it's definitely broken. Glass and water all over the floor. I saw it."

"If there's water everywhere, that would mean it was broken before Aunt Christine got there. It would have happened sometime during the storm."

"No, Dad said it rained again early this morning, too. So it could have happened after the ambulance took them to the hospital. Anyway, Detective Kalra was focused on Dad, asking him about Grandpa Franklin and if they'd ever had any problems with vandalism before. That's when I noticed Aunt Christine wasn't at the table. She was wandering around the living room. She stopped in front of Grandpa Franklin's chair and stared at it for at least a minute and then she started mumbling. I don't know what happened to her—she just lost it."

"So looking at Grandpa Franklin's chair upset her?" The bird let out a loud screech and rocked from side to side. "He spent most of his day in that chair, right?" I spoke louder as the bird continued to squawk. "Maybe that's when it hit her. That he was gone."

"Could be," Mitch agreed, raising his voice over the bird's squawks and whistles.

"But that doesn't explain why she's talking about being sorry—" I broke off. "What is wrong with that bird? He's going to wake up Aunt Christine. Should we cover him up? I don't see a cover."

Mitch extracted himself from the couch. "Here, we can use my jacket." As I stood up, a movement through the front window caught my eye. The sun was going down quickly, casting long shadows across the driveway. In the fading light, a man was walking toward the house.

"Hey, do you know him?" I asked, because I didn't recognize the man, but there were plenty of relatives that I'd only met once or twice and they wouldn't look familiar to me.

"No," Mitch said. We could hear the man's footsteps as he came up the steps and across the porch.

The bird was now fluttering its wings and screeching double-time. The doorknob below the dead bolt moved slightly as someone twisted it, then we could faintly hear the rattle of keys.

"He's coming inside," I said, and realized I was whispering.

Mitch struggled to get his jacket off, which was hung up on one of his rolled-up sleeves. He finally yanked his arm out of the sleeve. I grabbed the other side and helped him strip it off. "What should we do?" I asked. The bird was flittering around the cage, shrieking at full volume. The knob shook as a key was inserted. The small lock in the center twisted.

"I don't know, but since Aunt Christine thought someone broke into Grandpa Franklin's house, this doesn't feel right to me," Mitch said, glancing around. Was he looking for something to defend us with, a weapon? Unless we were going to pelt the man with ruffled pillows, we were out of luck. I reached in my pocket for my cell phone, but realized it was in my purse, which I'd dropped on the snack bar when we walked inside. Mitch picked up a floor lamp. "Phone," I hissed to Mitch. "Give me your phone."

He pulled his phone out of the carrier clipped to his belt and tossed it to me, then yanked the lamp's cord out of the plug and advanced on the door as the dead bolt swung from horizontal to vertical. I was already punching numbers and backing toward Aunt Christine's door when the front door opened and Mitch raised the lamp.

A small man in his late fifties opened the door. "Christy—," he called out, then stopped with one foot inside and one foot outside the door as soon as he saw Mitch. The man had a washed-out quality about him and looked like he'd fit right in with the folks in the turn-of-the-century photos on the wall. Maybe it was his clothes, a white long-sleeved shirt, brown tie, and brown dress pants, or maybe it was the way his sparse gray hair was parted and pressed down to his skull. I'm not sure why I had that impression, but with his monochrome clothes, round glasses, and thin, receding hairline, he didn't look threatening at all.

Mitch must have felt the same way because he set the lamp down and said, "Can I help you?"

As if he found floor-lamp-wielding men every time he opened a door, the man said, "You must be Mitch. I recognize you from the pictures of the family reunion. I'm Roy Martin, a friend of Christine's." He stepped inside, closed the door, and extended his hand to Mitch. "So good to meet you." It wasn't just Roy's soft, rolling drawl that indicated he was a Southerner. His manners and his instant friendliness marked him as being from the South, too. The bird continued to flap and squawk, but not as frantically as before. "Calm down, Einstein. I'll talk to you in a minute," Roy called, and the bird stopped making noise and rocked back and forth on its perch.

Roy walked over to me. "You must be Ellie. Christine says your children are delightful," he said as he shook my hand.

"Oh, well, thank you," I said, surprised that Aunt Christine had been able to sort out which kids had belonged to us at the reunion. Roy glanced back at the kitchen and then to the closed bedroom door. "Is Christine here? I came as soon as I heard."

"She is, but she's sleeping. She was up all night," I said, not sure if Roy knew only about Grandpa Franklin's death or if he knew about the police investigation as well.

"Poor thing. She's probably done in. I can stay here, if you folks have something you need to do."

Before I could reply, the bedroom door opened. Aunt Christine looked bleary-eyed and slightly confused. Her hair was flattened to her scalp on one side and she had a crease across one cheek from sleep. "I heard voices," she said, then saw Roy, and her face crumpled into tears.

Roy opened his arms. "Darlin', I'm so sorry."

She flew across the room to him and he closed his arms tightly around her.

I glanced at Mitch with raised eyebrows.

"Looks like Aunt Gwen doesn't need to come over. I'll give her a call."

"Do you think we'll be able to get to her car?" I asked as we pulled way from Aunt Christine's house.

"Dad said it shouldn't be a problem," Mitch said as he followed the curve of the road. The van's headlights cut into the night and lit up the trees and undergrowth lining the side of the road. We'd left Aunt Christine and Roy a few moments after they'd embraced. I wasn't actually sure they were aware we'd left. We were on our way to pick up Aunt Christine's car and bring it back to her. We'd left Roy and Aunt Christine sitting on the couch. With his arm around her shoulders, she had been recounting the events of the day while daubing at her eyes with a tissue. She'd been speaking in full, coherent sentences and I felt okay about leaving her.

"What did you think of Roy? He's not at all what I expected."

"How did you picture him?" Mitch asked. In the light from the dashboard, I could see a slight grin on his face. "George Clooney, only older?"

"No," I laughed. "It's just the way everyone described him . . . I guess I was picturing someone kind of like Ricardo Montalban. Someone suave and debonair and . . . I don't know . . . with more hair." I hadn't realized I'd formed any sort of idea of what Aunt Christine's beau would look like, but when I'd seen him, I'd realized how different my imagined picture was compared to reality.

Mitch laughed and said, "Well, it's obvious that Aunt Christine has fallen for him, hair or no hair."

"He seems to feel the same way about her. And he has a key! I wonder if anyone else in the family knows how close they are."

Mitch shrugged. "No clue," he said as we turned onto the gravel drive. It was a good thing he was driving because I would have missed the turn in the darkness. Mitch slowed at the curve in the driveway, but this time it was empty of extra cars. He parked in front of the garage.

"Where's the yellow tape? Wouldn't they leave that up?" I asked as I twisted around to check each side of the house. As my eyes adjusted to the blackness around the house, I could see it was all gone. "It's kind of weird," I said, scanning the empty yard, driveway, and porch. "A few hours ago, this place was crawling with people and now it's deserted."

"I guess the police are done. It must have been the storm that broke the window," Mitch said as he opened his car door. "Let me check and see if Aunt Christine's car is in the garage."

I climbed out and followed him, flicking through the keys on Aunt Christine's key ring, looking to see if there was anything that looked like a key to the side door of the garage, in case the car was in there. I glanced around the gloomy yard. There was no moonlight because the clouds still hung thick and heavy across the sky. With the porch light off and all the windows in the house dark, the yard was a sea of deep blackness. It felt late and I wanted to get back to the kids and see how their swim went and if they were tired. They were probably starving by now if they'd been swimming. Everything that had happened during this crazy day couldn't override the mom schedule in my head. Baths, bedtimes, meals, and even snack times were ingrained in my schedule.

I picked up my pace, so we could drop off her car and get back to Mitch's parents' house. As we approached the garage, I said, "I thought he used it for storage. Last time I talked to your mom on the phone, she said something about how they needed to clean out Grandpa Franklin's garage this spring and have a huge sale to get rid of all the extra stuff he had in there."

Mitch peered into one of the small windows on the side. "No, not in here. Man, cleaning that thing out is going to be a job."

"It's probably around on the other side of the house. There's a cleared area over there by the kitchen door." We turned and re-traced our steps and Mitch said, "Let me have the keys. If the screen is unlocked, I'm going to turn on the porch light so it won't be pitch black."

I handed them over and quickly followed him up the steps. There was no way I was hanging around the yard by myself. The porch swing creaked on its hinges. There was a flicker of movement on the edge of the porch. I squinted in the dimness and I could just make out the faint outline of a fat yellow tabby cat as it sprung lightly off the porch railing. It padded across the driveway and disappeared into the night. "Must be a stray," Mitch said. "Grandpa Franklin didn't have a cat." He opened the screen and braced it against his shoulder as he tried a few keys. He found the right key, opened the door, and flicked on the porch light.

A shriek sounded from inside the house.

Ellie Avery's Tips for Preserving Family Treasures

As you make your game plan for organizing family memorabilia, two important things to consider are:

- Accessibility—how often will you need or want to access the material? If you're putting away a selection of papers and certificates that you plan to hand off to your children when they leave home, you probably won't need to get to the items more than a few times a year. Store them in an out-of-the-way place like a high closet shelf. On the other hand, if you're tracing your family tree, you probably want your genealogical records within easy reach.
- Preservation—papers, photos, and fabrics last longer if preserved correctly and stored in a dry, low-humidity area.

Chapter
Four

I jumped backward, banging into the screen with my shoulder. Mitch flicked on an inside light, flooding the entry area with light.

"Gawd, you scared me to death. Mitch Avery, what are you doing here?" The female voice was coming from the far side of the room, which was still in shadow.

"Felicity?" Mitch asked, advancing into the living room. He found another light and turned it on. I stepped inside the front door, which opened into a living area that extended all the way across the house to a row of windows along the back wall.

I blinked a few times in the brightness and saw Felicity's compact, petite form, which her new pixie haircut only emphasized, emerge from the galley kitchen that ran along the left side of the room. She hurried between the mix of mission-style furniture and recliners in the living room and enveloped Mitch in a quick hug, then shifted to embrace me. I raised my eyebrows at Mitch over her shoulder. I'd never seen her so affectionate.

"Ellie, how are you?" she asked heartily.

"Fine." I rubbed my shoulder. "Now that my heart rate is back to normal."

"I came by to check on Buddy," Felicity said.

Mitch frowned. "Who?"

"The cat. He was sleeping on the porch swing. You probably scared him away."

Mitch said, "Grandpa Franklin didn't have a cat."

"No, Buddy dropped by to see him every day or so," Felicity said breezily. "I wanted to make sure Buddy hadn't been shut up in the house with all the comings and goings. He lives with a woman about three houses away, but he's an outdoor cat and if he doesn't come home, she worries." There was a smug undertone in her words that indicated she was the one in the know about Grandpa Franklin's life and we were the interlopers here.

She linked her arm through mine and tried to turn me back to the front door. She was strong—her job as a fitness instructor involved several hours of teaching aerobic, weight training, martial arts and yoga classes each day—but I had a height advantage. Okay, I had a weight advantage, too, which wasn't due solely to my extra inches. I knew she had more lean muscle mass than me, but I definitely had more, er—total mass. I braced my boots on the large braided rug that covered most of the hardwood floor. In the few seconds it had taken her to cross the room, I'd noticed a few interesting details. She was dressed in a black microfiber jacket and black jeans. There was a flashlight on the kitchen counter beside a brown grocery bag and a pile of opened newspapers. Two cabinet doors were open as well. She widened her green eyes. "What are you two doing here? I didn't even know y'all were in town."

"Obviously," Mitch said as he strolled into the kitchen. Felicity tugged on my arm again. I didn't budge. I was sure she could have used some of her martial arts moves to get me outside, but I guess she wasn't willing to go quite that far to get us out of the house. Mitch casually peered inside the bag and made a tsking sound. "Robbing the dead already, Felicity?" he said as he pulled out several newspaper-wrapped bundles and peeled the paper away to reveal pink glass serving bowls and platters.

Felicity yanked her arm away from mine and advanced on Mitch. "Those are mine. Grandpa Franklin wanted me to have them."

Mitch nodded and continued to remove bundles from the paper sack and unwrap them. "That so," he said, mildly.

I watched the interchange with interest. Felicity was not a person I wanted to cross, but Mitch seemed unaware of her darting around him like an angry wasp. "Be careful with that piece. Don't break it—it's valuable." She had quite a temper and could hold a grudge forever, something I'd discovered at the reunion. How could he have ever dated her? I suppose her diminutive frame might bring out the protective instincts in some guys, but Felicity was about as helpless as a Komodo dragon. Mitch managed to keep her hands away from the dishes and snapped a few quick pictures with his cell phone camera. "There," he said and began rewrapping the glass-ware. "Just in case."

"Just in case what?" Felicity demanded.

"I'm sure you'll take good care of all this. But if there's any question, any concern about where it is, or what it looked like, or how many pieces there are . . . well, we've got photos of what you already have."

Felicity gaped at him for a moment, then sputtered, "But, I wasn't taking—I mean, it's mine." I had to hand it to Mitch. His matter-of-fact tone was probably the only way to deal with her.

"Of course," Mitch said as he replaced the last bundle in the bag and picked it up. "I'll just help you carry this out to your car. It's around the side, isn't it?" He took her elbow and guided her to the kitchen door. As he went outside, I heard him say, "Don't worry, Ellie and I will lock up."

I could still hear her protesting as Mitch escorted her outside. His calmness didn't rub off on her. If anything, it was like throwing grease on a fire. She was sputtering and protesting more loudly than before.

I went to the far end of the room and began closing the curtains. I moved into the kitchen and pulled the shade that was over the sink. I took a quick look in a few cabinets, but didn't see any gaping holes in them, so apparently Felicity had just begun when we arrived. I ran my hand over the newspaper that was still on the counter and looked around the house. It was so sad and quiet. I folded the news-paper stack and shoved it in the trash can, then went back into the living room, my gaze on a large recliner. I'd only visited this house a few times but nothing had changed—the same furniture, the same arrangement, the same framed pictures of family scattered over the tabletops.

I walked over to Grandpa Franklin's recliner and frowned. Something here had bothered Aunt Christine. Something had caused her to descend into incoherent mumbles and that made Mitch and his dad so concerned that they'd bundled her out of here as fast as they could. The deep tufts, padded arms, and thick cushions were covered in a dark brown fabric, which had a bit of a sheen on the arms of the chair from years of use. A lightweight brown throw dangled from one arm, its fringe brushing the braided rug on the floor. An end table on the other side held everything Grandpa Franklin could possibly need: a stack of books, his reading glasses, a mug, the remote control, a notepad and pencil, the phone, and a narrow plastic pillbox marked with the days of the week. A floor lamp perched behind the chair within easy reach.

My throat prickled as I looked at the reading glasses and the books. I swallowed and blinked a few times to clear my watery eyes. It did look like he'd just stepped into the kitchen and would return in a minute. Maybe seeing the empty recliner with all his familiar bits and pieces around it had brought home to Aunt Christine that he was gone. I could picture him clearly—his mass of white hair, still thick despite his age, his bushy eyebrows and his slightly watery brown eyes. By the time I met Mitch, Grandpa Franklin was somewhat stooped and walked with an uneven gait. He was one of those people who had the gift of storytelling. He could spin a story, even something as simple as a trip to the store, into a tale that held everyone's attention and had us all laughing at the end. The stories I'd enjoyed the most were the ones from his past—scrapes he'd gotten into as a kid and his time in the military.

I walked over and shifted the books so I could see their covers. A new biography of Thomas Newton was on the top. A western, a memoir, and a mystery were sandwiched between another biography and a history of the fall of the Berlin Wall. The notepad was blank. Mitch returned to the room and came to stand beside me. "When I think of him, I always think of his stories," I said. "Especially that one about driving to Macon."

That made Mitch grin. "Yeah, he really had you going there for a few minutes, didn't he?" Grandpa Franklin had told me he drove from Montgomery to Macon when he was fourteen because he wanted to see his uncle who lived there.

"Well, that was when I first met him. I was an easy target, I guess. I wised up after that." Grandpa Franklin had a huge stock of true, fascinating stories, but he'd also been able to tell a whopper of a tall tale with a straight face that always sucked in unsuspecting people, like me.

"I never was sure about that Will Rogers story. Did he really meet him on a train to California?"

"I think that one was true."

I looked over the scene again, the chair and the end table scattered with items. "I wonder if there's something specific here that bothered Aunt Christine?"

Mitch studied the chair and table and shook his head. I saw his jaw clench. I wrapped my arm around his waist. "It is kind of hard to look at without seeing him there, isn't it?" I said.

Mitch nodded, then cleared his throat. "Maybe that was it—the emotions overwhelmed her."

"Could be," I said, resting my head on his shoulder. "But why would she be sorry? She took good care of him. Remember how hard she worked at the reunion to make sure he didn't overexert himself in the heat and how she made sure he kept drinking water so he wouldn't get dehydrated?"

I felt his shrug. "I don't know. It really doesn't make sense." He squeezed me closer for a moment, then said, "Come on, let's close the rest of the curtains and get out of here."

On the opposite side of the house from the kitchen, there was a short hallway that led to two bedrooms, a bathroom, and a staircase to a third bedroom in the half story upstairs. Mitch took the master bedroom and I went into the extra bedroom at the back of the house.

I could tell right away that this was where Aunt Christine sometimes slept. There were little feminine touches around the room— lace throw pillows on the bed, a comb and curling iron along with makeup on the dresser, and a flowered robe and gown hanging on the back of the closet door.

It was also the room with the broken window. A rectangle of particle board covered the bottom portion of the window where the lowest panes of glass would have been. The floor had been mopped up and the furniture had been moved to give easier access to the window. As I pulled the curtains closed, I could see that the window locks were simple crescent locks, the kind that you pushed open or closed with your thumb. Definitely not the most burglarproof locks. The window that was boarded up was locked and I couldn't see any damage to the lock itself or the sash around it. It didn't look like anyone had forced their way inside. I wondered why Aunt Christine had automatically called the police when she saw the broken window.

I heard Mitch trotting down the stairs and I met him in the hallway. As we made our way back through the house, turning off lights, I asked, "So Aunt Christine's car is out back?"

"Yes," Mitch said as he clicked on the front porch light, then closed and locked the front door. "Let's go out through the kitchen."

"You handled Felicity really well," I said.

"If there's one thing I've learned in the military, it's that there's only one way to fight stealth . . . more stealth."

"Did she have anything else in her car?"

We walked outside into the cool, dark night. "No. I think she was just getting started when we arrived. I'm surprised she didn't hear us drive up."

The back porch light threw a weak puddle of light over a white VW Golf parked close to the house. "She was on the other side of the house, so she wouldn't have seen the headlights, and if she was wrapping things in newsprint—that can be noisy." I'd done enough packing and unpacking of newsprint bundles that I knew all too well the racket it could make. It was enough to wake a sleeping baby or, in some cases, drown out a temper tantrum.

"I suppose," Mitch said as he waited for me to unlock the car and get in. "It's a stick shift—do you want me to drive it?"

"Are you kidding?" I said as I turned the key. "It's like riding a bicycle—you never forget."

"Okay, I'll see you at Aunt Christine's house," he said as he closed the car door.

"Wait, Mitch," I said, rolling down the window. "What kind of car did Felicity have?"

"It was an Eclipse, I think. Small, sporty."

"What color was it?"

"Red. Why?"

"Oh, no reason. Just wondering," I said, rolling up the window. "See you in a few."

I heard the clank of silverware and smelled bacon. I rolled over and glanced around the dark room. Everything was in the wrong place—the door, the window, even the furniture was wrong, I thought groggily. Then I remembered we were in the guest room at Mitch's parents' house. I listened, but didn't hear any noises from the rooms down the hall from us. Nathan and his cousin Jack were sleeping on sleeping bags on an inflatable mattress in Mitch's old room, which had been transformed into an office. I wasn't sure, but I think they'd smuggled in a rather large supply of Legos shortly before bedtime. Livvy was in the "blue room," a room decorated in blue toile. From the way her eyes lit up when she walked in the room, I had a feeling she was going to want blue toile in her room back home. She was sharing the room with her tomboy cousin, Madison. I wasn't sure if they'd get along since Livvy's current favorite color was purple and she was very interested in reading, but we'd come back from Grandpa Franklin's house and found them playing an intense game of Battleship. I didn't hear shouting or giggling, so I burrowed back into the pillows after checking the clock. Mitch was still breathing heavily, but he shifted toward me.

It felt weird, trying to go back to sleep again at six-thirty in the morning. If we were at home at this time on a Thursday morning, I'd already be in the kitchen fixing breakfast and packing Livvy's lunch for school. But we weren't at home. We were here in a weird state of suspended animation. We'd spent yesterday, Wednesday, receiving flowers and food while we waited for word from Detective Kalra about the status of the investigation into Grandpa Franklin's death and the break-in. Until the detective received the word from the county coroner about whether the death was natural or suspicious, everything was on hold. Those exact words were not mentioned, but they seemed to hover in the air, like the trace of wood smoke from the fireplace or the aroma of freshly brewed coffee that came from the kitchen all day because Caroline kept making pot after pot for the visitors who dropped by and the family who lingered, waiting for news. Caroline hadn't attended the awards ceremony yesterday, either. She'd sent an employee from her office to accept the award, instead.

I squeezed my eyes shut and tried to banish thoughts of the casseroles that had filled up the refrigerator and the sound of the phone ringing constantly with curious friends and neighbors wanting to know the day and time of the funeral. Caroline and Bill had managed to put everyone off with vague assurances that they would get the word out as soon as something was decided. I'd even heard Caroline putting off the local obituary writer. Her tone of voice had never changed as she explained that the family was still debating which funeral home they were going to use, so they couldn't put anything in the paper yet, but her face had looked stiff and agonized as she spoke the words. She'd hung up the phone and paused a moment with her hand on her collarbone. Uncle Kenny had said, "Don't see why you're even trying to keep it quiet, Caroline. You know the word will get out."

A steely look came into her eyes and she said, "Kenny, you know as well I as do that I'm doing the right thing."

Uncle Kenny was not a man to let anyone have the last word, but Caroline had sent him a scorching look and he'd closed his half-open mouth.

I sighed and opened my eyes. It was no use. I wasn't going to get back to sleep. I gazed at the ceiling fan and wondered again about the secrecy. Smarr wasn't a tiny town, so it was possible that their friends wouldn't find out about the investigation, but if it went on any longer, the news would spread. What I couldn't figure out was why it mattered if people knew about the investigation. Aunt Christine and Caroline had been back over to Grandpa Franklin's house yesterday and confirmed that nothing (except the Depression glass) was missing. And the word "murder" hadn't been mentioned again by anyone associated with the investigation. What was there to hide? Aunt Christine's weird remarks? She hadn't said anything else like the mumbled words I'd overheard and, interestingly, Roy wasn't with her yesterday. I'd expected him to be glued to her side, but she had spent the day with us, waiting for news about the autopsy. *Autopsy* was another taboo word. When it was mentioned, it was in low tones. The family hadn't requested an autopsy. The order had come from the county coroner to see if there was foul play involved in his death. We didn't even know how long the process would take.

I gently pushed back the covers and eased out of bed. Mitch continued to sleep like a kid after an exhausting day on the playground. I think I could have been slamming doors and shouting and he would have slept right through all the noise, but I moved carefully because I didn't want to wake the kids. I found my workout pants, a T-shirt, and a sweatshirt in my suitcase. I slipped into the clothes in the bathroom and pulled my hair back in a ponytail. I'd eaten so much yesterday and not really done anything except sit around and talk to the adults and occasionally run interference with the kids. I could use a brisk walk around the neighborhood.

The guest room was at the back of the house next to the sunroom, which opened to the backyard. The living room and sunroom were empty. A platter of bacon and pancakes sat on the long kitchen table beside a bowl of chopped melon and a stack of plates. The Realtor of the Year plaque that Caroline's employee had accepted on her behalf yesterday was sitting on the counter. The awards banquet, the main reason for our trip, had been pushed aside and was barely thought of now. A note tucked under a row of coffee mugs read, "Had to run to the office. Help yourself to breakfast. Juice and milk in the fridge." I recognized the elegant cursive as Caroline's handwriting. I didn't see Bill, or anyone else, but most of the family had gone home to their own houses last night since almost everyone else lived in the area. Only Mitch's older sister Julia and her husband, Wes, Jack and Madison's parents, had stayed overnight here with us.

I scribbled my own note under Caroline's and headed through the French doors into the sunroom. I stepped onto the deck and heard the gentle ripple of water from the pool. So that's where Bill was. The gray clouds had moved out overnight and now the sun was sparkling on the wake flowing out behind him as he cut neatly through the water. He did a smooth flip turn and I decided not to interrupt him. He was pretty focused. I set off around the house, my breathing sending out wispy white puffs in the chilly air.

The neighborhood was quiet, my quick footfalls the only sound besides the occasional car as it passed me. I normally worked out several times a week with the Stroller Brigade, a group of moms who met for a morning power walk interspersed with strength and toning routines. I wasn't about to stop and do push-ups or squats, since I was by myself—I would have felt silly—but I could keep my pace up. Without the stroller, I felt light and fast as I strode around the neighborhood.

By the time I circled back to the house, I was breathing hard and had taken off the sweatshirt and tied it around my waist. The sun was higher and the frosty bite was receding from the air. I slowed my pace to cool down, but then I spotted an unfamiliar car, a dark four-door sedan, parked behind our van in the already full circular drive. I picked up the pace again because it had the unmistakable look of an unmarked police car.

As I walked up the driveway, I saw Detective Kalra walking along the curve of the drive. I hurried up to her and asked, "Is there any news?"

She paused and looked at me for a moment before answering, as if she was trying to place who I was. "You're the Averys' daughter-in-law?"

"Yes, Ellie Avery," I said, not sure if I should put my hand out to shake hers or not.

She watched me for another second or two and I got the feeling that she was one of those people who very rarely said anything rashly or flippantly. She nodded and said, "I've informed your father-in-law that Mr. Franklin's body has been released to the funeral home and burial can proceed."

She made a move to open the car door, but I asked, "What did the autopsy find?"

"It was a natural death, a stroke," she said with the same careful, measured delivery.

"So what does that mean for the investigation?" I asked, and she tilted her head and narrowed her eyes slightly.

"It's closed. No evidence of an intruder was found, or even of a break-in. The damage to the window most likely occurred during the storm."

I was cooling down from the workout and the air felt icy on my arms. I untied the sweatshirt and slipped it over my head. "So . . . there's no sign of foul play, then?"

She opened her car door and rested her arm along the top of it. "No, there's no sign." The intensity of her examination of me went up a notch. It was like a spotlight had suddenly zeroed in on me. "Do you have something you'd like to tell me? Or perhaps your aunt has something to add?"

"No, I just wanted to know what had happened," I said, thinking that she must have picked up on Aunt Christine's strange shift in behavior.

"Then, in that case, you have your answer." She turned to slide into the car, then stopped and looked back at me. "I know about you—that you're a . . . well, I'll call you a tipster. You like to get involved in police investigations. Refrain from that while you're here. There's nothing to indicate that this situation is anything more than a natural death that happened to occur on the night of a severe thunderstorm. But if there's anything else, anything the family is trying to cover up, I'll find it. If you know something, you might as well tell me now."

Was she threatening me? And calling me a busybody, too? I felt my cheeks flush. I took a breath and reminded myself that she didn't seem like the type of person to throw words out without thinking. Her statements had a purpose—to throw me off guard and get me riled up. "I have passed along important information I have found out to the police in the past." I said, trying to match her measured tone.

Her face broke into a grin. "Oh, I'd say you were more than a mere informant. 'Instrumental' was the word I heard, if I remember right."

I ignored that statement. She was just letting me know she knew about my past involvement in a few police cases. And if she thought I was truly a busybody, she was assuming that if I knew anything further about Grandpa Franklin's death, I'd be dying to share it. "You just said the investigation is closed," I countered, hopefully taking us away from the subject of me.

"But it can always be reopened." She handed me her business card before she sat down in the driver's seat and buckled her seat belt. "Keep that in mind. And you might want to pass that fact along to any other family members who would be interested."

Chapter
Five

I entered the house through the sunroom and walked into a bee-hive of activity. Mitch's dad had showered and changed and now stood in the kitchen rolling out biscuits. Mitch's mom had also just arrived back and was putting her coat away in the hall closet. The kids were zipping around the house like miniature meteorites. They were blurs of bed-head hair and pajamas as they dodged into the room, then out again. The television was announcing the five-day outlook, all suns and cool temperatures, while Mitch looked on with the remote control in one hand and a glass of juice in the other.

"There you are," he said, tossing the remote on a chair and walk-ing over to me. He planted a kiss on my cheek, then whispered, "No fair disappearing on me this morning. It's no fun waking up alone."

"Tell me about it," I said. "I was definitely alone when I woke up this morning."

"I had to break up a pillow fight at six-fifty."

"Oh, that's terrible. I feel so sorry for you," I said. "Doesn't look like you would have gotten to sleep much longer, anyway," I said, nodding to the activity in the kitchen.

"Sad, but true. The kids have already eaten. They've found a box of toys that my mom keeps in the guest room." The teasing smile dropped off of Mitch's face. "Did you hear the news? The investiga-tion's closed and Grandpa Franklin's body has been released. Dad's called everyone and they're on their way over here now. He's already been on the phone to the funeral home."

"Yes, I saw Detective Kalra as I was coming inside," I said. "Did you get the impression she wasn't . . . satisfied with the autopsy?"

"No. She was straightforward. Told us the results and that the case was closed, then she left."

"So she didn't have any more questions for anyone?" I asked, glancing around the room, looking to see if Aunt Christine was here, but I didn't see her.

"No. What are you saying?"

I shrugged. "When I talked to her, she hinted that the case could be reopened."

"Why?"

"I don't know why. She said if anyone knew anything else—"

"Ellie!" Mitch's dad called as he slid a tray of biscuits into the oven. "Come on in here and have some breakfast. The grits are coming right up."

"Great, you know how I love those grits."

"Bill, stop teasing her," Caroline admonished, and shoved the platter of bacon and pancakes at me. "Help yourself, dear." It was a running family joke. On my first visit to Smarr, Mitch's dad had pretended to be shocked when I told him I'd never eaten grits. "Well, you can't marry Mitch until you've had some grits," he'd declared, and said he'd cook some for me himself. Caroline had rolled her eyes and told me "to pay him no mind." She had leaned closer and said, "You do see what you're getting yourself into, don't you? He's always like this. And he's just *one* member of the family."

Caroline looked better today than she had for the last few days. She had on her full complement of jewelry—thin sliver hoop earrings that matched her silver necklace, bracelet, and ring. In her black sweater and herringbone pants with low-heeled pumps, she looked every inch the successful Realtor.

"I'll clean up first," I said. I didn't want the whole family to see me without makeup and in sweaty workout clothes. By the time I'd showered and changed into jeans and a white turtleneck sweater, the kitchen and living room were crowded and opinions were flying in a lively discussion. I filled a plate—no grits—and sat down at the table next to Aunt Nanette, amazed at the transformation in the atmosphere of the house. Yesterday it had been tense and quiet, today it was noisy and . . . relieved, I realized. Bill had the coffee pot in his hand and was walking around the room, refilling cups.

"The Twenty-third Psalm," Aunt Nanette declared. "That has to be one of the readings."

"Yes, but that's so short," Aunt Christine countered. She was alone again today and I wondered again about her relationship with Roy and if she was deliberately keeping it from the family. She sat in the living room, a wrinkled tissue in her hand. She had on a faded baby blue sweatshirt, but she was wearing her boot-cut jeans. I did a double take at her boots. They were at least two inches high. I avoided heels whenever I could, but if she wanted to wear them, then that was fine by me. I was proud of her for branching out and trying new things.

Felicity was sitting at the kitchen island, breaking off pieces of a croissant and scattering flaky bits all over the counter. Felicity's antics hadn't escaped the family's notice, but in the uncertainty surrounding the investigation of Grandpa Franklin's death and the break-in at his house, they'd avoided an all-out confrontation with her. "What about one of those letters from Addison McClure? He certainly talked about them enough and she's, you know, famous," Felicity said.

I shook my head, "I'm still surprised that's true. I thought that was another one of his tall tales."

Bill paused, coffee pot poised over Aunt Nanette's mug. "Oh, no. It was true. She knew everyone around here back then and babysat for most everybody in Smarr."

"Wow," I said, trying to picture one of the world's most well-known yet reclusive authors changing diapers. Nope, I couldn't do it. The only thing that came to mind when I thought of Addison McClure was *Deep Down Things*, a coming-of-age story about a young girl, set in the South during the Civil Rights era.

"I can't wait to read those letters," Felicity said as she ripped off another piece of croissant and stuck it in her mouth.

Aunt Nanette lowered her chin and sent Felicity a disapproving stare. "You know he always said those were private letters and that he'd—"

"Take them to the grave with him. I know, I know," Felicity snapped back. "But he's not here. Those letters are important. Addison McClure is famous. People want to know more about her."

Aunt Christine sucked in a breath. "Felicity, I cannot believe you're talking like this. Of course, we will respect what he wanted. It doesn't matter what people *want* to know. Sometimes they don't need to know everything."

"It's her own fault," Felicity said, sullenly. "If she'd give a few interviews or write some new books, people wouldn't be so crazy to find out more about her. You saw the ruckus last year when all those news crews came to town for the book festival." Felicity seemed to sense that she didn't have—and wasn't going to win—the approval of most of the room, so she swiveled toward me. "It was the fiftieth anniversary of the publication of her first book. She was the guest of honor at Book Daze that year, and would she give a speech? No. Even with all those camera crews hanging on her every word, all she came up with was two sentences. Two sentences and she was done!" Felicity's eyebrows were up near her hairline. "I mean, can you imagine? All those people wanting to talk to you, put you on TV, and she mutters 'thank you,' and walks away."

I was sure Felicity would love to be in the spotlight. In fact, she'd be perfect for one of those reality shows. She'd thrive on the attention and act outrageously, too.

Bill said firmly, "We will abide by what Dad wanted. We're not discussing the letters now."

Felicity shrugged, "Doesn't matter, anyway. He always said he'd take them to his grave, so he probably burned them or something stupid like that."

"Felicity," Bill said sharply, "that's enough. Caroline, where were we?"

"The readings," she said.

"Wait." Aunt Christine pulled at the neckline of her blue sweatshirt as she said, "We've got to do something about his casket. I was there during his prearrangement meeting and of course he picked out the cheapest one—everyone's going to think we're cutting corners if we use that casket. We have to upgrade it or it'll be an embarrassment."

Bill leaned against the counter and crossed one scuffed loafer over the other. "Now, Christine, he picked what he wanted. We've got to leave it at that. Be glad he didn't pick a plain pine box—that's what he threatened to do, you know. He didn't see the point of spending a lot of money on the casket."

"That's true," Aunt Nanette confirmed, her long nose bobbing up and down as she nodded. "Always said he wasn't actually going to be in it, so what did it matter?"

"Not in it?" Felicity said, shocked. "Of course, he's going to be in it."

"His soul," Aunt Nanette clarified with disdain, and called Queen over to her side. She didn't say it aloud, but her expression clearly conveyed that she thought young people these days were barely worth talking to.

Caroline pressed her lips together and I wondered if she was counting to ten . . . or maybe twenty. Finally, she spoke. "We can't change the casket at this point. If it will make you feel better, we'll have Pastor Davis mention Dad's thrifty ways or something like that. We must finalize the funeral service. We already have 'Amazing Grace' and 'The Old Rugged Cross' for the hymns, which were two of his favorites," Caroline said. "Back to the readings. We need one more."

"I've always been partial to 'Remember,' " Uncle Bud said. He was a rough, tough kind of guy and reminded me of the illustrations of lumberjacks from storybooks. He was tall with broad shoulders and had a heavy brow that jutted out over his eyes. He tended to scowl. Today, his flannel shirt was a blue-and-black plaid and, since it was cold, he had the sleeves down, covering his phoenix tattoo. It was his only concession to the weather. I'd never seen him wear a coat, much less gloves. He hadn't shaved today and stubble covered his face.

"Don't know it," snapped Aunt Nanette, and Queen turned her head to check and make sure she wasn't in trouble.

Uncle Bud, who was leaning against the kitchen countertop holding a mug of coffee, promptly began to quote,

Remember me when I am gone away,
Gone far away into the silent land;
When you can no more hold me by the hand,
Nor I half turn to go, yet turning stay.
Remember me when no more day by day
You tell me of our future that you plann'd:
Only remember me; you understand
It will be late to counsel then or pray.
Yet if you should forget me for a while
And afterwards remember, do not grieve:
For if the darkness and corruption leave
A vestige of the thoughts that once I had,
Better by far you should forget and smile
Than that you should remember and be sad.

He finished, then looked down quickly at his mug and took a sip of coffee. And his eyes, were they glassy? I have to say hearing Uncle Bud quote poetry was about the last thing I'd ever expected, but the way he spoke the words had affected everyone. The room was completely still. The faint chatter from the kids was the only sound.

Caroline cleared her throat and said, "That's lovely, Bud. Would you like to recite that at the funeral?"

He nodded. "Of course."

"Well, that's settled then," Caroline said, and I noticed Aunt Nanette was discreetly wiping the corner of her eye with her napkin. Caroline glanced at the clock and said, "Grisholm's can have the order of service printed for us." She turned to Mitch. "You can drop off the final version and catch up with Dermont, or was it Jake you went to school with? I always get those Grisholm boys mixed up." I looked at Mitch with raised eyebrows.

"It was Dermont," he said. Then he explained to me, "The Grisholm family owns one of the local funeral homes. All their kids work there and I went to school with Dermont."

Caroline said, "Also, you'll need to stop by Grandpa Franklin's house and pick up a tie. Grisholm's called and left a message earlier. They need a tie to go with the suit."

"I forgot the tie?" Aunt Christine said. "I thought I picked one out."

"It didn't make it to the funeral home, so Mitch can take one over there," Caroline said.

"But I'm sure I . . . well, maybe not. I remember coming out of his room with the suit and that was when I noticed the breeze, from the window, you know. After that, it was so confusing."

Aunt Nanette said, "Good grief, Christine. It doesn't matter. They need a tie. We'll get the tie over there."

Aunt Gwen called out, "Oh, that's okay. We took care of it. Grisholm's called us this morning when they didn't get an answer here, so we ran by his house and picked up the tie we gave him for his birthday. We took it to the funeral home. You can mark one thing off your list, Caroline."

Aunt Christine stiffened. "It wasn't that awful one with the football helmets on it, was it? You didn't take that one, did you?"

Aunt Gwen looked a little uncertain. "Well, of course it was. You remember," she said, cajolingly. "Crimson banner and a football."

"Of course I remember it and he's not going to be buried in that tie," Aunt Christine declared. Everyone in the room stopped what they were doing to look at Aunt Christine, whose cheeks were flushed.

Aunt Gwen was the only one who didn't notice how upset Aunt Christine was. "But he liked it. He wore it the very next Sunday and it goes really well with the suit."

"He hated that tie."

"Do you have it mixed up with—"

"No, he hated that tie," Aunt Christine repeated. "But he wore it to be nice. Nice! He did not attend the University of Alabama and he had no interest in your slavish following of their athletic program."

Aunt Gwen looked as if someone had slapped her. "Are you sure . . . ?"

"Yes, I'm sure. I knew him better than anyone else in this room. Don't tell me I didn't. I was the one who spent whole days with him."

Aunt Gwen opened her mouth to interrupt, but there was an inflexibility in Aunt Christine's voice that I'd never heard before. But she had been a teacher. I'm sure she had to be firm with her students. She stood, her gaze scanning the rest of the room as she continued. "Sure, the rest of you'd drop in for an hour or two. Or call to talk for a few minutes, but I was with him every day. I was the one who took him to the doctor and to the grocery store and the library. I knew what he liked and didn't like. And he detested that tie, but he was too much of a gentleman to let you know how he felt. He'll be buried in his favorite blue tie with the yellow stripes. I'll take care of it now," Aunt Christine said as she picked up her purse with trembling fingers and marched out of the room.

"Well," Caroline said, a bit uncertainly. "I guess that's settled."

Aunt Gwen said, "I didn't know . . . I didn't mean . . ."

Uncle Kenny, usually so blustery, was uncharacteristically quiet as he said, "Let it go, honey. Christine deserves to have the last word. She's right. She did know him best."

Caroline looked at Bill. "Do you think someone should go with her . . . make sure she's okay?"

After exchanging a quick glance with Mitch, I hopped up. "I'll go," I said, and dashed out of the room. I wanted to talk to her and this looked like the perfect opportunity to get her alone. It wasn't always easy to have a private conversation with everyone around.

I jogged quickly down the driveway and caught up with her at her car. "Wait, Aunt Christine. Would you like some company?"

She shrugged and unlocked her small white car. I slid into the passenger seat. As she pulled out of the driveway, her hands fluttered over the steering wheel. "I really shouldn't have said that to Gwen. I feel terrible. Oh, my."

"I'm sure Gwen will get over it. Everyone is a little emotional right now," I said. Aunt Gwen was the type of person who'd steamroll over people and didn't even realize what she'd done. Creating that little scene was probably the only way to get through to her.

"Yes, but to say those things . . . I shouldn't have." She sighed. "They don't understand what it's been like taking care of him. It was so hard." Her voice wavered and she swallowed hard. "They didn't want to admit it, but I knew. I knew he wasn't going to last much longer."

"How did you know?" I asked.

"It's hard to put it into words," she said slowly. "He'd changed. His mind . . . I could tell things weren't right. And then when he started talking about Momma and his dead brother . . . well, I just knew. Here we are." She stared at the house for a moment, then bit her lip. "I think it's a good thing you came with me. I'm such a silly old lady. I'm nervous about going in there. Well, best to do what has to be done quickly," she said as she shut off the car and stepped onto the gravel driveway.

She'd parked at the side of the house and we entered through the kitchen. The curtains were still drawn and in the light of day the rooms looked gloomy. She flipped on a light in the kitchen. "I suppose we'd better leave the curtains closed," she said as she moved quickly through the living room and clicked on a table lamp for more light. "I'll just be a moment," she said, and disappeared down the hall to Grandpa Franklin's room. I walked into the living room, studying Grandpa Franklin's chair again. It still looked just the same.

Aunt Christine reappeared with a blue tie and came to stand beside me. "Makes me sad, just looking at it." Something on the floor had caught her attention. "Now, that's not right," she murmured as she leaned down and straightened a stack of books on the lower shelf of the table. She picked up a magazine that had slipped between the table and chair. "And look at this. Who left this out?" She opened a small drawer in the table and froze in place.

I leaned around her shoulder and saw the drawer was a jumble of paper crammed inside. "Oh, this is all wrong," Aunt Christine said as she pulled out several magazines and a newspaper insert with the television schedule. A remote control slipped out of the middle of the pile and thudded to the floor.

She dropped into the recliner and began to straighten the papers, her hands perfectly steady now. "This is just not right. Dad would never have a mess like this in his drawer. He was very tidy."

I reached down and picked up the remote control. "Maybe the police messed it up during their investigation," I said.

"No," she said, shaking her head. "I was here, right at the table in the kitchen, and I watched them. I remember a nice young police lady looking around this room. She had on plastic gloves and she opened this drawer and glanced at the papers, but didn't take anything out. They weren't smashed into the drawer then. And he never kept the remote in there. He was very particular about where everything went." She glanced up at me. "Of course, you know all about that."

I put the remote control down on the tabletop and realized I'd missed something she'd said, "I'm sorry. What did you say?"

"That you'd know something about keeping everything in its place."

"Oh, yes. Right," I said with a smile. Everything In Its Place was the name of my part-time organizing business. Sorting, organizing, and paying attention to detail were integral parts of my life. I looked at the remote control again. "You know, I don't think the remote was in the drawer when Mitch and I came by here the other night."

"No, Dad never put it in the drawer. It was always right there on the corner, so he could reach it easily." She patted the edges of the magazines into line and replaced them. "I imagine someone could have stopped by yesterday and watched TV. Or, Kenny might have watched sports while Gwen was getting that awful tie . . . ," she trailed off uncertainly as she looked around the room. "That's odd," she said. "Look at the couch cushions. They're on backwards. They weren't like that the other day. Would have driven Dad crazy."

"Here, I'll fix them," I said, and went over to switch the cushions around so that the zippers weren't facing out. "There. All done," I said.

"What in the world?" Aunt Christine said. I turned and saw she was running her hands around the cushion of the recliner she'd been sitting in. "It's been slit."

Ellie Avery's Tips for Preserving Family Treasures

Sort and Purge
This step may take some time, but you don't want to think you've finished organizing your family photos and then find another box you've overlooked.
  • Gather all the items you want to organize.
  • Divide the items into groups such as photos, school papers, etc.
  • Begin thinning at this stage, as well. Make separate piles for trash and donate.

Chapter
Six

The recliner had been dissected. There was no other word for it. Someone had taken a sharp blade and very carefully slit the seams in the deep recesses of the chair—under the seat cushion and below the puffy layers that padded the back. All the cuts were small, only about the width of a hand.

I sat back on my heels and put my hands on my hips. "Why would someone slit the covers on the recliner, but be so discreet that you wouldn't be able to tell unless you looked closely?"

"I don't know," Aunt Christine murmured. "It's a good thing the couch cushions had zippered covers or they'd be slit, too, I'm sure. That's why they were turned the wrong way." She was slowly pacing around the room, looking at bookcases. She went in the kitchen and opened cabinet doors. "Someone has been looking around. The coffee filters have been moved and some of the books aren't in alphabetical order."

"Grandpa Franklin always kept them in alphabetical order?"

"By author, yes." Aunt Christine picked up the tie from the recliner and shook it at me. "I bet it was Felicity, looking for those letters. You and Mitch found her here already once. She knows where the key is. Why wouldn't she come back? She wants those letters—thinks they're valuable."

Her words jogged my memory and I thought of the blond jogger who said she'd seen a red car here the night Grandpa Franklin died.

"Oh, I'm going to have to talk to her about this. We cannot have this. It's just plain wrong." Unlike the indignation that bordered on fury she'd shown when talking to Aunt Gwen earlier, now she seemed more annoyed than livid. "That is just like Felicity. So inconsiderate."

"Where are the letters?" I asked as I smoothed the fabric of the seat cover back into place.

Aunt Christine ran one hand over her forehead. "I don't know. No one knows. We tried to talk Dad into returning them to Addison McClure, but he wouldn't. Said he'd do it later. Stubborn does not begin to describe him. It took all the persuasion I had to get him to give up his car, which seemed, at the time, to be the most important battle. Lord knows, we tried, but Dad got agitated every time the letters came up, and we decided to leave it alone. I think he liked having them—said they were a part of history and he liked that. He was a big history buff, you know. He was always telling me some odd fact. One time he told me that the White House had once been called the President's Palace—can you imagine? Anyway, the letters didn't seem important, but I can see that they're going to be an issue, especially with Felicity. She'll never let it rest."

"Well, did he have a safety-deposit box?"

"We cleaned his deposit box out a few years ago. Transferred everything to my box. They weren't there and I know they're not in his desk because I do—*did*—his taxes. I cleaned out his desk a few weeks ago and didn't see them." She looked down at the tie and seemed to finally notice it. "Oh, we better get this to the funeral home," Aunt Christine said as she moved to the door. "The locks will have to be changed. Ruining perfectly good furniture, I tell you . . ."

She continued in that vein during the drive to the funeral home and I wasn't able to break into her monologue. She parked in front of Grisholm's Funeral Home, which was located in a large red brick, plantation-style building with white trim and a two-story pillared portico that extended over a large circle drive. It was a modern building and it looked quite a bit like some of the houses in our neighborhood in Georgia, except for the size—it was much larger. The exterior had the same traditional architectural touches that dominated our neighborhood: dormer windows in the second story and black shutters bracketing the windows. I wasn't sure if I found the similarity comforting or creepy.

A sign informed us that the entrance under the portico led to the chapel. We followed the arrow to the funeral home entrance at the opposite end of the building. A woman in her early twenties with heavy-framed rectangular glasses was sitting behind a desk in the black-and-white tiled entrance area. "May I help you?" she asked in tones so smooth that they were almost tranquilizing.

Aunt Christine was suddenly mute and looked a little pale.

"We need to drop this off for Franklin Avery," I said, gesturing to the tie that Aunt Christine held.

"Of course." The woman stood up. Two long gold necklaces swayed across her pale pink cardigan as she moved around the desk. Her face was as serene as her voice. "You must be part of the Avery family."

Aunt Christine pressed her lips together and I could see it was an effort for her to even speak. "Yes," she said in a barely audible voice. She swallowed and continued in a stronger voice. "I'm his daughter, Christine."

"So nice to meet you. I'm Rosanna," the woman said as she took the tie. "He was a lovely person. I remember him. I was in training when he came to do his prearrangement details and he was so nice. Now, let me just check . . ." She reached over the desk for her phone. After a short conversation, she turned back to us. "We'll get this taken care of," she said, raising the tie, "and then he'll be in the Tranquility Room after ten o'clock."

Aunt Christine nodded and I said, "Thank you so much. We'll let the rest of the family know." I guided Aunt Christine to the door. Once we were outside in the sparkling sunshine, I asked, "Would you like me to drive back?"

"No, I don't want to go back to Bill and Caroline's right now. I want to see him," she said, straightening her shoulders and raising her chin.

"Are you sure?"

"Yes, I think I need to see him—it's what I'm dreading, seeing him in the . . . casket. I need to see him and I'd rather do that now, alone."

"Okay," I said, checking my watch. "It's nine-thirty now. Why don't we get a cup of coffee or something and then come back."

"Fine. Except no coffee for me—my high blood pressure, you know."

"All right, juice then?"

I took the keys and drove until I found a Krispy Kreme and pulled into the parking lot. I ordered us two fruit smoothies. Normally, I'd jump at the chance to have one of the warm glazed donuts, but I figured the smoothies probably had enough calories and sugar in them to last us all day. At least there was no caffeine. I sat down opposite her at the table and said, "I've got orange or berry. Which would you like?"

"Thank you, Ellie. Orange would be wonderful." She took a few sips, then said, "It really is an odd feeling. We're going to bury my dad tomorrow, but when I look around, it's a gorgeous day and people are out smiling, eating donuts, laughing, like nothing has happened. It feels unreal."

"Yes, it is an odd contrast." I swirled my straw around my drink and said, "Aunt Christine, can I ask you something?" I wasn't sure if this was the best time to bring up the subject, but I didn't think I'd have another opportunity.

She set her drink down and folded her hands on the table. Her eyes were the exact same color as her faded baby blue sweatshirt and I realized that I'd never really looked at them. They were beautiful. "Of course, dear. What is it?"

"When Mitch and I took you home after you talked to the detective, you were saying some rather strange things."

Her gaze dropped to the table. "Yes, well, I don't quite know what I was saying then," she said with a feeble laugh. She glanced up at me quickly and I knew that she did remember and was hoping that I wouldn't press her on it. She pushed a few flakes of donut glaze on the table into a pile with her fingertip. "Ellie . . . it's hard to explain and I'd rather not go into it. It's too difficult to talk about."

"The only reason I'm asking is because I saw the detective who investigated the break-in and she seemed to think that someone is holding back information. She asked if my aunt had anything more to share. She must have heard you."

Aunt Christine gave a small shrug as she concentrated on sweeping the crumbs into a napkin. "It doesn't matter now. Best not to go into it."

"She said the investigation could be reopened."

"Reopened? Why?" Her gaze jerked up to meet mine and she looked scared.

"I don't know, but she seemed to think she hadn't gotten all the information." I leaned forward and touched her hand. "Was there something else you didn't tell her?"

"No, of course not," she said quickly.

She already seemed fragile and I didn't want to upset her any more. I paused, thinking how much more traumatic it would be for Detective Kalra to return and ask more questions. "You kept saying you were sorry and that it was your fault," I said gently.

She sagged back against the booth. "Oh, Ellie. I was doing fine, holding myself together, but then I looked over at his chair. It was so empty. He would never sit there again, and then I saw his glasses. It was like grief washed over me, like . . . a wave. I couldn't stop it. I was flooded with it. I should have been there that night. It was stormy and I shouldn't have left him alone. If I'd been there . . ."

Her distress was so genuine, so raw. I squeezed her hand and said, "Aunt Christine, you can't know that. You could have been there and the same thing could have happened."

Her face crumpled. "But it might have made a difference. It might have." Tears welled in her eyes and overflowed past the crinkles at their corners.

Oh, Lord. What had I done? I'd reduced her to tears. I pulled some napkins out of the holder and realized people were staring at us. "Aunt Christine—"

"And do you know what makes it worse? I wanted the family to hire a home-care nurse so I could have more time with Roy. If I'd known Dad was only going to live a few more months, I would have spent every day with him. *Every day.*" She took the napkin and patted her eyes as she spoke. "I've been so selfish—that was why I was sorry."

I believed she was being completely honest with me. She looked so miserable. "Aunt Christine, you did so much for him."

"Yes," she said, and took a ragged breath. "Yes, I did, but I was beginning to resent it and that's wrong. It's just plain wrong to resent your own parent."

"You were there for him and there's nothing wrong with wanting your own life, too."

"I suppose," she said, doubtfully. Her tears had stopped flowing and she wiped her eyes with the scratchy paper napkin. The aroma of warm yeast and sugar rolled out of the kitchen and engulfed us. You could probably gain weight just by breathing the air in here. Aunt Christine took another small sip from her half-full drink, then set it firmly on the table. She seemed somewhat restored to normal, except for her red eyes. She looked at her watch. "Let's go back to Grisholm's. It's after ten. It's time."

During the short drive, she was silent. I glanced at her face before we went inside the funeral home and saw a resolve that hadn't been there earlier. The desk at the entry area was empty. Aunt Christine stood stiffly, her arms held tightly to her sides and her hands clamped together at her waist. I looked around the desk for a bell or buzzer, but there was nothing there. A long L-shaped corridor branched out behind the desk. A plaque beside a doorway in the longer corridor read SERENITY ROOM. "Let me look along here and see if I can find him," I said to Aunt Christine. She gave a jerky nod and remained with her feet planted in the entry area.

Instrumental music played softly in the corridor. It was the only noise except for the muted sound of my footsteps on the low cream-colored carpet. Goosebumps rose on my arms as I glanced in door after door, casket after casket. So many dead people. A few rooms had small smatterings of people, talking quietly, but the hallway was long and empty. Sconces glowed with soft light, and oil paintings of landscapes decorated the wallpaper between the doorways. I'd already passed rooms labeled Peaceful Rest, Quiet Interlude, Reflec-

tions, Zen Meditation, and Calm Serenity. How many synonyms
were there for the word "peaceful"? My stomach clinched as I
caught sight of a small white casket through one of the doorways. It
was half the size of the ones I'd been seeing. A child's casket. I hurried on to the next doorway, the last one.

Finally, the Tranquility Room. I turned on my heel and hurried
back to the entry area. Aunt Christine was still glued to the floor exactly where I'd left her. "I found the Tranquility Room. Are you
ready?"

She gave an almost imperceptible nod, but didn't move. I put an
arm around her shoulders and took a step forward. She moved with
me and we progressed down the hall. I'd always thought of Aunt
Christine with her squat, chubby figure as solid and robust, but right
now she seemed delicate. I kept my gaze on the room at the far end.
I didn't want to think about all those bodies in the other rooms. In-
tellectually, I knew death was part of life and the process of grieving
for and burying the dead shouldn't be creepy. Everyone died, but
somehow the thought of all those bodies lying in caskets in room
after room freaked me out.

Get a grip, I ordered myself. It just feels weird because as a cul-
ture we push death away and never consider it, never want to even
think about it. Well, I certainly couldn't escape the reality of death
here, I thought, as we reached the last room.

"Here we are," I said, and cringed at the heartiness of my voice. I
removed my arm from her shoulders. I noticed she was hunched
over slightly as if to ward off a cold breeze. She reached out and
gripped one of my hands in both of hers as we stepped into the
room.

It was decorated in shades of pale blue and cream with couches,
chairs, and tables ranging around the room. There were more glowing sconces and oil paintings of smooth rivers. It would have been a
pleasant room to spend time in, except for the fact that it was in a funeral home. A tabletop water fountain burbled in one corner, almost
drowning out the muted music.

We both looked around the room and then looked quickly at each other. There was a large gap in the furnishings on one wall. "Where's the casket?" Aunt Christine asked, looking bewildered.

"I don't know. I didn't look in here before, just came back to get you as soon as I saw the room name. Let me check," I said and led her to one of the chairs where she perched uncertainly. I went back to the door. Below the name of the room was a printed card with the name Franklin Scott Avery on it. "This is the right room," I said to Aunt Christine. "I'll go find someone."

I hurried back down the hall and emerged into the entry area as Rosanna pushed open a white wainscoted door at the end of the shorter corridor that was set at a right angle to the longer one. She was carrying a mug of tea in one hand and a stack of papers in the other. "Oh, hello. You're with the Avery family, right?"

"Yes. Ellie Avery. My aunt and I are here to see Franklin Avery, but he's not in the room."

"Not in the room?" she said, her head rearing back a little as if I'd said something completely absurd. "Maybe you're not in the right room. He's in the—"

"Tranquility Room, I know. That's where we were and there's no casket in there. My aunt is waiting there."

Rosanna frowned as she set down the mug and papers on the desk. "Well, let's just go have a look, why don't we?" she said in an extra chirpy voice, and I knew she thought we'd just looked in the wrong room.

We hurried down the longer hall. The whisper of her fluttering pink skirt was the only sound besides the muted music. "Here we are. *This* is the Tranquility Room." Her voiced died away as she took in the empty space and Aunt Christine, looking puzzled and distraught. "Well, let me . . . um . . . check." She recovered her composure and said, "He must have stepped out. I'll be right back."

Stepped out? He *stepped out*? I stifled a giggle. Where had he gone? For coffee?

"Oh, Ellie. This isn't good. Where is he?"

I fought off the giggles because Aunt Christine looked so upset. I said, "I'm sure it's just a little mix-up. They probably told us the wrong room."

I walked over to the water feature that bubbled in the corner, then paced back to the door. I looked out and saw Rosanna and a man in a dark suit popping in and out of the rooms along the corridor. They met at the end and conferred, then glanced back my way. The man disappeared down the shorter corridor and she walked back down the hall toward me.

"I am so sorry. There's been a little . . . ," she looked for a moment like she didn't know what to say, then seemed to decide, as she continued in a slightly firmer tone of voice, ". . . a little delay." She shot me a quick glance from behind her thick-framed rectangular glasses and then smiled. "So sorry about this. Why don't you come with me? We have a nice room, a lounge for families. You can wait there while we sort this out."

We trooped back down the long corridor again, and by this time I wasn't feeling quite so uncomfortable about being in the building and seeing all the caskets. There's nothing like familiarity to drive away the creepiness factor. Once we were back at her desk, Rosanna turned to the left and led us a few feet down the shorter corridor to a room that was more utilitarian than the viewing rooms. "Here you go," she said as she pulled out a chair from a round wooden table so Aunt Christine could take a seat. "Help yourself to any of the refreshments. I'll be right back."

While the viewing room had felt almost like a living room with its upholstered couches and chairs and fine paintings, this room felt more like a kitchen. It had the same black-and-white checked tile floor I'd seen in the entryway. Cabinets with Formica countertops ringed the walls and a refrigerator hummed quietly in one corner. There was a television mounted in one corner with a set of instructions posted beside it so people could watch the funeral services in the chapel on closed-circuit TV. Thankfully, the television was turned off right now.

"This is dreadful," Aunt Christine declared, and I was glad to see some of the spark coming back into her eyes. "I'm calling Caroline. She's the one who insisted on using Grisholm's, although we used Besley's when Cousin Maureen passed and they did a perfectly good job."

A flash of pink whipped by the doorway and I drifted in that direction as Aunt Christine powered on her cell phone. I leaned out the door slightly and saw Rosanna and the man in the dark suit whispering. The man, who had extremely curly dark hair, was talking quickly. They were standing in front of the white door at the end of the short hallway that I'd seen Rosanna emerge from earlier.

The man's voice rose slightly and I caught a few words. ". . . told you . . . not *there*."

Rosanna shook her head. I could see the impatience on her face as she said, "That's impossible."

I missed the man's next words, but he seemed to be arguing with her.

"Fine," Rosanna said, "you do that. I'll double-check," and pushed the white door open.

The man turned and hurried toward me. I slipped back into the room as he strode by. Aunt Christine was dialing as I looked out the doorway again. The white door hadn't closed completely. "I'll be right back," I said. She waved her hand distractedly as she punched numbers on the keypad. I wasn't about to wander all over the funeral home on my own, but I had the distinct impression that Rosanna and the dark-suited man were scrambling to cover something up and they weren't going to be straight with us.

A group of people were filing by Rosanna's desk and leaving the building as I crossed the hall and peered into the crack of the open door. No black-and-white tile, or wallpaper back here, just plain white industrial tile and drywall painted white. There was a bulletin board with notices pinned to it and a poster about proper hand washing technique. I edged the door open and saw a smaller office with an array of papers stacked on a desk and farther down the corridor, more offices. This area had a utilitarian feel to it. This was the behind-the-scenes area of the funeral home that customers—clients?—family members?—didn't see. I noticed a floor plan with fire escape instructions tacked to the bulletin board. If there was a fire, I was supposed to walk down the hall directly in front of me, past another office, a prep room, and an anteroom, then exit into the garage. I could guess what the prep room and anteroom were for and there was no way I was going down that hall, even if there was a fire at my back.

Rosanna came out of one of the offices as a male voice inside called out, "Of course he's not back here. We sent him out at nine forty-five. We don't have anyone else—check for yourself, if you'd like."

She froze when she saw me, then walked forward quickly, a fixed smile on her face. "Mrs. Avery, if you'll step back into the lounge—"

"Where is he?" I asked, not budging.

"There seems to have been a small mix-up," Rosanna said. "Now, if you'll just go back to the lounge—"

At that moment, a man came barreling through the doorway and crashed into my back. I lunged forward and my shoulder banged into the wall. It was the curly headed man. "Oh, excuse me. So sorry," he said. Up close, I could tell he was much younger than I'd realized. He was probably either in his late teens or early twenties. His face was flushed and I supposed he normally had ruddy features. But his rushing around and the anxiety that clearly showed on his face had heightened his normal coloring. He grabbed my elbow and helped me stand back up before turning to Rosanna. "I don't know where he is." Rosanna looked at him sharply, but the man continued, his voice urgent. "He's gone. Franklin Avery's gone."

Chapter Seven

"How can he be gone?" Mitch asked.

I pressed my cell phone closer to my ear so I could hear over the raised voices. "I don't know. But they can't find his body anywhere. They've . . . lost him."

The white door was open and when Aunt Christine heard our voices, she'd come into the hallway to see what all the fuss was about. Rosanna got a panicked look on her face and had herded everyone back into the lounge and shut the door. She was now standing with her back to the door, guarding it as if her life depended on keeping us inside. I suppose, more accurately, it was her job that depended on keeping the disturbance we were making away from other quietly grieving families. "That's impossible. You can't just lose a body," Mitch said.

"You wouldn't think so, would you? Apparently, they've looked everywhere and he's not in the funeral home. I think you should come down here. If you have any pull at all with the Grisholm family, it might help us figure out exactly what's going on."

"Okay. Who's there now?"

"A young woman named Rosanna, who earlier in the day was very serene—" Rosanna's voice screeched, "Police? No, you cannot call the police," as she tried to maintain her blocking strategy at the door and push the cell phone away from Aunt Christine's ear, as I said, "—and a young guy in a suit with really curly dark hair."

"That's got to be Jake, Dermont's younger brother. They're actually letting him work there? I can't believe it. I'm on my way."

I pulled the phone away from my ear and stared at it for a second. I'd never known Mitch to hang up on me and he usually didn't leap into action. Thoughtful contemplation mixed with a big dollop of patience was usually more his style. Now I was *really* worried.

Rosanna had left her post by the door and pried Aunt Christine's phone from her hand. "We'll sort this out. I'm sure it's just a mix-up," she said.

The man with the curly hair—Jake—was sitting at one of the chairs at the table with his head in his hands. I could hear him saying, "Pick up. Pick up the phone. I swear, if you've gotten me in trouble, you crazy b—"

I must have registered in his peripheral vision, because he twisted toward me and I saw that he was on his cell phone. He yanked it away from his ear, then ended the call. He stuffed the phone in a pocket, then stood quickly.

"Jake? You are Jake, aren't you?"

He ran his hands over the suit coat and adjusted his tie. "Yes, ma'am," he said, his smile falsely automatic.

"Would you happen to know something about where Franklin Avery is?" I glanced down at the pocket where he'd stashed his phone.

"No, ma'am," he said, but his expression looked exactly like Nathan's when I've caught him lying to me about brushing his teeth, evasive and guilty at the same time.

"Are you sure?"

"Oh, yes, ma'am. Most unusual thing I've ever seen. Nothing like this has ever happened."

"Young lady," Aunt Christine's imperious voice, which had corralled and cowed generations of unruly students, rang out. "Give me back my phone. I do not care that you don't want me to call the police. If you cannot find my father's body, it must be reported. Now, give it back," she said, and held out her hand.

Rosanna looked queasy as she reluctantly handed the phone

back. "Please, let us check again. I'm sure it's just an error. He'll turn up," she finished weakly.

"This is a very serious situation. Instead of trying to cover it up, I suggest you call your boss," Aunt Christine said sharply before turning back to her phone. Jake slipped out of the unguarded door.

Rosanna closed her eyes briefly, then said, "Yes, of course. You're right. I'll call Mr. Grisholm," and left the room.

"I'd like to report a missing body. At Grisholm's Funeral Home. . . . Yes, it's an emergency. No, we don't need an ambulance. Didn't you hear me? A body is missing." Aunt Christine listened for a moment, then rolled her eyes and said in an undertone to me, "This may take some time." She spoke into the phone again and said, "Christine Avery. C–h–r–i–s–t–i–n–e . . ."

I remembered Detective Kalra's business card. I'd tucked it into my purse this morning after I'd returned to the house. I dug it out to use my cell phone to call her office. Aunt Christine had spelled her last name and was saying that she didn't know the funeral home address, but that they didn't need an exact address because it was on Waverly and anyone would be able to see it from the road. I could see that it was going to take a long time before Aunt Christine got through to anyone who could help her. I had a feeling Detective Kalra could make things happen and she was familiar with Grandpa Franklin's death. Of course, she already thought there was something off about his death, and I hoped I wasn't putting anyone in the family in a bad position by calling the detective, but finding Grandpa Franklin seemed to be the most important thing right now. I dialed the number.

"Rickets."

"Oh, sorry," I said. The voice was gruff and definitely masculine. "I must have the wrong number. I was trying to reach Detective Kalra."

"She's out," he said.

"I talked to her this morning about Franklin Avery—"

"Whoa, whoa, whoa. Let me stop you right there. I know she had some bee in her bonnet about that case, but it's closed. You want to leave a message?"

"Yes . . . well, when will she be back?"

There was a heavy sigh. "Look, lady, I don't have time for this. I don't have her exact ETA, so you want to leave your name and number or what?"

Irritated at his tone, I said, "Well, no, I don't want to unless she'll be back in the next few minutes, because there's a dead body that's missing."

After a pause, he said, "Dead body? Missing, you say?" His choppy, irritated tone had vanished.

"Yes. Franklin Avery's body is missing from Grisholm's Funeral Home."

"Oh, boy," he said, sounding resigned. "I'll be right out."

Mitch arrived before the police. He was alone when he walked into the lounge area. "Where is everyone else?" I asked.

"Who else?"

"The rest of the Avery family. I figured you'd arrive as part of the Avery family motorcade."

"No, I didn't tell anyone else, just came straight here. Hello, Aunt Christine," he said, pausing to give her a peck on the cheek. "How are you doing?"

"Good, now that Ellie's got the police on the way. Never in my life have I seen such incompetence. And I worked in the public school system, mind you."

"Incompetence. Right. That brings us to Jake. Where is he?" Mitch asked.

"I don't know. He was in here with us for a few minutes. He made a phone call. He was saying something about someone getting him in trouble and then he left."

"Typical. All right, let me see if I can find him. Have you already looked around, Ellie?"

"Are you kidding? This is a funeral home. I'm not looking around."

Mitch frowned at me. "Really? You? You're afraid you might see a dead body?"

I ignored that comment and said, "They've looked in all the

viewing rooms, the chapel, the . . . prep room, and even in the, what did she call it, Aunt Christine?"

"The selection room." At Mitch's puzzled frown, Aunt Christine added, "The rooms where they display all the different caskets and urns."

"Oh," Mitch said. "And . . . ?"

"Empty. All empty, according to Mr. Grisholm." Aunt Christine's hands fluttered up to pat her mouth and she got a funny look on her face.

"Are you feeling all right, Aunt Christine?" I asked. She'd held up remarkably well, considering the situation. From some of the things Aunt Nanette had said about Aunt Christine, I'd had the impression that she was ditzy, but she hadn't gone all spacey and helpless. She was the one who took charge and demanded the police be called in. And now that I thought about it, I doubted you could be silly or ditzy and survive as a teacher for thirty years. "Yes, I'm fine," she said, her eyebrows lowered and a frown on her face. "Where's his casket?"

I looked at her for a moment, then realized what she was asking. "That is an excellent question. Where is the casket?" I turned to Mitch to explain.

"The viewing room where Grandpa Franklin was supposed to be was empty. It's not just his body that's missing . . . it's the casket, too. The coffin."

"Casket," corrected a voice from the doorway. "We call them caskets," Rosanna said. She still looked shaken and pale as she stepped in the room. "Mr. Grisholm wants me to let you know we are double-checking everything right now."

"Rosanna, did the funeral home have any burials or cremations scheduled for today?" I asked.

Aunt Christine let out a little gasp. "Oh, Ellie, you don't think—"

"Sorry, Aunt Christine, but we have to ask."

As comprehension dawned, Rosanna grabbed the back of a chair to steady herself. "No, we don't have anything on the schedule until tomorrow."

"Thank goodness," Aunt Christine said as I breathed a sigh of relief.

"Where's Jake?" Mitch asked.

Rosanna seemed to get back a little of her warmth as she asked, "Oh, do you know him? He's helping his father look, I'm sure. Although, I haven't seen him in a while."

"I'd like to speak to him," Mitch said. "I'm an old friend from school."

"How nice," she said uncertainly, and picked up a phone mounted on the wall. She dialed and listened for a moment, then replaced the phone. "He's not at his desk. Let me look outside," she said, and glanced out the window that looked over the front parking lot. "No, his car is gone. He must have stepped out."

"That's convenient for him," Mitch said. "Do you know where Mr. Grisholm is?"

"Yes, he's in the garage, checking the cars."

"Then let's go."

She looked like she wanted to argue, but instead she gave a small nod and led him out of the room.

Out the window, I saw a dark blue four-door sedan pull into the parking lot. I looked closely and saw the light bar mounted inside the car. It was an undercover car. I went out to meet him, since the entry area would be empty. I pushed open the heavy door and squinted in the glare of the sunlight. Detective Rickets was about my height. His head was shaved and he had close-set, gray-blue eyes. His dark suit was blue and would have fit in perfectly at the funeral home, but there was something about him, a confidence in his walk and a command in his gaze, that conveyed he was in charge. I walked toward him and we met on the sidewalk.

"I'm Ellie Avery," I said as I put out my hand.

"Detective Rickets," he said as he shook my hand briefly, then pulled a small notebook and pen from his pocket. He flipped it open and had me spell my name and give him my contact information. After he'd written down my address, he raised his eyebrows and said, "Georgia?"

"Yes. We're here for Franklin Avery's funeral. He's—was—my husband's grandfather."

"Okay. So, you say the body's missing?"

"Yes." I told him everything that had happened from the moment Aunt Christine and I had discovered the viewing room was empty. "My husband, Mitch, is here. He had one of the employees, Rosanna, take him to find Mr. Grisholm. I think they're in the garage area—oh, wait. Here they are," I said as I saw a group of people in dark suits flow out of the building. Mitch was at the back of the group, talking with a man who I thought was Jake's older brother. He had the same reddish tinge to his face and dark hair. The differences were that this man was taller, had a slightly slimmer build, and instead of having the unfortunate corkscrew curls his brother had, his dark hair only had a slight wave to it. He and Mitch were in conversation and walking quickly behind another, older man who had to be Mr. Grisholm. The family resemblance was there in the ruddy cheeks and dark hair. He was tall, much taller than Detective Rickets. "I can assure you there's no need for you to come inside, Officer . . . ?"

"Detective Rickets. You're the owner." He said it as a statement, not a question.

"Thomas Grisholm." He spoke in the same low, soothing tones that Rosanna had used earlier in the morning. "Now, as I was saying, we've had a slight error and don't need—"

Detective Rickets bounced on his toes and said, "Found him, did you?" There was a moment of silence, then Detective Rickets asked, "The missing body. You found it?"

Mr. Grisholm cleared his throat. "Unfortunately, we haven't located Mr. Avery. But I assure you it's only a matter of time—"

"So then the answer is no. If a body is missing, Mr. Grisholm, then you do, indeed, need me here. It is a police matter." A small group of people exited the funeral home and looked at us curiously as they walked to their cars. The unmarked police car also got a few long glances from the group.

Mr. Grisholm again explained how everything was just fine. I took a few steps to where Mitch was standing. "Did you find anything?"

"No," Mitch said, shaking his head. "This is Dermont," he added.

Dermont stepped forward and shook my hand. "Ellie, so good to see you again. We met at your wedding, but I'm sure you don't remember me. I can't tell you how sorry I am about all this. We've looked everywhere." Dermont's voice didn't have that smooth veneer that Rosanna and Mr. Grisholm spoke with. He looked genuinely distressed. "If Jake has anything to do with this—and this has his fingerprints all over it—well, then, there's going to be hell to pay," Dermont said, glancing at his dad. It seemed Mr. Grisholm was wearing down. He was telling Detective Rickets that if he had to stay, then to please move his unmarked car around back.

Mitch leaned toward me and said, "Dermont has checked every room in the funeral home. No sign."

"What about the garage?"

"Nothing."

"That's so strange," I said, looking out over the parking lot. With the sun shining, you could almost forget it was winter, except for the bare trees and faded monotone brown of the grass. The branches creaked and stirred as the wind whipped through them.

The group of people who'd left the building were getting in their cars, which were parked in the row nearest to the funeral home. It was also the row where I'd parked Aunt Christine's car. A clump of cars filled some spaces down at the end of the building and I assumed that was where the employees parked, because Rosanna had looked in that direction to check for Jake's car. As the trees danced in the wind, I saw a flash of white through the shifting branches. There was a lone vehicle, a white van at the farthest corner of the parking lot. A swell of landscaped grass and evergreen bushes blocked out the traffic from the busy road a few feet away and another island of landscaping partially shielded it from view. I stepped to the side so I could see around the cluster of trees and stared at the van.

"Ellie, we're going inside," Mitch said.

"Just a second," I said, and set out across the parking lot at a brisk pace.

I heard Mitch call to me, but I kept moving. It would only take a few seconds . . . I dodged around the landscaped islands of trees and bushes that were spaced across the parking lot. The sides of the van were solid, no windows. I hurried to the back doors and leaned close to the tinted window.

I turned and shouted, "I think I found him."

Ellie Avery's Tips for Preserving Family Treasures

Organizing School Papers and Artwork
One of the biggest organizing challenges families face is organizing all the paper and artwork that comes home from school. Here are a few ideas to help:

- Enlist your child to help you decide what to keep. You may be surprised at which items are special to your child. If you don't ask, you won't know what they value. If your child wants to keep everything, then you'll have to explain that they don't need to keep everything, only the things that are the most special. It's an opportunity to help kids learn how to sort and thin out their belongings. It may be a lot of work in the beginning, but you'll be teaching them a skill that they'll use again and again.
- Three-ring notebooks with plastic sleeves are an easy way to save special papers and awards. Accordion files are another good way to store paper. You can label each slot by year or activity.
- Plastic bins or cardboard office storage boxes are great for holding nonpaper items like ballet shoes, T-ball pennants, hand-knitted baby blankets, and sports trophies.
- Decorate with artwork. Frame those watercolors or fingerpaint drawings and hang them on your child's wall. The clay pot your child brought home from art class might be a good place to store pens or paper clips.

Chapter
Eight

The van wasn't locked, but I hung back. Mr. Grisholm wrenched the doors open and climbed inside. Detective Rickets followed him. With two people in the modified interior and a casket, the back of the van was full and I had no desire to cram myself in there with them. The casket was a dark wood with simple hardware.

Mitch, Dermont, and I looked on as Mr. Grisholm folded back the lid, revealing the padded and ruched white fabric inside. Mr. Grisholm and Detective Rickets looked back to us, questioningly. Mitch stepped on the bumper, took a quick look, then nodded his head. "Yes, that's Grandpa Franklin," he said. His voice sounded funny, almost compressed. I stepped on the bumper and looked into the casket. Grandpa Franklin's body had been jostled to one side of the casket and the pillow was angled under his shoulder. I stared for a moment before Mr. Grisholm quickly closed the casket. The lanky body gone frail and the thatch of thick white hair did look like Grandpa Franklin, but the face was so blank—no sharp gaze, no quick smile after I fell for one of his tall tales. I stepped down and moved away from the van, thinking that he was truly gone and I'd miss him so much.

Dermont was talking quietly to Mitch around the side of the van and I moved in their direction. "We use it to transport remains from the hospital or coroner's office to the funeral home. Again, Mitch, I'm so sorry."

"So the van is kept in the garage, unlocked, with the keys available?" Mitch asked in a tight, controlled voice.

"Yes. There's never been a need to lock anything down," Dermont said, and I wandered to the driver's door and peered inside. The keys were still in the ignition. The interior was spotlessly clean except for a small piece of paper on the driver's seat and a pair of work gloves. I opened the door, setting off the dinging sound that warned the keys were still in the ignition. I pulled the paper, which was folded into a small square, out of the crevice where the seats came together. I opened the creased paper. It was a flyer for a spin class at Smarr Fitness Center. I felt a presence looming at my shoulder and realized Mitch was behind me. He took the paper from me and shoved it into the pocket of his leather jacket. "What are you doing? The person who took Grandpa Franklin's body could have dropped that by accident."

"I know," he said, grimly.

"You have to give that to Detective Rickets," I said as I looked over his shoulder and saw the detective approaching. Mitch took my elbow and moved us a step back from the van. As Detective Rickets glanced inside the van, Mitch casually looked away and said so quietly that only I could hear, "Felicity works at Smarr Fitness Center."

"I know, but that doesn't mean she's involved. Besides, she was at Bill and Caroline's house with the rest of the family this morning."

"She got a call and left right after you did," Mitch said.

"You've got to give that . . ." I trailed off when I looked at his face.

"If she's involved, the family will deal with it."

The driver's door was still open. "Looks like there won't be any prints because of the gloves," Detective Rickets said, then shouted toward the back of the van, "You can take it back to the garage." Mr. Grisholm closed the back doors with a thud and came around to climb into the driver's seat.

"Is it going to be searched for fingerprints and hairs . . . all that CSI stuff?" I asked.

Detective Rickets placed his hands on his hips as he said, "Afraid not. The sheriff's department only has so many resources. Right now, we've got a vehicle theft, a home burglary, and a report of a man trying to lure a kid into a car at the convenience store out on Highway Twenty-seven. Those things have to take priority over this situation."

"I'll send a car back for the rest of you," Mr. Grisholm said, and I could tell he was focused on getting the van back and fixing what had happened. There was a tension in his expression and I wasn't sure if he was embarrassed or furious. Probably both, I decided.

"I'll just ride along with you," the detective said easily and went around to the passenger side.

"We'll walk. It's not far," Mitch said, and we turned back to the building. The van gave us a wide berth as Dermont fell into step beside Mitch.

I heard a car approaching. A silver Honda Accord had driven into the parking lot. It pulled alongside of us and Jake's curly head appeared as the window rolled down. "What are you doing out here?"

"Where have you been?" Dermont asked. "I can't believe you left—you knew what happened and you left?"

"Well, Rosanna said you and Dad were on it and I had to pick up those envelopes at the printer."

"You left to go to the *printer*?" Dermont stepped away from the car and rubbed his hand across his forehead. "God, Jake, I can't believe you'd be that stupid. Even you should see that—" He broke off, stared at Jake for a moment, then lunged to the car and gripped the door frame. "You know something. What is it? What's going on?"

Jake rotated the wheel and let the car roll a few feet as he said, "Nothing. Don't know what you mean."

Dermont didn't let go of the car door. "Jake," he said warningly, as he walked beside the car. Jake broke eye contact and glanced in the rearview mirror before bringing the car to a stop.

Mitch and I exchanged a glance.

"Okay. Okay." Jake held his hands up. "Calm down. I don't know anything for sure, but I . . . might . . . know what happened." Jake's gaze flicked back to us, then he looked at his brother questioningly.

"Go ahead," Dermont said scathingly. "We lost their grandfather. I doubt it can get worse."

"Oh. Well, last week, the English prof was late for class." Jake ran his hand around the steering wheel as he talked. "We waited around for a few minutes, then some of us went over to the student union. One of the guys recognized my name when I introduced myself. He asked all these questions about the funeral home—stuff about the remains and other weird things. I didn't think about it until today, but he asked about joyrides in the hearse, stuff like that." He was still running his hand over the steering wheel as he said, "When I realized that a casket was gone, I checked the garage and didn't see the van." His hand faltered, then stilled on the wheel as he shifted so he could look at his brother. "Look, I don't know for sure, but I think he did it."

"And so as soon as you remembered this, you hopped in your car and took off?" Dermont asked, his voice disbelieving.

"Hey, I went to look for the van. It's not my fault—I went out the back way and didn't see it parked in the front parking lot. It was here the whole time, wasn't it?"

"We don't know," Dermont said, his grip on the car door still tight. He dropped his head for a moment, then looked up at Jake. "Who was it?"

"The guy who asked all the questions? I don't know."

"He's in your English Lit one-o-one class." Dermont released the car door and stood up. "It shouldn't be too hard for the detective to find him."

"No, he's not in my class. It was just some kid that I talked to at the student union. I don't know who he was."

"Well, can you describe him?" Dermont asked.

"Sure . . . brown hair. Kind of long. Black shirt, baggy jeans, and I think Converse shoes." Jake paused, then said, triumphantly, "And he had a skateboard."

Dermont groaned. "That could be half the student body at Smarr Community College. You better get in there and tell Dad what happened."

"Yeah, I should go tell them," he said, and nodded. He drove off slowly as if he wanted to put off the event as long as possible.

Dermont turned back to Mitch and me. "Again, I'm so sorry." He rubbed his forehead, looking as if he had a headache. "But you know Jake. He always was . . . ," he glanced at me and amended what he was going to say, "an accident waiting to happen. I still can't believe Dad's making him work here. It would be so much better to keep him away from here. As far away as possible."

I don't think he actually meant to speak the last part aloud and looked a little startled when Mitch clasped him on the shoulder and said, "I know all about younger siblings—remember, I have Summer and she's able to create chaos with a couple of words." They began walking back to the funeral home. After looking back at the now empty corner of the parking lot where the van had been parked, I fell into step with them.

"I can't believe Detective Rickets isn't going to investigate," I said, and burrowed my hands deeper into my coat pockets.

Mitch, sitting on the wrought-iron chair beside me, moved his feet as a splatter of pool water landed near his shoes. "Watch me, Daddy! Watch me! Watch me!" Nathan shouted. He and Livvy were again wearing their floaty bathing suits. Livvy laboriously paddled over to us and gripped the edge of the pool. "Why won't you come swim? The water's lovely."

"Lovely" was Livvy's latest new word. She had a tendency to latch onto certain words or phrases and use them to death. She'd heard the word from a classroom assistant at school, who'd pronounced Livvy's drawing of the continents "lovely." So many things in Livvy's world were lovely now.

"You and Nathan have a good time. I'll swim another day," I called, and she frowned before bobbing back over to Nathan. They began splashing gallons of water as they tried to outdo each other with their antics. The pool was sheltered from the breeze and the sun was still shining, so I'd figured swimming was a great way for the kids to burn off their energy. Nathan ducked into the water and blew bubbles, then emerged with water streaming down his face. I knew the kids were warm enough in the heated pool, but the chill of the wrought-iron chairs was making me shiver.

"Good job, buddy," Mitch called. To me, he said, "You heard Jake—it was a prank."

Once Jake repeated to the detective what he'd told us, Detective Rickets had taken a brief look around the funeral home and declared that the incident was a result of the funeral home's inattention to securing entrances coupled with juvenile mischief. He'd summed it up by saying, "It appears that the person who took the casket entered the funeral home through an unlocked door to the garage area, and discovered the casket containing Mr. Avery's remains in the anteroom where it was left unattended before it was to be moved to the viewing room. The person moved the casket to the van in the garage, which had the key in the ignition." Detective Rickets speculated that the person drove to the end of the parking lot, had second thoughts, and ditched the van. "All he had to do was slip over that berm of landscaping between the funeral home and the strip mall that's under construction next door and he'd be out of sight. No video cameras over there, so no recordings."

At that point, Detective Rickets had swung toward Mr. Grisholm and said, "You have any video cameras set up in this place?"

Mr. Grisholm shook his head. "The—ah—nature of our business has proved a deterrent to burglary."

"All righty. I'll check the other businesses along the street here, see if they noticed anything," he said after taking down Jake's rather general description of the guy who'd asked questions about the funeral home. His tone indicated he didn't think there would be any results.

A splash of water brought me back to the present. Livvy squealed as Nathan flung water at her. I snuggled my chin into my wool scarf and looked at Mitch. "So now you don't think Felicity had anything to do with it?"

Mitch shook his head. "No, you were right. Anyone could have picked up that flyer. I jumped to a conclusion," he said as he ran his shoe along the line of bricks that edged the pool.

I blinked. "You never do anything like that." Between Mitch and me, he was always the thoughtful, reasonable one.

Mitch lowered his voice as he said, "You saw her taking things from Grandpa Franklin's house. Who knows how much she would have bundled out of there if we hadn't shown up. If she thought Grandpa Franklin had something valuable on him—jewelry or even those letters, she'd steal a casket, no question."

"Wow," I said. "That's pretty harsh. She's that moneygrubbing?"

"Yes," Mitch said without hesitation. "She's selfish." Mitch glanced over his shoulder at the house, where the family was still discussing the incident at the funeral home in rather loud tones. They were debating about switching to another funeral home, but I thought it was probably too late for that.

"But to steal a body? That's crazy."

"She'd do it," Mitch said emphatically.

"That still sounds crazy to me, but Felicity was Aunt Christine's first thought today at Grandpa Franklin's. Oh! I haven't told you about that. Someone had searched Grandpa Franklin's house. Things aren't in the right places and some of the cushions are slit. I wonder if Aunt Christine has told everyone about it. She thinks it was Felicity."

"I wouldn't put it past her."

I shook my head. No matter how much I wanted something, I don't think I could bring myself to vandalize someone's house. Mitch's eyebrows crunched together as he asked, "So the cushions were slit?"

"Yeah, but it was done in a way that's not noticeable when you first look at it. Aunt Christine wants to change the locks. When would Felicity have time to do all this stuff? Doesn't she have to work?"

"She's off today and she could have gone by Grandpa Franklin's house anytime yesterday. No one is staying there all the time."

"Speaking of Aunt Christine," I said, "I asked her why she said she was sorry."

"You did what?" Mitch sat up straight.

"I asked her why she said she was sorry," I repeated, a bit defensively. "She said it was because she thought she should have been there with him."

"Ellie, why do you do this?" Mitch said, his tone laced with frustration.

"Do what?"

"Have to know every little detail." He frowned. "Of course, she was upset because she wasn't there. Don't make such a big deal out of it."

He rarely got upset. He was one of those people who rolled with the punches. Almost always, he was unflappable and composed. But every once in a while, when something really bothered him, his imperturbable air faded. It was like watching the fizz erupt when Livvy added vinegar to baking soda for her Show and Tell project. I felt stung. "I just wanted to know why she said she was sorry. It was kind of odd. And that detective insinuated that she thought there was more to be investigated. She could reopen the case. Isn't it better to know what we're dealing with? Have everything out in the open?"

"Saying she was sorry isn't odd," Mitch said, ignoring my last arguments. "Not odd at all when you consider her father had just died. She was in shock. Why do you always push and push? Why do you always have to know everything?"

That hurt. I said quickly, "I don't have to know everything."

Mitch twisted to me and said, "Yes. Yes, you do. And if anything appears the slightest bit unusual, you want to know more and you keep picking and prying." His words were like shrapnel, each one a tiny wound, inflicting pain. I always thought I had a knack for picking out things that didn't fit. I did it all the time in my organizing business. I could look at a room, a closet, or a schedule and just *see* what needed to go to organize things. And, sure, I had a healthy sense of curiosity. At least, I'd always thought of it that way. There had even been a few times when I'd been able to ferret out the truth from under layers of lies.

I was getting worked up, my heart pounding, as I said, "Well, at least I'm not like you—burying my head in the sand and saying 'everything will be okay, there's nothing to worry about.'" I stopped abruptly at the wounded look on Mitch's face, realizing my words had hurt him as much as his had hurt me. Normally, I'm not so quick on the mark verbally, but there's something about fighting with your spouse—some of those barriers that usually prevent me from saying the first thing that pops into my head are down and I know him so well that he's an easy target.

I realized there weren't any splashes coming from the pool and twisted in that direction. Livvy and Nathan were both standing motionless in the shallow end, their wary gazes trained on us. The water lapped against their still bodies. Great. Now we were arguing in front of the kids—something we try to avoid.

"Nathan, where's the ball you were throwing?" I called out, and Nathan high-stepped through the water to get it, still watching us out of the corner of his eye. Of course, Livvy saw an opportunity to get the ball from Nathan, so she swiped it and then he went after her. All was normal in the pool again, so I turned back to Mitch and said in a quieter voice, "Besides, even you have to admit that my . . . ," I paused, trying to think of a word besides nosy, "inquisitiveness has paid off in the past."

"Ellie, I don't want to argue with you." I could tell by the care he took in choosing his words that his flare of emotion was fading and he was reining in his anger. He sighed and said, "Tonight after the viewing, I'll ask Dad about a locksmith, which will keep Felicity out of the house."

It didn't seem like a very good solution to me. Was anyone going to talk to Felicity? Aunt Christine had said she would, but after the scene at the funeral home, I didn't know if Felicity would be at the top of her list.

It's hard to argue with someone who refuses to argue back. Even though I wanted to defend myself and my actions, I leaned back against the cold wrought-iron chair and tried to relax my tight shoulders. "You never want to argue," I said. He didn't take the bait, just leveled a glance at me that said he was backing off and I'd be smart to do the same, but I continued, "Why wait to call a locksmith? Do it now before something else happens."

"No, everyone is stressed out as it is. I'm not going to make it worse. After the viewing, I'll take care of it."

I shook my head. "There are too many weird things going on," I persisted, leaning toward him. "The broken window that still hasn't been fully explained, and someone searched Grandpa Franklin's house. We're assuming it was Felicity, but it might not be her."

"No," Mitch crossed his arms. "We're not going off on a wild goose chase here. The broken window was from the storm and Felicity is trying to discreetly ransack Grandpa Franklin's house. That's all that's going on."

I checked the kids. Their arms were cranking as they energetically splashed each other. I lowered my voice and said, "Mitch, your grandfather's body *disappeared* from the funeral home. We need to contact Detective Rickets and tell him about the search at Grandpa Franklin's house, except . . ." I frowned, thinking of how quickly he'd closed down everything this afternoon. "He seemed like he didn't want to look into anything too closely. It would probably be better to talk to Detective Kalra. I've got her card," I said, making a move to get up.

Mitch put his hand on my wrist. "Ellie. We're not calling a detective—any detective. What happened this afternoon with Grandpa Franklin's body—that was incompetence on the part of Grisholm's. They should never have let Jake work there. He's a magnet for trouble."

I watched the kids splash for a few moments. I knew that tone of voice. Mitch was usually so easygoing, but every once in a while he could be so stubborn. Like his temper, his stubbornness didn't show up very often, but when it did, well, there was no changing his mind.

"Fine. Ignore it, write everything off." I stood up. "I have to get ready for the viewing. Can you bring the kids in?"

"Sure," Mitch said, and I could feel his gaze on me as I pushed in the chair. "Ellie," he said, his voice quiet, "this is my family. If there's something wrong, the family will take care of it."

"Will they, Mitch? Will they really try to get to the bottom of what's going on? Or will they close ranks and hide it?" I strode away before he could answer.

Chapter
Nine

"Thank you so much for coming," I said to an older man who was moving around the room, speaking to each Avery family member. Most of the Avery family was here for the funeral, except for a few relatives who lived far away, like Dan's mom, Jenny. He shook my hand and moved on to Mitch, who was standing in a cluster of people near the casket. We hadn't really talked since our argument at the pool. There had been the rush to get ready for the viewing and get the kids settled with the babysitter, a part-time employee from Caroline's office.

We'd decided earlier in the day that the viewing and the funeral might be too upsetting for Livvy and Nathan. Both of them seemed relieved when I told them they didn't have to go if they didn't want to. "Good," Livvy had said. "I don't want to see a coffin." Livvy's cousins, Madison and Jack, were staying with them as well. Madison had brought the newest installment of the Infinity Mystery series, which was Livvy's all-time favorite book series. Livvy had said, "Wasn't that lovely of her?" The books followed three friends as they used math to solve mysteries. I'd left her curled up on the corner of the couch already halfway through the first chapter of *The Spiral Secrets*. Nathan and Jack had been alternating between building with Legos and playing with dump trucks. With a Disney movie as backup in case everyone got bored, I knew they'd be fine.

I shook another person's hand and accepted more condolences. The room was crowded with people who'd come to pay their respects to the family. Unlike this morning, everything was running smoothly. The casket had been in place when we'd arrived. I'd edge over to look inside and was relieved to see that Grandpa Franklin's body had been repositioned. The soft music played, the water feature burbled, and people circulated, speaking in low murmurs. The funeral home was being obsequiously polite and deferential. We probably could have asked for a bagpipe serenade and it would have happened in an instant.

"Thank you so much for coming," I said as a woman reached out to shake my hand.

She clasped both of her hands around mine and said, "I had to come. Mr. Avery was such a wonderful person." As I focused on her face, I realized she was the jogger who'd stopped at Grandpa Franklin's house to see if he was all right. Dressed in a black wrap dress and with her blond hair loose around her head, she looked completely different. "So sad that he's gone," she said in her distinctive nasal tones.

"Yes," I said. I still had the feeling I knew her from somewhere. "I'm Ellie Avery. I'm married to Mitch, Franklin Avery's grandson." She'd mentioned her name when she was at Grandpa Franklin's house the day we arrived in Smarr, but I couldn't remember it and she obviously didn't remember that I'd been there at the tape line beside her.

"Maggie Key," she said. As soon as she said her name, I had it. At least, I thought I did. Could it be her?

"Margaret Key, the author?" I asked hesitantly.

"Why, yes. That's me," she said, smiling widely.

"My daughter loves your books. In fact, she's just started *The Spiral Secrets* and I know she won't put it down until she finishes it," I said, trying to reconcile this woman in front of me with the picture on the back flap of the books in the mystery series. She looked about fifteen years older than her photo. I wondered if she hadn't updated her photo in years or if she'd had some serious air-brushing done. In real life, wrinkles radiated out from the corners of her brown eyes and she had the beginnings of a double chin. Instead of the silky, smooth blond hair that framed her face in the photo, she had slightly frizzy blond curls with dark roots.

"Oh, that's wonderful! It's so important for children to be readers—that's why I write middle-grade chapter books. If kids fall in love with reading, then it's a lifelong love."

"That's true. I'm so glad you've written the Infinity mysteries. Livvy can hardly wait for the next one. She'll be so excited when I tell her I met Margaret Key!"

"Oh, call me Maggie. Everyone around here does. Here, let me give you some bookmarks for your daughter." She unzipped her slouchy leather purse with her small, delicate hands and dug around inside.

"I can't believe my husband didn't tell my daughter that her favorite author lives in the town where he grew up."

"Well, he probably has no idea I live in Smarr. Here we are!" she said, and pressed a stack of brightly colored bookmarks into my hands. "And take some stickers, too." She settled the purse on her shoulder and said, "I only moved here after the book festival last year. I fell in love with Smarr during Book Daze—such a rich literary history and so quaint—have you seen the downtown? No? Well, you must go. It's quite revitalized now with little craft shops and antique stores and bistros. I'd spend all day downtown, if I could. But, of course, if I did that, I'd never get any writing done. And Quincy House, have you been there?"

"Yes," I said, and before I could elaborate that it had been one of the first places Mitch had shown me during my first visit to Smarr, she said, "Oh, good. It has the *best* Sunday brunch. Have you had it?" I nodded and she continued, "The crepes! They're so—" She broke off as a rotund man with round glasses and a brown goatee going gray joined us.

He extended his hand. "Sorry to intrude, but I couldn't help overhearing. I have to agree that Smarr's downtown area is one of the most picturesque that I've seen. That's where I'm going to open my pizzeria. Authentic, oven-fired pizza, mind you." Maggie was staring at him and made no move to take his hand. He reached out and grabbed her hand as he said loudly, "I'm so thrilled to meet a famous author. You should come by after we open! I'll put a signed photo of you on the wall."

She smiled weakly, then withdrew her hand. I was a little surprised at his boisterousness. I know I'd just said almost exactly the same thing, but his voice carried across the room and people were turning to look at us. "Oh, pardon me. I've completely forgotten my manners," he said as he reached out to shake my hand. "Stan Anderson. New in town." I introduced myself and he continued, "I never met your grandfather—just arrived a few days ago—but my dad was a buddy of his and wanted me to convey his sympathies to the family."

"How did your father know Grandpa Franklin?" I asked, stepping back slightly. Stan Anderson was one of those people who didn't seem to have any regard for personal space. He leaned toward me as if to keep me from getting too far away. He had a narrow forehead, but his face widened at his chin into heavy jowls. With his egg-shaped body, triangular head, and thick neck, he reminded me of the oval-shaped Weebles toys that the kids liked.

"The war. They served together," he said, then leaned—wobbled?—toward Maggie. "And you? How did you know Franklin Avery?" Was there something else there in his question? A hint of accusation? No, I decided as I searched Stan's round face, which was open and guileless.

Maggie said, "I'd talk to him at the end of my run. During the spring and fall, he was always outside, puttering about in the yard or sitting on the porch. At first, I waved to him, but eventually, I stopped to chat almost every day."

Stan nodded and said, "I can see why you'd do that." Again, there seemed to be a whiff of some extra layer of meaning in the air, but only for a second. "Well," Stan pivoted toward me and tilted forward in a small bow. "Pleased to meet you. And Ms. Key, delighted. I must say that meeting you today has brought joy to an otherwise distressing and sad day."

He walked to the casket and Maggie and I exchanged a look. I said, "Well, that was . . . interesting. You must get tired of being accosted by strangers."

"No, not really. Being a writer is lonely, you know. That's why I had to come today. I spend most of my days communing with my laptop and to talk to someone—an actual real, live human being—as opposed to a virtual conversation like e-mail or Twitter or Facebook, well, chatting with Mr. Avery was often the highlight of my day." Her words faltered and she swallowed. "I will miss him," she said as she opened her bag again and found a tissue.

"We all will," I said.

Maggie nodded and said, "I should talk to the rest of the family." She moved on and I noticed Stan Anderson leaving the room. I went to check on Aunt Christine. I wasn't sure how she'd react to seeing the casket after this morning's fiasco, but she'd been relatively calm. Roy was with her and she'd gripped his hand as she viewed Grandpa Franklin's body. She'd cried a little bit and then recovered. Now she was standing beside Roy, talking to some neighbors that I'd met earlier. Interestingly, except for holding his hand earlier, she and Roy were maintaining at least a foot of space between them. It looked like Mitch and I were the only people who knew how close they were.

The crowd shifted and I saw Mitch staring down into the casket. I went over and slipped my hand into his. "Hey," I said, softly. "How are you doing?"

He squeezed my hand instead of speaking. We stood that way for a while. Finally, he let out a deep sigh and we moved away from the casket. He put his arm around me and dropped his head down to my ear to whisper, "Thanks for being here."

"Of course," I said. I leaned back so that I could look at his face as I said, "About earlier, at the pool, I feel bad about what I said . . ." I trailed off because I really did think that the Averys would close ranks to protect their own, but I hated the tension between us. "Look, I don't want us to fight."

"Me either—well, unless we get to make up. That's the only good part about fighting," he said, and I could have sworn he waggled his eyebrows.

"Oh, I see what you're trying to do. You're trying to use your charming personality to distract me—get me to forget that something strange is going on."

"I'd hoped more than my personality would be involved."

"Mitch," I said, glancing around the room. "I can't believe this. Are you actually flirting with me during your grandfather's visitation?" The corners of his lips turned up as he gave a small shrug. "Maybe," he said.

"You *are* trying to distract me. How about a truce? You open your mind to the possibility that something . . . problematic . . . is going on and I'll see if there's anyone who doesn't have the last name of Avery who might be doing these things."

He looked at the ceiling for a moment, then locked back onto my gaze. "Deal. I'm always open to possibilities."

The next morning, I was again the first one awake. The house was completely quiet. No kids giggling and no aromas wafting from the kitchen. I made an effort to relax back into sleep, but I gave up after fifteen minutes and crawled out of bed, careful not to wake Mitch. I pawed through our jumble of clothes and decided I had to do some laundry, as I pulled on sweatpants and one of Mitch's Air Force Academy sweatshirts.

Five minutes later, I was standing in the driveway in the weak morning sun, twisting my hair up in a clip. The air was frigid and I wished I'd thought to grab my gloves. I shoved my hands in my pockets and set off at a near run to try and warm up. After a block, I was warmer and relaxed my shoulders, which I'd had shrugged up near my ears in an effort to maximize my body heat. I pulled my hands out of my pockets and settled into a steady stride, arms pumping, breathing out clouds of white air. A trash truck rumbled in the distance and a hound barked a few streets over. I turned the corner at the end of the block. A strip of dead grass planted with old-growth maples separated the sidewalk from the street. Most of the houses along the street had waist- or shoulder-high bushes lining the sidewalk. I'm sure in the summer it was a shady, leafy haven from the heat, but now it was a dim, dormant corridor of twisty brown branches interspersed with gaps of leaf-strewn concrete driveways. A few feet in front of me where the tall hedge stopped at the edge of the concrete driveway, someone stepped into my path.

Instinctively, I veered to the side, making for the street, and then it registered: the person was Detective Kalra. "Hello, Mrs. Avery. Do you have a moment?" she asked. She wasn't wearing the bulky jacket with the official logo. Instead, she had on a purple cashmere sweater, gray slacks, and black boots. She was holding a newspaper.

"Detective Kalra," I said, moving back to the sidewalk. "You surprised me."

"Sorry. Would you like to come inside for a moment?" she asked, pointing up the driveway with the newspaper toward a brown brick rancher with pale yellow shutters. "I've got coffee, if you'd like a cup."

"No, thanks. I didn't realize you lived in the neighborhood," I said slowly, wondering why she was being so solicitous—it was quite different from her almost antagonistic approach last time we'd spoken. And no matter how nice she was right now, I didn't want to share a cup of coffee.

"Since I saw you walking yesterday morning, I thought you might be by today. I'd like to talk to you."

"Oh," I said, surprised. She certainly hadn't been giving off a let's-be-friends vibe the last time we'd talked. Was this some sort of one-person version of the good cop–bad cop routine? "Thanks again, but I really do have to get back. The funeral is today," I said, and moved to step around her.

"I think the sheriff's department was too quick to close the investigation into the Franklin Avery situation."

"You made that quite clear the last time we spoke," I said, over my shoulder.

"I didn't get your message until late yesterday. Rickets tried to make sure I didn't get it at all." I turned and walked back to her as she said, "I didn't find out about the situation at the funeral home until last night. Look, I didn't want to do this on the street," she said as she gestured up and down the tree-lined avenue with the newspaper she held, "but I think something is wrong."

The frosty air was seeping back into my body, and my ears, face, and fingers were beginning to tingle. "Why are you telling me this? And why the friendly approach? Is it because you didn't get anywhere being intimidating and now you're trying to be my buddy?"

"No. I'm being straight with you." She gazed at me with her dark eyes, her face frank and open. A slight frown wrinkled the skin between her arched brows. She looked troubled. Her mouth quirked down and she hesitated a moment before plunging in and speaking quickly as if she wanted to get the words out in a rush. "Yesterday, I thought I could get the case reopened if I uncovered new evidence, but the pushback I got when I asked about your message and the way the funeral home incident was handled . . . well, I'll just say that Bud Avery has some good friends in this town. He wanted the case wrapped up and he got it."

"Uncle Bud put pressure on the police to close the case without investigating?" I asked, momentarily forgetting about my increasingly numb fingers.

She nodded, her dark gaze holding mine. "Yes, that's what I'm saying."

"Grandpa Franklin didn't die a natural death?"

"No, I'm not saying that," she said quickly as her frown deepened. She looked away at a car moving slowly down the street.

"Well, what do you mean? You can't just throw that out there."

"I know. I'm sorry. I shouldn't have put it that way. His autopsy came back clean—nothing. No unexpected drugs, no unusual bruises, marks, or cuts. And the scene at the house—no footprints outside the window. No unexpected fingerprints, nothing to indicate a struggle or intruder except the broken window, which could be a result of the storm. It's all very clean and tidy—on paper." She shook her head. "But there's something. I don't know what it is. The whole situation doesn't feel right."

"So you were fishing yesterday when you asked about my aunt?" I said, still wondering why she was sharing all these details with me. The case was closed, but I'd found out that trying to get investigators to share information was about as easy as getting the kids to confess to marking on the wall with crayons.

She sighed and slid the newspaper out of its protective plastic sleeve, then tucked it under one arm. "You could call it that, I guess. I was thinking more along the lines of following up my last hunch."

"You think Aunt Christine murdered her father?" As soon as I said the words aloud, I realized how ridiculous they sounded. Even though I'd thought something strange was going on with her rambling words, deep down, I didn't want to believe she'd hurt Grandpa Franklin. "That's absurd."

She carefully folded the plastic sleeve into thirds. "I agree with you," she said as she stuffed the plastic into her pocket and shifted her gaze to my face. "But Mr. Avery did take up quite a bit of her time. Maybe her boyfriend was tired of waiting."

"You think Roy—"

"It's a possibility, is all I'm saying," she said, interrupting me. "That's what we do, explore possibilities, at least when we're able to do our job properly," she said with more bite in her tone, but I realized her frustration wasn't directed at me.

"So what are you going to do? You can't just drop this bombshell and walk away."

"I never intended to do that. I have a conference in Memphis I have to attend, or, more accurately, have been ordered to attend. I'll be back on Monday. In the meantime, you have my card. I'd like you to call my cell phone if anything else unusual happens."

I didn't answer right away. I let my gaze drift to the black Camry in the driveway behind Detective Kalra where her rolling suitcase sat waiting beside the open trunk. She was asking me to side with her instead of the Avery family. I chewed my lip, thinking about it. Mitch would be furious if he knew. He'd already made it clear that any dirty laundry should stay inside the family. But this wasn't some family squabble. This was a possible murder. And if it was murder, I couldn't keep quiet. It was better to find out the truth. I gave her a quick nod, then said, "But what will you do? You've already said the case is closed."

She swallowed. "I can go over a certain person's head to get the case reopened, but I need more than I have right now." She looked slightly nauseous at the thought.

I said, "That would have to be a risky step, career-wise, I mean."

She pressed her lips together in a line as she nodded. "Yes. Yes, it would be, but I can't stand by and let someone get away with murder. If it was murder," she added quickly. "You see it's too big a question to leave open, don't you?"

"Yes, I certainly do. But what I still don't understand is why I'm suddenly your confidante."

She pulled the newspaper out from under her arm and cocked her head to the side as she studied me. "Well, you're part of the Avery family, but you're not."

"Pardon?"

"You're inside their circle, but you're not part of the circle. Not quite. You married into the family. You didn't grow up here. There's a division between you and them."

I stared at her, partly offended and partly irritated that she'd read the situation so accurately.

She frowned. "I'm sorry if I've upset you, but it's quite clear to an outsider like me that you haven't been completely absorbed into the Avery family. I get the sense that you're resisting total submersion," she said. "You're my way inside, the best I've got with my limited abilities right now."

I blew out a breath. "Well, if all your hunches are as dead-on as that assessment, then I can see why you'd want to follow up on them," I said.

"Oh, I'm good at my job, I will admit that." She released a small smile as she acknowledged the compliment, then her face turned serious. "Thank you for listening, Mrs. Avery. I know this is not what any family member wants to hear. I'm sorry my unorthodox methods have pulled you into this."

I shrugged. "I'm quite familiar with unorthodox methods, Detective."

She raised her eyebrows and said, "So I've heard."

Ellie Avery's Tips for Preserving Family Treasures

Unusual Ways to Preserve and Organize Artwork

- Oversized items—take a photo of items that are too large to store, like oversized paintings, a model volcano, or rock collections.
- Change the format—you can have children's artwork reproduced on everyday items like refrigerator magnets, coffee cups, calendars, or T-shirts.
- New art from old—create a collage with pieces cut from several different art projects. Use a collage frame with individual framed sections, or overlap the projects in a single large frame.

Chapter
Ten

"**D**idn't the soloist sound beautiful?" one woman asked as she dipped a baby carrot in a pool of ranch dressing on her small plate.

"Oh, yes," the woman beside her said, her highlighted blond bangs bobbing as she nodded. "The best rendition of 'Amazing Grace' I've heard in a long time," she agreed before she speared a sausage ball with a toothpick and popped it into her mouth.

I picked up a discarded plastic cup and plate from the fireplace mantel and edged around the women who were wearing dark suits. I assumed from the way they'd greeted Caroline that they were Realtors and knew her from work. The funeral and graveside service were over and we were back at Caroline and Bill's house. The funeral had been held at Grandpa Franklin's Baptist church, which had been packed with mourners. The service had gone quickly and I hadn't caught all of it because my mind kept drifting to my encounter with Detective Kalra. The music had been superb. The soloist did have an excellent, effortless voice. Uncle Bud's reading of the poem had also been moving simply because he didn't seem the type to recite poetry. He'd looked slightly uncomfortable in his suit and kept pulling at his tie, but now that the service was over, he'd lost the jacket and rolled up his sleeves, revealing the phoenix tattoo, and he looked more like his normal self. Not as many people came to the graveside service, which was even shorter. A small contingent of family and friends had returned to Caroline and Bill's house for food. I drifted around the room, picking up trash, hearing snatches of conversation.

". . . and then there was that story he used to tell about how he talked his younger brother into jumping off the barn with a bedsheet as a parachute," Dan said.

Laughter sounded from the group of men gathered on the couch holding cups of coffee, then one of them shook his head and said, "Lucky for Frank, his brother landed in a pile of hay."

I stacked a few more discarded cups and moved to the dining room where Felicity was staring at Aunt Gwen as she said, ". . . You don't mean that was true? He really did travel to China? I thought that was just one of his stories."

"Oh, no . . . I think it was when he was in his twenties. You know that ornate brown box on the shelf under the windows? He brought that back . . ."

I moved back into the kitchen to dump the trash, thinking that Felicity was the last person she should tell about old—which in Felicity's mind probably equaled *valuable*—Chinese boxes. I made a mental note to check and see if they were still there the next time we went over.

Aunt Christine and Roy were sitting beside each other on the couch. He stretched his arm across the back cushions and Aunt Christine inched away, looking uncomfortable.

The kids circled through the living room again and I shooed them back to the bedrooms. All we needed was for one of the kids to come skidding down the hall and run into an adult carrying coffee and a plate of food. They seemed to be handling the events of the day okay. I didn't think Nathan fully understood what had happened, but Livvy did. She'd cried that morning, when we left for the funeral.

"Oh, there you are. I've been looking for you."

I turned and saw Maggie. She was wearing a dark tunic sweater in a loose weave that came down to her hips and partially covered a crinkly black skirt. A flowing multicolored scarf was wrapped around her neck and hung almost to the hem of her skirt. She was digging around in a large shoulder bag. "Is your daughter here? I brought . . . well, I thought . . . oh, where is it? Here we go," she said as she pulled out a book. I recognized it as the newest book in the mystery series, which Livvy had borrowed from her cousin.

"Livvy will be so excited. I'll go find her."

When I returned with a curious Livvy in tow, Maggie crouched down to her level. She had a pen uncapped and poised over the title page. "Hi, Livvy. Your mom told me how much you enjoy my books. Can I sign this one for you?"

Livvy's eyes widened as her gaze ricocheted from the book to Maggie's face and back again. "Oh! You're—you write the books—my favorite—"

Since it looked like it might be awhile before Livvy was capable of a coherent sentence, I leaned down and said, "Yes, I'm sure Livvy would like that very much."

Maggie signed her name with a flourish under a note, then handed the book to Livvy. "I know this has to be a sad day for you. I thought this might help you feel a bit better," she said.

Livvy nodded, then quickly read the inscription. She closed the book and clutched it to her chest as she grinned at Maggie. I was about to nudge Livvy and remind her to say thank you, but she did me proud. "Thank you so much. It's lovely to meet you."

"Delighted," Maggie replied as she stood back up. Livvy gave her one more shy smile, then sprinted down the hall.

"Thank you. I can't tell you how much that means to Livvy."

"I'm glad to do it. I was just thinking about what a difficult day this is for her—and the whole family, of course. I was devastated when my grandmother died." She let out a sigh. "I was about Livvy's age when it happened." She'd been looking down the hall after Livvy, but seemed to gather herself and focus on me as she said, "Now, I really must leave. Pages to write, you know."

I made another circuit of the living room, gathering empty plates. The crowd was thinning as several people moved to get coats from the pile in one of the bedrooms. As I walked behind the couch, I heard Roy say, "Ready to leave?"

Aunt Christine stiffened. "No. We can't leave together. You go on."

"But I want to run you home. I know it's been a long day. Besides, I drove." He stood up and extended his hand to her.

"No," she shook her head and said in a voice so low that I could barely hear her. "You go. I'll get someone else to run me home."

Roy dropped his hand back to his side. "What is this, Christine? You've been acting strange all day."

She didn't look up at him. Instead, she focused on the plastic cup she held. "I can't be gallivanting around with you on the day of his funeral. It's not seemly. You go on."

"Christine, no one is going to think twice if I give you a ride home." He waited a moment and when Aunt Christine didn't respond, he went and spoke to Bill and Caroline, then left. I helped Caroline put the extra food away, then I returned to the living room. Aunt Christine was still sitting on the couch with a pensive look on her face. Aunt Nanette and Uncle Bud were sitting in chairs beside the couch and were leaning toward each other as they talked.

"You doing okay?" I asked as I sat down beside Aunt Christine.

She started and then glanced at me. "Yes. Sorry. Lost in thought. Just thinking of what needs to be done. Dad's icebox needs to be cleaned out—hadn't even thought of that. And I left a stack of his envelopes sitting on the kitchen counter."

"I'm sure next week will be soon enough. You're probably ready to go home." She did look limp with exhaustion. "You've already done so much," I said, thinking of her scurrying around making phone calls and laying out food, making coffee and tea, then setting out extra chairs. "Maybe someone else can do that," I said, and looked over to Aunt Nanette and Uncle Bud.

"Do what?" asked Aunt Nanette.

"The refrigerator needs to be cleaned out at Grandpa Franklin's house," I said.

"I can't," Aunt Nanette said without a hint of apology. "I have to get home and let Queen out—she's been shut up in the house all day. And the next few days are full. We're in the final countdown to Book Daze."

Aunt Christine nodded, like it was a done deal, but I looked at Uncle Bud with raised eyebrows.

"Me?" he said. Clearly, the idea that he might be expected to clean out a refrigerator had never crossed his mind. "I can't do it, either. Got to get back to the office. Check in. Meetings all weekend, too," he mumbled.

I said, "Well, maybe Uncle Kenny or Aunt Gwen—"

"They have a business to run, as does Caroline," Aunt Christine said flatly. "I'll take care of it."

"You do have more time," Uncle Bud said. Looking relieved that he wouldn't be checking expiration dates, he said heartily, "Yep, not all of us are lucky enough to be retired."

"Yes, I do have all the time in the world," she said dryly. Uncle Bud totally missed the underlying sarcasm. I got the feeling that the "you're retired" card had been played many times as duty after duty had fallen on her as Grandpa Franklin aged.

Uncle Bud stood up. "More coffee, anyone?"

"None for me," I said. Aunt Nanette declined, but she wanted more cheese and crackers and followed him into the kitchen.

Aunt Christine was tapping her finger against her lips. She'd already moved on from the irritation she'd shown toward Uncle Bud. She said thoughtfully, "You're right, I can leave the icebox until later, but I forgot to mail the envelope with the electric bill, too. It's due in next week. Tuesday, I think. I really should go by there and pick it up along with the rest of the envelopes. If it goes in the mail today, then it won't be late." She pressed her hands against her thighs as she stood up with a sigh. "I'd completely forgotten about all these little details, but now that the funeral's over, I'm remembering them."

"The bill probably isn't that urgent. They'll just send another bill with the late fee and that will go to the executor of his estate." I stood up beside her as she moved slowly around the couch.

"Dad *never* missed a payment—that was another thing that signaled something was wrong. He forgot to pay a whole stack of bills. When I saw those bills with their due dates just a few days away, I nearly fainted. Dad never, ever missed a payment. No, I really should go over there and put the envelopes in the mail. I wonder if Nanette is ready to leave." She leaned down to pick up her purse, her movements slow and laborious like she was weighed down.

"How about I run you home and we'll pick them up on the way?"

She looked up, surprised. "Ellie, that would be so kind."

I found her coat and mine, then went to check in with Mitch, but he'd rounded up the kids and was playing a game of flag football with them in the backyard. I told Caroline I was going to run Aunt Christine home and she said, "Oh, thank you, dear. She does look like she's almost asleep on her feet. She never would admit that she's tired, but I think the whole thing—discovering him and the investigation—has taken a toll on her."

We were barely out of the driveway before Aunt Christine's eyes drifted closed, so I drove her straight home. Her eyes popped open as I stopped behind her small car, which was sheltered in the carport. The honeysuckle vine on the side of the carport looked thicker and the flowers seemed to be a deeper red. "Oh! Did I fall asleep? How embarrassing. I hope I didn't snore."

"No, nothing like that," I said. "I'll run back to Grandpa Franklin's and pick up the envelopes, if you'll give me his key. I can drop them in the mailbox on the way back to Bill and Caroline's house."

"You don't have to do that. There's a post office just a little ways back up the road. It'll just take a few minutes—"

"No, I insist. You're tired and I have to drive right by Grandpa Franklin's house on the way back. I saw the post office and I can drop the envelopes there. Besides, you need to let someone do something for you every once in a while."

She blinked and said, "Well, that's a new thought. I'm usually the one who . . ."

"Does everything," I said, finishing her sentence. "I know. I can tell. You go on and get some rest. I'll help with the refrigerator, too. Just give me a call and tell me when to meet you there."

"That's nice of you, Ellie," she said as she worked a key off her key ring. "Mitch picked a good one when he picked you."

"Oh, I don't know about that . . . ," I said, suddenly feeling guilty as I thought of the speculation Detective Kalra had cast on Roy and Aunt Christine. And I'd wondered about her strange behavior, too. I didn't think she'd feel so charitable toward me if she knew that. Sure, I wanted to help her out. I knew what it was like to have people dump things on you. Being a part-time, stay-at-home mom meant I was very familiar with the neighbors who expected to be able to leave their kids with me when school was cancelled or when they had a dentist appointment. What else could I have to do except watch their kids? After all, I was home all day, anyway.

"Oh, I'm right about you, Ellie. No one else would offer to help me clean out an icebox. You're a good one." She levered herself out of the car, then leaned back down to speak to me. "Let's see, Monday . . . it'll have to be before the meeting with Gus."

"Who?" I asked.

"Gus Wallis, the attorney," Aunt Christine said. "The reading of the will. It's at one."

"Oh, right. I don't think Mitch and I are going to be there."

Aunt Christine said, "You and Mitch have to be there. All the seconds have to be there."

"Seconds?" I asked. Was she more tired than I realized?

"You know, the second generation of Averys. My brothers and sisters, we're the first generation. You, Mitch, Felicity, and Dan, and so on, are the second generation. Your kids are the third. Much easier to say firsts and seconds have to be at the reading of the will, if you see what I mean."

"Oh. Of course." I'd forgotten the special terminology the Averys used. I'd found out it was pretty common in the South to refer to different generations of a family with unique names. After years of being a military spouse, I should be good at decoding jargon, but the lingo of the Avery family still got the best of me at times. "All right. How about we meet at Grandpa Franklin's house at ten on Monday? I'll return the key to you then." It had already been decided that we'd be attending church with Bill and Caroline on Sunday. Aunt Christine went to a different church closer to her house, so I wouldn't see her until Monday.

"Good idea. See you then. The envelopes are on the kitchen

counter, already stamped. Thank you for the ride," Aunt Christine said before she shut the minivan's door. I waited until she was inside, then drove to Grandpa Franklin's where I parked beside the kitchen door and retrieved the key from the minivan's empty cup holder where I'd tossed it.

I trotted up the steps and unlocked the door. It stuck a little, so I shoved it and stumbled into the kitchen when it finally opened. I caught my balance, then switched on the light. The curtains were still closed and the room was gloomy. I shivered. The house felt extremely drafty. Someone—Aunt Christine?—must have turned down the heat. I chafed my hands together as I crossed the kitchen and picked up the stack of envelopes. My heels clumped loudly across the hardwood floor. I'd dressed up for the funeral, breaking out my little black dress and heels. I wore them so rarely that I was amazed they still fit. I was more used to wearing T-shirts, tennis shoes, and jeans, only occasionally throwing on business casual pants and a nice blouse for consultation appointments with potential organizing clients. I also had on a black cardigan under my thick wool double-breasted pea coat, but I still felt shivery and wished I'd grabbed some gloves or a scarf.

I glanced through the stack of outgoing mail to make sure the electric bill was there. It was, but with the temperature in the house so low, I didn't really see why Aunt Christine was worried about it. The furnace clicked on and I felt a gush of cool air hit my ankles before a blast of warm air followed. I frowned and stuck the envelopes in my pocket. If the heater was on, it certainly wasn't doing much good. Maybe I should check to see what the temperature was set at? I glanced around the murky darkness of the living room, wondering where the thermostat might be. I stepped out of the kitchen and noticed a light in the small hallway off the living room was on. I didn't see a thermostat as I crossed the room, but the air grew increasingly colder as I neared the hallway.

I don't know what it was—the icy air or the contrast between the dark living room and the bright hallway—but something made me move more slowly as I neared the hallway. The slice of braided rug, mirror, and open bedroom door looked completely normal. But I could feel the cold air on my face now and I could see the light wasn't emanating from the overhead fixture in the hallway. It was coming from the right, shining up at an angle. The hairs on the back of my neck stood up.

It's nothing, I told myself—probably just a night-light. But as I got closer to the door frame, I saw the light was a narrow beam, splashing up the wall, widening as it neared the ceiling. I was suddenly aware of my heartbeat rushing in my ears as I leaned cautiously around the door frame.

There was a man sprawled at the end of the hall.

Chapter
Eleven

My heart slammed into overdrive as disjoined thoughts formed. Definitely a man. No one I recognized right off, but his face was turned away from me toward the stairs. He wasn't moving at all. Was he okay? I couldn't see his chest moving, but it was pretty dim in the hallway, even with the light from the flashlight.

Get out. Get out now. Don't look. Just get out.

I walked backward a step, but I couldn't do it. I couldn't leave without seeing if he was all right. I stepped back into the doorway, then inched a bit closer to him.

My stomach lurched at the unnatural angle of his head. There was no way he was alive. Blood had pooled under the side of his face on the floor. I looked away and I forced myself to breathe in and out. *Don't be sick. Don't be sick.*

I gazed at the stairs, fighting down the surge of bile in my throat. I focused on the rug at the top of the stairs. It was wrinkled and twisted so that the edge of it lapped over the top step. There was a glove on a step about halfway down the stairs. My gaze was pulled back down the stairs. I didn't want to look, but I couldn't help it. I stumbled backward and caught the door frame to the hallway. *Police.* I needed to call the police. *Fingerprints*—I jerked my hand away from the door frame.

A groan sounded behind me. I whirled toward the extra bedroom, then swiveled back so that I could see both the bedroom and the man's body down the hall. I didn't want my back to anything. As impossible as that was, that's how I felt.

The eerie noise came again, this time fainter, and I saw the door to the extra bedroom shift an inch. It was open and I could see the room was empty. I leaned to the side and looked down the tiny strip of space on the side of the door where the hinges were. Through that sliver, I could see there was no one behind the door. The door wavered again, letting out another creaky moan as the hinges shifted. I released a jerky breath that sounded loud in the stillness of the house. A gust of cold air brushed my face as the door creaked and shifted another inch, revealing that the board that had covered the broken window was gone. The window was wide open.

I backed out of the hallway and hurried across the living room. I was running by the time I got to the kitchen. It's amazing I didn't fall as I skidded down the steps outside the kitchen door. I fumbled with the key fob and unlocked the van door with a click. I scrambled inside, locked the doors. My cold fingers trembled as I dug my cell phone out of my purse and punched in the three numbers that would bring the police back to Grandpa Franklin's house.

After I'd given all the details to her, the 911 operator told me to stay on the line.

"I can't. I've got to make another call," I said.

"We need you to stay on the line," she countered.

"I'm not going anywhere. I'll be here when the police get here," I said, and hung up. I dialed Mitch's phone number. He wasn't going to like this one bit. The wind whipped a few dry pine needles against the windshield and I flinched. I realized I was shivering and turned the ignition key, then cranked the heat. The phone line rang as I watched the wind sweep some brown leaves across the driveway and into an eddy before they caught in the undergrowth of the bushes surrounding the back of the house. I knew the body inside the house was going to stir up everything that had been so carefully smoothed over. The questions about the disappearance at the funeral home would be looked into further and the Avery family wouldn't be happy about that, Mitch included.

The call finally went to voice mail and I left a quick message with the basic facts. As I hung up, a sheriff's car pulled into the driveway and Officer Taggart emerged. I stayed in the van and rolled my window down as he came around.

"Hello, ma'am. You called nine-one-one?"

"Yes, I did. There's a body in the house. At the foot of the stairs."

"A body?"

"Yes. A dead body. I don't know who it is."

"And why were you in the house . . . ?"

"I was picking up some mail for my aunt, Christine Avery. She gave me the key."

"You were here the other day. You're the daughter-in-law from out of town."

"Yes, I'm Ellie Avery."

He wrote down my name and contact information, then told me to stay in the car. "Is the door locked?" he asked, looking at the door that opened into the kitchen.

"No. I didn't lock it when I ran out, just called nine-one-one." A second car from the sheriff's office pulled into the driveway and another officer joined Officer Taggart at the steps leading up to the kitchen door. I watch, fascinated, as they drew their guns and held them, arms stiff, and pointed the barrels to the ground. They exchanged nods and then went through the door. I blinked and shook my head. I felt like I was watching a cop show. The few windows on this side of the house reflected back the banks of trees and bushes with a slice of sky. I couldn't see anything inside. I didn't think there had been anyone else in the house, but I supposed you couldn't be too careful when you entered a crime scene.

I shifted the heat to a lower setting and flexed my fingers around my phone. I was finally warm, but I wondered if Mitch had picked up my voice message. I glanced at the clock on the dashboard. Five more minutes. I'd give him that before I called Bill and Caroline's house. I couldn't put it off longer than that.

They should have found the man by now. I watched the door,

which they'd left open, but no one appeared. I'd seen the dead man—before, when his face was whole and normal. I swallowed hard and forced myself to think about the clothes he'd worn—tan barn coat over a brown plaid shirt, tan slacks, and suede lace-up boots.

The jacket had been large and had probably covered up his heftiness when he was alive, but with him sprawled on the floor, the jacket had fallen open and showed the man's pudgy stomach straining against the fabric of the brown plaid shirt. There had been a second glove, a match to the one on the stairs, hanging halfway out of his coat pocket. My mind flashed back to the man's face. I didn't want to dwell on that image, but I took a steadying breath and made myself think about his features. His face—the side that had been turned up toward me—had been plump and rounded. His sparse hair was brownish gray. And there had been some facial hair—not a beard, but a goatee. I'd only been able to see a small bit of it because his head had been turned away, but I remembered the goatee. It was brown going gray.

I'd met someone recently who had a goatee. Had he been at the funeral? I didn't think so. Earlier? Had I met him at the visitation? That was it! I sat up straighter—the Weebles guy. What was his name? Sam? No—Stan. Stan . . . Anderson. Stan Anderson. I'd only talked to him briefly at the visitation, but he'd said he'd never met Grandpa Franklin. I flipped my phone around and around in my hands, trying to figure out why he'd be in the house in the first place.

Officer Taggart came out the door. His gun was in his holster and the other officer moved behind him at a regular pace. So the inside of the house must be empty except for Stan Anderson. The second officer moved off around the back of the house and Officer Taggart came over to my window. I rolled it down.

"Describe to me what happened when you arrived here."

I took him through each thing I'd done and when I finished, the second officer had come back and drew Officer Taggart aside. They were only a few feet away and I could hear the second officer reporting, "No sign of footprints. There's a thick ground cover under the window and with all these leaves, there won't be anything in the woods."

"Check anyway," Officer Taggart said, and the other officer nodded and left to search the woods behind the house.

A flash of reflected light in the mirror shined in my eyes and I turned to watch an F-150 pickup roar into the gravel beside me. It was followed by another car, this one a dark blue four-door sedan with tinted windows. Uncle Bud swung down from the pickup's driver's seat and Mitch climbed out of the other side. Detective Rickets emerged from the unmarked car. He braced his hands on his hips and stretched his shoulders back, then went to greet Uncle Bud with a hearty handshake.

Mitch trotted over to the van and I unlocked the doors. "Ellie, you're so pale. Are you okay? I came as soon as I got your message."

"Yes. A little shaken up, but okay. It's Stan Anderson in there," I said, tilting my head toward the house. "He was at the visitation. I met him."

"Why are you even here? Mom said something about you taking Aunt Christine home."

I explained what had happened as I pulled the bills out of my coat pocket and set them in the console between us. "I ran out here and called the police," I said as I wound up my story.

"You're sure he was dead? Not just passed out?"

"Oh, he was dead all right," I said, catching sight of my face in the rearview mirror. Mitch was right. My skin looked chalky. "His neck's broken."

Mitch took my hand and squeezed. "You're okay now. Everything's going to be okay now."

I smiled at him halfheartedly. "I don't think so."

"Why?" Mitch asked.

"Don't you see? This is going to reopen the investigation into Grandpa Franklin's death. Even though he's already buried, they'll have to try and figure out why Stan broke into his house."

Mitch frowned as Detective Rickets ambled down the steps from the kitchen door and rounded the corner toward the back of the

house. There was a tap on Mitch's window and we both jumped.
Uncle Bud loomed beside the window. Mitch rolled the window
down and a frigid breeze coursed through the two open windows.
"So, Ellie, what's the story here?" Uncle Bud asked. He might have
been asking me if I thought it was going to rain later today.

"A man's dead," I said flatly.

My abrupt answer didn't seem to bother him. "Know who it is?"
he asked conversationally.

"His name was Stan Anderson."

"Stan Anderson? Who the hell is Stan Anderson?"

Before anyone could answer him, Detective Rickets came around
the corner of the house and walked up to Uncle Bud. "It's the new
guy, Stan Anderson. Was going to open up some sort of restaurant."

"A pizzeria," I said, and everyone turned to look at me. "I met
him at the visitation. He said he was opening a pizzeria in downtown Smarr. He didn't know Grandpa Franklin, but his father did.
That's why he came to the visitation."

Detective Rickets studied me for a moment, then turned back to
Uncle Bud, a deliberate dismissal of me. "It'll take us awhile to get
the body out. Coroner's on his way."

"What happened?" Uncle Bud asked.

Detective Rickets shrugged a shoulder. "Funeral was today,
right? Announced in the paper?" When Uncle Bud confirmed both
things, Detective Rickets said, "Anderson probably saw the notice
and figured it was the best time to break into the house. Pick up a
few valuables before the relatives take everything away."

"But it didn't look like he'd taken anything," I said, and Detective Rickets leaned down so he could see me inside the van. "Was
there anything in his pockets?" I asked, thinking of the large pockets on the barn coat.

"No, well, nothing you wouldn't expect. Wallet, keys, that sort of
thing."

"Then how could it be a robbery?" I asked.

"He didn't have a chance to take anything before he died."

"But he was at the foot of the stairs. The rug at the top of the
stairs was rumpled and one of his gloves was on a step. He'd been

upstairs. If he was looking for valuables, wouldn't he have taken something from there and have it with him on the way back down?"

Mitch pressed my hand and I shot him a look. Detective Rickets said, "Probably doing a quick run through to get the layout of the house. He takes the stairs too quickly, trips, and, well . . . that's it. Down he goes, pockets empty."

I supposed it could have happened that way, but it wouldn't have been my first assumption. "Why would Stan break into Grandpa Franklin's house, anyway? It's not like he was extremely wealthy or had lots of valuables lying around."

"You'd be surprised what some people consider valuable, Mrs. Avery," Detective Rickets said. "A jacket, a pair of shoes. Even one of those fancy digital music players all the kids have now. Heck, Mr. Avery had a TV and that's probably all it took."

"But the TV is still there. He didn't take it. He hadn't taken *anything*."

Mitch gripped my hand tighter and I glared at him. Detective Rickets stepped back from the window and turned so that his back was to us, and he spoke to Uncle Bud. Mitch powered up his window, then twisted around to face me. "Ellie, what are you doing? Are you trying to irritate him?"

"No! I'm trying to get him to do his job—investigate—but it doesn't look like that's going to happen." Detective Rickets shook hands with Uncle Bud, who looked satisfied. "Uncle Bud wouldn't look like that unless Detective Rickets was doing exactly what he wanted."

"What are you talking about?"

"Uncle Bud pressured the sheriff's department to close your grandfather's case. And he's doing the same thing here."

"How could you even know that? Did Uncle Bud tell you himself?"

"No. Someone in the sheriff's department told me." Mitch opened his mouth and I quickly said, "And that's all I can say right now, but this person is someone who would know."

Mitch ran his fingers through his hair, a sure sign of frustration. Under his breath, he said, "Contacts. She has contacts in my hometown. How is that possible?" He took a deep breath and turned to me. "Okay. Let's leave that for now. Let's stay focused on what's really important here. Why? Why would Uncle Bud do that?"

"I don't know—that's what my . . . my . . . source is trying to figure out. Look at it this way, Uncle Bud is pretty powerful around here, right? How many times have you told me how he influenced zoning changes and county decisions? He's got connections and he's not shy about using them to get what he wants."

"But why would he want the case closed?"

"I don't know. Maybe he's got something to hide. Maybe someone in the family has something to hide."

"Are you serious?" Mitch's gaze was cold. "You really think a relative is involved in this? That is the most absurd thing I've ever heard. I thought you were letting go of the Avery family as prime suspects."

"No, I'm not saying an Avery is involved. I don't know what happened. But Uncle Bud got the investigation of Grandpa Franklin's death shut down. Now there's a dead man in Grandpa Franklin's house on the day of the funeral. And that's not even taking into account the whole missing casket fiasco. Yes, I'm serious about this. What I don't understand is how anyone wouldn't be seriously looking into what's going on."

My cell phone rang and I snatched it up. I listened, then said, "Okay, I'll be back in a few minutes."

I turned to Mitch and said, "That was Caroline. Livvy's not feeling good. We need to get back."

"Why don't you go ahead," Mitch said stiffly as he opened the door and stepped out. "I'll catch a ride back with Uncle Bud."

"Fine," I said shortly, and put the van in reverse.

"Fine." He shoved the door hard.

"Fine!" I managed to get out before the door slammed. He turned and walked to Uncle Bud's truck without a backward look.

Ellie Avery's Tips for Preserving Family Treasures

Organizing Photographs
If you have hard copies of your photos, thin your photographs before placing them in albums or photo boxes. You don't want to regret throwing away photos later, so err on the side of caution. There are many ways to organize photos:

- Chronologically by date—this is the most popular.
- By individual—a photo album or collection focused on a single person. Some families like to keep both chronological albums as well as a running album for each child. A photo collection that focuses on a child is a wonderful graduation or wedding gift.
- By location/event—since we tend to take more photos on special occasions, you could organize photos around holiday celebrations or family reunions.
- Scrapbooking—this hobby takes photo albums to the next level and allows you to showcase the most interesting and unique photographs by combining them with decorative papers, text, and embellishments that reveal the story behind the photographs.

Chapter Twelve

"Aunt Nanette, why do you think Stan Anderson was in Grandpa Franklin's house?" I asked. A furry head loomed beside me and I reached up to rub Queen's ears. I was riding in the front passenger seat of Aunt Nanette's Mini Cooper, Queen's usual seat, and she wasn't pleased with the situation. She ducked her head under my arm and tried to wiggle into my lap.

"Queen, back," Aunt Nanette commanded, and Queen retreated to the backseat where she paced from window to window while whining softly. Aunt Nanette came to a complete stop at the corner of the residential street, then drove slowly across the intersection. At this rate, Aunt Christine would be completely finished cleaning out the refrigerator before we even got halfway to Grandpa Franklin's house.

Aunt Nanette sneezed, a tiny feminine sneeze that was completely at odds with her brusque personality and appearance. There was nothing girly about Aunt Nanette's black trench coat, gray sweater, tan corduroy pants, and clumpy boots. "I hope you're not getting sick, too," I said. I'd returned to Bill and Caroline's house late on Friday to find Livvy sitting limply on the couch. Her eyes were watery and she was sneezing. She had a cold and had spent most of Saturday and Sunday sleeping in our bedroom. On Sunday evening, she'd perked up and said she felt like eating and watching

TV, which I knew meant that she was on the road to recovery. Not wanting to spread her cold to the rest of the family, I'd stayed home with Livvy while Mitch and Nathan attended church with Bill and Caroline on Sunday. Nathan had been sick a week ago with the same symptoms, so I figured he was in the clear and could interact with people.

It amazed me that the presence of so many people actually made it easier for Mitch and me not to talk. He spent a lot of time with his dad, which was a good thing. Bill had looked pretty devastated at the funeral service and I hoped that having Mitch around helped him a little as he grieved. They'd spent quite a bit of time in the sunroom at the back of the house. They'd alternated between watching basketball and playing checkers. Mitch also met Dan at the neighborhood park for a game of one-on-one basketball yesterday.

Mitch had stayed at Grandpa Franklin's house on Friday until Stan's body was removed. Except for a few brief conversations about going to the store to pick up medicine for Livvy and whether or not Nathan had to eat his sausage links at breakfast, Mitch and I had hardly spoken to each other. I knew he was upset with me for insisting that something odd was going on around Grandpa Franklin's death. I'd called Detective Kalra and left her a message about Stan's death. She'd called me back Sunday, but I'd missed her call and her message had only said she would do what she could to look into the situation and she'd be back Monday.

Apparently, any inquires Detective Kalra had made hadn't changed the situation around Stan's death. Uncle Bud had come by for coffee early this morning and informed Bill and Caroline that Stan's next of kin had been notified and that the sheriff's department told him the case was wrapped up. Aunt Nanette had also dropped in on Sunday to check on Livvy, which surprised me, because I hadn't noticed her paying much attention to the kids during the last few days. In fact, I'd have thought she'd find it a challenge to match all the names to faces. Nothing against Aunt Nanette—I still have trouble keeping all the Avery relations straight. But she arrived with a stack of word puzzle books, a picture book about English castles, and a carton of orange juice, which she told Livvy would fix her right up. She dropped in again this morning, Monday, with another book—this one was a kid's graphic novel about King Arthur. "The kids love these—comic books with a newfangled name," she'd said to me, pointing to the graphic novel. She didn't stay long since she was on her way to prepare for Smarr's book festival, and she'd offered to give me a ride when she realized I was going to Grandpa Franklin's house to help Aunt Christine.

Mitch and I had a brief conversation—well, more an exchange of one-line sentences—that morning about me going to help Aunt Christine. He'd told me he was okay with keeping an eye on Livvy until the reading of the will. The same babysitter was returning to watch the kids and since Livvy didn't have a fever and she kept bouncing out of the bed instead of lying there listlessly, I knew she'd be fine, but I was worried that she'd already passed her cold onto the rest of the family.

Aunt Nanette wiped her nose with a tissue and said, "I'm not sick. I haven't had a cold in fifteen years. Allergies, nothing else." She sounded like she would take it as a personal affront if she came down with a cold. "Now what were you asking about? That unfortunate man who died?"

"Yes, did you know him?"

"No. Never heard of him," she said dismissively. "Apparently, he was a thief."

"You don't think it's a little strange that he died in Grandpa Franklin's house on the day of his funeral?"

Aunt Nanette sighed as she turned into the driveway to Grandpa Franklin's house. "Honey, I think almost everything that goes on nowadays is strange."

"What do you mean?"

"I'm old—out of touch, I suppose you'd say, but so many people are just plain loony. Like Felicity suddenly deciding she can't eat eggs and milk. A vegan, she called it," she said with a snort as she pulled the car to a stop at the foot of the kitchen steps beside Aunt Christine's car. "Sounds like something out of a science fiction movie. Eating an egg isn't going to hurt anyone. And all this caterwauling about polar bears and the ice caps. Seems to me that a polar bear is one animal that can take care of itself as long as people aren't hunting it. It's not like they're marooned on ice floes. They can swim, can't they? And these people who dress their dogs up in clothes like dolls. I'll be the first to admit that I spoil Queen, but I never forget that she's a dog. I draw the line at frilled dresses for dogs." Aunt Nanette broke off abruptly, then smiled at me. "See, you've got me up on my soapbox. Forget about my rants—those things are neither here nor there. The man was a thief or he was just plain loony. Either way, being able to understand or even guess why he was there—well, I don't think I'm the person to ask."

I glanced back at Queen as I climbed out of the car. She'd already hopped into the front seat, obviously glad to see me go. "I don't think Queen would look good in ruffles, either. Not dignified enough," I said. "Thanks for the ride. Do you have time to come inside?"

She glanced at the house and her face softened slightly. "No. I can't. If I go in there . . . ," she broke off, and shook her head before saying, "all I'll be able to think about is that he's gone." She cleared her throat and said, "So I'm off. Lots of work to do today."

I nodded and climbed the steps. I'd assumed Aunt Nanette was using her volunteer work to get out of helping Aunt Christine, but from the vulnerable expression that had flitted across her face when I mentioned coming inside, it looked like staying busy was her way of coping with grief. I rapped on the kitchen door and Aunt Christine opened it. "Ellie! You remembered!" she said as I stepped inside and shut the door behind me, making sure to lock it. Not that I thought we had anything to worry about . . . but it didn't hurt to be cautious.

Aunt Christine was in her boot-cut jeans and a sweatshirt with the slogan "I dig treasure hunting" embroidered on it. "I just started," she said. She'd pulled out a cabinet drawer to hold open the refrigerator door. Brown grocery bags sat on the countertop. In the living room, she'd opened the curtains, but left the lamps off and, with the deep overhanging eaves of the bungalow, the room was mostly in shadow.

"Okay, what would you like me to do?" I asked.

"Why don't you take the food out and I'll bag it. There's a garbage bag over there for anything that's spoiled."

I handed her a stick of butter and a jar of peach jam. "So you looked around when you first got here?"

"Oh my, yes. I still can't believe what happened to you last week," she said, shaking her head. "I'm so sorry that happened. You're probably still shaken up, aren't you? You didn't have to come today, you know."

"I'm all right, but I wouldn't want to be here alone." I sniffed a half gallon of milk and reared back. "This has gone bad." Christine took it from me and emptied it into the sink. "You're certainly braver than I would be. I wouldn't have come in alone. How did you get in here?" I asked as I dug in my pocket and pulled out the key she'd given me last week so I could pick up the envelopes.

"I used the one that's hidden outside. Dad always kept a key on the front porch in one of the porch pillars." She took the key from me and put it on the counter beside her purse. "There's a crevice around one of those rocks and a key fits right in and you'd never notice it unless you knew where it was. I walked through the whole house as soon as I arrived. The window is boarded up again and everything else was locked up tight. Bud had one of his crews come over and . . . clean."

"Oh, he did, did he?" I asked, and couldn't keep the sarcasm out of my tone.

"Yes, he's got connections all over town—painters, framers, electricians, plumbers. After all his years in real estate, if it's got anything to do with home repair or remodeling—Bud's the man to talk to."

I opened the vegetable tray and pulled out a plastic bag of what had once been lettuce, but now resembled sludge. I tossed it in the garbage bag. "I see. Has he got connections in the sheriff's department, too?"

"You mean, Joel Rickets? He's known Joel for years. They drink coffee together most every morning down at Krispy Kreme."

"That explains it," I said as I handed her some shiny Gala apples.

"Explains what?"

"Why Rickets closed the case so quickly on Stan Anderson's death."

As Aunt Christine placed the apples in one of the bags, she tilted her head. "But what else could he investigate? The man was a stranger, an opportunist, who was stealing from us during a traumatic time. I don't feel sorry for him at all." Aunt Christine tucked a loaf of bread onto the top layer of one of the brown grocery bags. "It looks like he had a pattern of this type of behavior."

"Breaking and entering?"

"No, Joel said something about embezzlement. Charges were filed, but the case was dropped before it went to court . . . or something like that. But still, embezzlement is stealing, just a different way of going about it."

"But you haven't discovered that anything's missing here, right?" I asked.

"No. Joel came and got me and I looked through the whole house. Nothing's gone—except that Depression glass that Felicity took, but we'll sort that out as a family, so there's no need to tell him about it. That man probably hadn't gotten to the actual taking part. He was casing the place."

"Did Grandpa Franklin have anything small that was valuable? Anything that could fit in his pockets?"

"No . . . nothing like that. He gave us girls all of Mother's jewelry when she died. The only other valuables were the TV, stereo, and computer. They were too old to interest a thief. "

"Well, he must have been after something small because he didn't have a car. How did he get here? This isn't exactly in town."

"He probably had an accomplice. Someone dropped him off and was going to pick him up, but when he returned and saw all the activity, he hightailed it out of here." Aunt Christine pointed a carton of eggs at me to emphasize her point.

I said, "Well, a possible accomplice is worth investigating, don't you think?"

Aunt Christine shrugged. "Needle in a haystack, probably."

I stifled a sigh, realizing that the odds of changing her mind could probably be measured in fractions—fractions with very large denominators. Could I be completely off base? Was Stan Anderson just a clumsy opportunist?

"This can certainly go in the trash," I said as I handed her a Styrofoam take-out box. She opened it and shook her head. "I should have known he wouldn't eat it all." She put it in the trash and said, "Barbeque brisket. I picked it up from Sonny's and dropped it by here on my way to dinner last Monday night."

I pulled out the last thing in the fridge, a tub of yogurt that had been shoved to the back, and turned to see Aunt Christine was staring off into space with a distressed look on her face. I checked the date on the yogurt and tossed it in the trash without opening it. "Did you go out with Roy that night?" I asked, realizing that I didn't know what Aunt Christine had been doing the night before Grandpa Franklin died. If she'd been with Roy, her comments about hurting Grandpa Franklin might not be so odd after all. Had Grandpa Franklin felt excluded from the new relationship in Aunt Christine's life? As far as I knew, Aunt Christine's love life had been pretty tame. Had she ever had a serious boyfriend before?

She looked back at me and blinked. She looked like she'd forgotten I was in the same room with her. "Roy? Oh, no. Not that night. He was working the late shift. I had dinner with my teacher friends at Benito's. Even though I'm retired, we still get together every few months and go out to eat. Darcy was showing off her new baby—the sweetest baby girl. Here, let me show you." She grabbed her purse and pulled out a phone. "Roy talked me into this newfangled phone," she said, holding it out at arm's length and tilting her head back as she tentatively tapped the touch screen. "He showed me how to take pictures, so I gave it a whirl that night—oh, here they are."

She handed the phone to me. There was a picture of five women ranging in age from early twenties to probably sixties. They were gathered around a table with a red-and-white-checked tablecloth. Drinks and loaves of bread covered the table. One young woman with dark circles under her eyes and a large smile on her face was hemmed in by a stroller and a huge diaper bag. She was holding a tiny pink bundle. I touched the screen and moved to the next picture, a close-up of a yawning baby. The last picture was of Aunt Christine holding the baby. "So cute," I said, and felt that twist of bittersweet nostalgia. My kids were long past being infants. "Babies are always so precious, aren't they?" I said as I handed the phone back.

"They are when they're sleeping," Aunt Christine said. "Darcy said she hasn't slept more than two hours in a row since she came home from the hospital. She spent the whole dinner trying to wake up little Elise, but couldn't. She didn't go to the movie after, either. Said Elise would start crying and she'd miss the end." She slipped the phone back into her purse. "All right, back to work." She shook open another brown paper bag.

We finished the refrigerator and moved to the freezer, which didn't take long. Aunt Christine wiped down the shelves while I carried the grocery bags to her car. When I returned to the kitchen, she was doubled over, wiping the bottom shelves of the refrigerator.

"Here, let me do that," I said.

"Thank you. My knees are not what they used to be—all those years of sinking down to get on the same level with the kids have caught up with me. I can't forget to water the plants—the ivy by the front door looks sickly."

"You go ahead and do that. I'll finish in here," I said. I wiped everything down, wondering how grimy the shelves were in my refrigerator. They could certainly use a good cleaning. I stood, tossed the paper towel in the trash, and unhooked the refrigerator door from the cabinet drawer that Aunt Christine had pulled out to hold it open. As the door swung shut, I glanced in the narrow drawer. It held accumulated odds and ends, all neatly arranged in a plastic tray. There was an address book, pens and pencils, a few rubber bands, and a take-out menu for a barbeque restaurant. It was the stack of business cards that caught my attention. I picked up the top card for a better look. I read the name aloud, "Anderson Stanley."

"What did you say, dear?" Aunt Christine replaced a watering can under the sink and turned toward me.

"Who's Anderson Stanley?"

"I don't know." She saw the drawer and said, "If you found it in there, then it was probably someone who came to work on the house. Dad kept all their business cards in there. I know the tree trimmer's number is in there and that nice man we got to paint the eaves last summer—his card is there, too."

The flimsy paper of the card was plain white. There was one phone number with an unfamiliar area code in the bottom right-hand corner. A single word was centered under the name, *producer*. "It says he was a producer."

"Producer?" She frowned, then her face cleared. "Oh, Dad told me about him. He came by, let's see, it must have been about two weeks ago. He was making a documentary about the disappearance of small southern towns and wanted to interview Dad."

"Did Grandpa Franklin do the interview?"

"No, he didn't want that kind of attention."

"That doesn't sound like Grandpa Franklin. Didn't he always have a story about everything?"

"Yes," Aunt Christine said slowly. "There was something he didn't like about the fellow. I don't know what it was, specifically, but I could tell Dad wasn't too taken with him." She picked up the garbage bag. "We should have just enough time to drop the food at my house before we go to Gus's office."

"Don't you recognize the name?"

"No . . . sounds familiar, but I can't place it."

"It sounds familiar because that's the name of the man who died here—only reversed. Anderson Stanley. Stan Anderson."

She took the card from me, angling it at arm's length as she studied it. "That's got to be the strangest coincidence I've ever heard of."

Chapter Thirteen

"A coincidence? Do you really think that?" I kept my voice low as I spoke into my phone. I was following a sturdy middle-aged woman who was escorting Aunt Christine and me along a hallway to the conference room at the attorney's office. I'd taken the business card with me. After we'd put the food away at Aunt Christine's, I'd left another message for Detective Kalra while Aunt Christine changed out of her sweatshirt into a red corduroy shirt and black blazer.

I hadn't expected to hear back from Detective Kalra and had taken my phone out to put it on vibrate when her call came in. "No," she said. "I think the chances of two men with the names Stanley and Anderson, in any order, being connected to your grandfather are slim to none. Add the fact that 'Anderson Stanley' visited your grandfather shortly before his death and then a few days later 'Stan Anderson' dies in a botched robbery attempt at the same house . . . well, that situation is either fate or foul play, but I have to check everything out. Your aunt didn't see this 'Stan Anderson' at the visitation, or at Mr. Avery's house? She doesn't know what he looked like?"

"No, I described him and she said she didn't remember seeing anyone like that at the visitation."

"And you're sure no one else saw 'Anderson Stanley' visit Mr. Avery?" Detective Kalra asked.

"I don't know. Aunt Christine said that Grandpa Franklin told her about the man, but she wasn't there. He told her about it afterward." Static crackled on the line. "Oh, before I lose you—Aunt Christine says on Monday night she was at dinner with friends at a restaurant named Benito's and that Roy was working the night shift at the pharmacy."

"I'll check on it . . . back in town . . . sheriff's office . . ." The line went completely quiet and I switched the phone to vibrate, figuring it would be awhile before I'd hear from her again.

The woman stopped at a doorway. "Gus'll be along in a moment. There's bottled water, coffee, and tea on the credenza. Help yourself." Uncle Bud, Aunt Nanette, Uncle Kenny, and Aunt Gwen were already seated at an oval table.

The lawyers' offices were in a two-story brick building that had once been a home and had been converted to offices. The walls were painted a subtle yellow. Cream trim surrounded the windows with their wavy aged glass and framed a view of three massive oak trees. A painting of a man in his fifties with a Roman nose and gray at the temples of his dark hair hung at one end of the room. Aunt Christine and I slid into the padded swivel chairs at the table as Felicity burst through the door.

"Hello, everyone!" she sang out, and dropped into the chair beside me. She plopped a Dooney & Bourke purse onto the conference table with a small crash, then her keys clattered down beside it. She shrugged out of her leather jacket. "Where is everybody? Where's Gus? Isn't it time to get started? Dan's parking the car. He'll be here in a minute."

Aunt Nanette's glare was so focused on Felicity that I inched slightly away from her. "This may be a day that you've been looking forward to, but I'll remind you that this is not a happy event. It is a solemn occasion, the last time we will hear my father's wishes. Comport yourself accordingly or I'll see that you're removed."

Felicity tossed her head. "No one can make me leave. I have a right to be here. I'm family. And at least I visited him," she said as her accusing gaze slid from Aunt Nanette to Uncle Bud, then over to Uncle Kenny and Aunt Gwen, before finally resting on me. "I wasn't too busy to take some time to brighten his day."

"This is not the place for disparaging comments, Felicity. I will not have it," Aunt Nanette declared.

Felicity opened her mouth to respond, but at that moment Dan loped into the room, followed by Mitch, Bill, and Caroline. Felicity muttered a word under her breath and I glanced at her sharply, but no one else seemed to have heard it in the commotion as the last arrivals, Julia and Wes, Mitch's sister and brother-in-law, came in and took the seats at the other end of the table. Dan pulled out a chair beside Felicity. Mitch walked around and sat down opposite me. Caroline, in a casually dressy taupe sweater and black skirt, side-stepped into a chair, causing her long gold-chain necklace to shift back and forth as she smiled across the table to me. I knew she'd gone to the real estate office this morning, but Bill's stubbly beard, rumpled knit polo shirt, and worn jeans attested to the fact that he'd taken the day off from Smarr Electric Company where he worked in management.

A woman in a sea-foam green suit that matched her eyes walked to the head of the table. I could see the family resemblance, especially in her nose and the shape of her eyes, between her and the man in the portrait behind her. "For those of you who don't know me, I'm Gus Wallis," she said, arranging folders on the table.

I looked at Aunt Christine, questioningly. She leaned toward me and said, "Short for Augusta. That's her dad in the picture, Augustus."

"Looks like everyone is here," she said as she glanced around the room. "Let's get started." She took a seat and pulled out a set of papers. "Mr. Avery was very specific. He wanted this will read with all of you present." She cleared her throat and read, "I, Franklin Scott Avery of Culverton County, Alabama, being of sound mind, do make and publish this, my last will and testament. I hereby revoke all previous wills and codicils of every nature and kind. I nominate, constitute, and appoint my son Ernest Adrian Avery to be the sole Executor and Trustee of this my will and to serve without bond."

I glanced around the table, puzzled. Ernest? Who was Ernest? Mitch caught my glance and tilted his head in the direction of Uncle Bud. I raised my eyebrows and discreetly mouthed the word, "Ernest?" No wonder he went by "Bud."

Mitch shifted in his chair and propped his arm up on the table so that he could rest his chin in his hand, hiding his grin before anyone else noticed. I felt a bit of the tension between us slacken.

I returned my attention to the reading. Gus's voice, a mellow alto, was strong and carried clearly across the quiet room. She read that William Marcus Avery, Mitch's dad, was to be the sole executor of the will if Uncle Bud wasn't able to fulfill that position. As she read the instructions for dealing with funeral costs, taxes, and other financial matters, I glanced around the table. Everyone was focused on Gus. Uncle Bud looked stoic, his jaw set. Aunt Christine blinked rapidly and touched a tissue to the corner of her eye. Aunt Nanette looked sad and fierce at the same time. She kept shooting pointed glances at Felicity, as if her look alone could keep Felicity in line.

Gus read, "I hereby bequeath the landscape print in the hallway and all the contents of the guest bedroom to my daughter Christine Maria Avery along with a sum of seventy-five thousand dollars to be paid from my estate after all taxes, funeral costs, and other bills are settled. I give this amount to Christine because she deserves it."

Beside me, Felicity tensed and leaned forward slightly. Gus continued, naming who would receive which individual items from his possessions. Grandpa Franklin's antique pocket watch and roll-top desk went to Uncle Bud. Mitch's dad received the tools in the garage. The quilts stored in the trunk in the living room were to be divided among the women of the family. Aunt Nanette received all the photo albums and the china set. Uncle Kenny received Grandpa Franklin's guns. Julia and Wes received a box of family portraits and family charts because of Julia's interest in tracing the Avery family history. Summer received a painting and Aunt Jenny inherited a set of figurines. Felicity gripped the arms of her chair when Gus read, "To my grandson Daniel Benjamin Avery, I bequeath my computer and all the Depression glass, because Felicity has a fondness for it. To my grandson Mitchell Steven Avery, I bequeath my military memorabilia, including the Civil War sword that is stored in the attic, and the dirt bike in the garage."

Felicity's forehead wrinkled into a frown. "That's it?" she hissed. I ignored her and smiled across the table at Mitch. I knew from his quickly closing down expression that he was touched that Grandpa Franklin had remembered those days when he and Dan had ridden the dirt bike at his house.

Felicity was vibrating like a plucked string as she whispered something in a fierce tone to Dan. He put a hand on her arm, which she jerked away. I could tell Gus was nearing the end of the will. "And I hereby give all the rest and residue of my estate, including my house, to my grandson Mitchell Steven Avery."

Felicity exploded to her feet, the chair shooting out behind her. "What!"

Gus skewered her with a look sterner than the ones Aunt Nanette had been shooting at her. "Sit back down. I'll finish and I think any questions you have will be answered."

Felicity remained standing until Dan yanked on her hand and she collapsed back down into the chair he'd pulled back for her. "Not Mitch," she said under her breath. "Dan. It's supposed to be *Dan.*"

"I have arranged things this way because my children are settled and prosperous and I believe my house would be more of a burden than a benefit to them. My children have done me proud and are well established in their chosen careers. Mitch has the steady common sense to make good decisions regarding this bequest. He may keep or sell the house. There are no requirements on this bequest. I hope it provides financial security for him and his family."

"No!" Felicity said, jumping to her feet again. "Not Mitch! We were supposed to get the house."

The silence evaporated as excited chatter broke out around the table. Mitch? Grandpa Franklin's house? My thoughts didn't seem to be connecting too well. Mitch inherited the house? I looked at Mitch across the wide expanse of the conference table. He looked as stunned as I felt. Normally not one to show extremes of any emotion, his eyebrows were crunched down over his dark eyes and he was shaking his head from side to side as he said, "He never said anything."

Felicity's impatient whine grew louder. "There's been a mistake. He knew how badly we need that house. It should have been us!"

Mitch broke out of his reverie. He twisted toward Gus and pressed his hand down on the table. "You're sure? He didn't have another will? Another version?"

Gus stood up, speaking loud enough that she overpowered the swell of voices, even Felicity's shrill tone. "This is Mr. Avery's final will and testament and it conveys his express wishes. He did not make these bequests lightly. I know there was long consideration about the distribution of his possessions and assets." She looked directly at Felicity as she said coldly, "There was no duress involved and he was of sound mind when he made this will. He was absolutely sure of what he wanted to do."

Felicity sputtered, "There's got to be some mistake. I *know* he wanted us to have the house."

"There is no mistake, I assure you. This document was witnessed and signed in this office and it will hold up to the closest scrutiny."

Felicity dropped down into her chair and threw an evil look at Mitch, who didn't notice because he was still stunned. "How could he? How could he give it to you?" Felicity asked, switching her venom to me. "You didn't even visit him. He hardly knew you!"

Smarting at her vicious tone, I opened my mouth to reply, but Uncle Bud's deep voice said, "That's enough." At the same time, Dan leaned over and said, "Felicity, for God's sake, hush." His face was flushed and his gaze darted around the room. He looked like he wished he could be anywhere but in this room.

"No, I won't hush," Felicity said. "What about his money? Mitch gets the rest of it, too?" she demanded of Gus.

"What do you mean?" Gus asked.

"His money," Felicity snapped. "He had gobs of it. Besides the seventy-five thousand," Felicity seemed to choke on those words. "The rest of his cash goes to Mitch?"

Gus gazed at her steadily, her face completely blank and professional, but I could see a vein in her neck throbbing just above the collar of her suit. "There is no additional money. It is my understanding that Mr. Avery lost quite a bit in the recent economic downturn. He liquidated his assets, except for the house, then used the money to pay off debts and pay for the funeral preplanning arrangements." She turned to Bud, dismissing Felicity. "I'll have a packet to give you today."

"But that can't be right!" Felicity said. "He was rich. Rich! He had a lot of money."

Dan stood up and took her arm. "That's enough." I'd never heard him sound so firm.

She tried to shake him off. "Where's the rest of it? We'll hire an accountant and have you audited!" Dan pulled her forcibly to the door.

"There is no more," Gus said flatly.

Right before Dan managed to propel her out the door, Felicity shouted over his shoulder, "Then he took it to the grave! He always did like to have cash. It's probably in the casket—that's why it was stolen. We've got to call the police . . ."

Dan finally managed to get her out of the room. He banged the door shut behind them and the rest of us sat there in the sudden silence.

"Utter nonsense," Gus said, blowing out a breath that made her bangs flutter. "Now, I think we're about done here . . ."

Gus wrapped up the meeting and everyone began to stand up, except for me and Mitch. Aunt Christine made her way over to Mitch. He immediately stood up to talk to her. She hugged him and then said, "Congratulations . . . I don't know if that's the appropriate word, but I'm glad Dad left you his house. He was right. It would have been a burden to the rest of us. You and Ellie are young and have so much energy." She smiled across the table at me and said, "And what better person to coordinate everything than a professional organizer?"

I felt like a twenty-pound barbell landed on my shoulders. All that stuff. Except for the items listed in his will, we owned everything in Grandpa Franklin's house. From a long distance away, I heard more relatives echoing Aunt Christine's words as they trickled out of the room. Numbly, I moved around the table and met Mitch at the far end. Caroline was hugging him. "He made a good decision, I think," she said. "I have to run. I have a showing in half an hour, but let us know if there's anything you'd like us to do." Bill echoed Caroline's words as he patted Mitch on the back on the way out of the room. Gus was the last person to leave. She paused with her hand on the door. "I have some paperwork for you, but take as long as you want in here. Let it sink in a little before you make any decisions. Stop by my office before you leave." She closed the door behind her.

"He left me his house." Mitch still looked shell-shocked. He leaned against the table. "I didn't expect . . . I mean, I never even thought . . ."

"I know. It never crossed my mind, either. We own a house now." Our house in Georgia was a rental. "It was sweet of him to think of you. We own a house—a house that's got to be at least, what, fifty years old?"

"Probably closer to eighty. I think he told me it was built in 1930."

"An eighty-year-old house." I sank down beside him. "Think of the maintenance," I said, remembering the older bungalow we'd owned in Washington state. I loved the older homes with their loads of charm and character, but after living in one, I now knew they also came with old pipes and wiring, smaller rooms, and miniscule closets. "And it's in a city we don't live in. What are we going to do with it? And with all his stuff?" I closed my eyes at the enormity of the job we'd just been handed. "We can't live in it. Should we sell it? Rent it? Could it be a . . . a vacation home," I stumbled over the words because they were so absurd. Us owning a vacation home? I wanted to laugh, but sobered as another thought struck me. "Taxes. What will this do to our taxes?"

"I don't know." Mitch drew in a deep breath and said, "We're going to approach this as he intended, as a gift." He took my hand as he spoke. "A huge, unwieldy gift, but we're going to accept it in that spirit. We're going to take things step by step and figure out what's best."

"Okay," I said slowly, studying his face for a moment. He looked more like his old self, a bit calmer. Taking things slowly was his normal operating procedure.

His steadiness made me feel a little bit better, but the enormity of the whole situation . . . a house and everything in it. "It's such a huge gift, Mitch. What are we going to do?" I asked.

"First, we're going to follow my wife's excellent organizing advice. You always say to break the big projects into smaller jobs. We're going to divide this massive thing into smaller pieces and work on each one. What should we tackle first?"

"I suppose that would be making sure we find all the items Grandpa Franklin wanted to give to people. Once those things are out of the house, we can clean out . . . or sell . . . or give away . . . or store . . . everything else. What will we do with the rest of his things?"

"Don't know," Mitch said, and pulled me up to stand beside him. He wrapped one arm around my shoulders as we walked slowly to the door. "We're going to take care of the bequests. That's our first order of business. One thing at a time, remember?"

"Right. Good plan," I said as Mitch opened the door and we walked down the hallway.

"Hey, besides the house, you're also the owner of a sword and a dirt bike."

Mitch's face broke into a grin. "I know. Nathan is going to love that dirt bike."

"Oh, I don't think that's such a good idea."

"Not now. In a few years. Don't worry. He'll be fine."

"We'll see," I said, determined to keep that dirt bike stored in the garage. The garage! I hadn't even looked in there, but Mitch had said Grandpa Franklin was using it for storage since he sold his car. I shuddered. Who knew what had been crammed in there?

Ellie Avery's Tips for Preserving Family Treasures

Storing Photographs
- Organize photos into albums or boxes. Use archival quality plastic sleeves and boxes so that the photos will last longer. As you organize photos, jot down the time frame or theme of each album or box ("London trip" or "kindergarten through third grade"), then you can create a master list with the location of all your photos.
- Negatives will last longer if stored in special archival sleeves.
- Due to the extreme temperature variations of garages, attics, and basements, these are usually not ideal places to store photographs. Store photographs in a low-humidity area with a fairly constant temperature.

Another option is to scan your photos and save them digitally. Make sure you back up your data.

Chapter Fourteen

"Oh my goodness," I said, holding onto the heavy wooden garage door I'd just shoved open. Gus had given us a set of keys when we left the attorney's office and, after a quick stop for a sandwich, we'd driven straight to Grandpa Franklin's house. Mitch had unlocked the padlock and wrestled the other door open. He stood opposite me, his hands braced on his hips. "Yeah."

It wasn't that the garage was messy. Everything was arranged in tidy lines. Row after row of identical boxes took up the left side of the double garage. A cleared path ran down the middle from front to back. On the right side, groupings of items were arranged in exact order. The lawn equipment, a mower, leaf blower, edger, and various rakes and shovels were near the door. Tools were arranged on a peg board beside a large workbench. There were sections of lawn furniture, appliances, and bicycles.

"It's almost like being in a department store," I said as I walked down the cleared aisle, pausing to look at an arrangement of boxes labeled for the kitchen. I read the precisely lettered writing on the side of one box, "Backup toaster, coffeemaker, can opener." I looked back at Mitch, "He had spare appliances?"

"Yep. Always wanted to be prepared. If he found a deal on something, he bought it and saved it in case what he was using broke."

I spun in a slow circle, trying to take it in. I stopped and rubbed my hands over my eyes. It was too much. Too much stuff. I couldn't comprehend it all and that surprised me. I moved my hand down over my mouth and just stood there, dumbfounded. I'd helped people organize all kinds of different things and the size of the job had never made me feel like I'd been steamrolled.

"Ellie, you okay?" Mitch asked, walking toward me.

"Ah—not really. Mitch, all this stuff is ours," I said. "*Ours*." I worked hard to keep our lives light and sleek and efficient. There was no need to move extra stuff every time the military packed us up and sent us to a new address, but in just a couple of hours the things—the stuff we owned—had doubled. Maybe tripled. I turned to the rows of identical boxes lined up with military precision on the left side of the garage and read one of the printed labels. There was a string of numbers and the word "Avery." I read the final line aloud, *Stars Fall: Memoirs of an Alabama Boy*. Mitch, what is this?"

Mitch looked up from a paper he'd pulled from his back pocket. "Those? Copies of Grandpa Franklin's memoir. He wrote it a few years ago. Remember, he sent us a copy? It was pretty interesting. All about him growing up."

I did remember the book. I'd read it, too. I looked over the conglomeration of boxes. There were so many rows that I lost track when I tried to count them. Stacked to the height of my shoulder, the rows of dusty brown cardboard seemed to stretch out across the garage as numerous as the Xi'an warriors. "Why are there so many boxes?"

Mitch didn't look up from the paper this time. "He self-published. The company printed the books and he stored them here. Last year, he was trying to get the local big box bookstores to carry them."

I looked at the label again. "There's forty per carton . . . that's more than I can count."

"Probably a couple thousand copies."

What were we going to do with thousands of copies of the same book? I turned away from the stacks of boxes. I paced down to the far end of the garage, then back to where Mitch was standing by the open doors. Okay, it wasn't as bad as it could be, I told myself. It could be a jumbled mess that I had to sort out first. At least Grandpa Franklin had been an organized pack rat.

"I can't believe we own all this stuff," I said. I knew I was repeating myself, but I was really thrown for a loop.

"We don't own it *all*," Mitch said as he tugged open the flaps of a box. "For instance, this box full of photo albums goes to Aunt Nanette."

In the parking lot of Gus's office, Uncle Bud had given Mitch a list with all the bequests. He'd asked us to find and distribute the items. "Right," I said, dusting my hands off. "Let me see that list. What else can we get out of here?"

An hour later, I stretched and arched my back. My fingers were numb and my nose was running after being in the cool air so long. Inside the garage, the air was still chilly and I could see my breath, but the sun was beating on the stiff, yellow grass outside the garage doors. Mitch waved as he backed out of the driveway. Grandpa Franklin's will was a game-changer. It had pushed away the tension and stress between us and made us focus on working together instead of struggling with each other. I knew those differences, those conflicts, were still there, but for now, we had the house to deal with and that was our focus.

Mitch made a three-point turn, which kicked up a few bits of gravel and a little dust before the minivan lumbered away. Besides the photo albums, we'd also loaded the tools into the van. Mitch was going to drop those things off and return for another load.

I'd found a box of old newspapers and a stack of flattened boxes. I searched the area around the tool bench until I found a roll of packing tape. I avoided looking at the boxes as I left the garage. They still overwhelmed me.

What did you do with that many books? Could you give them away? I hated the thought of throwing books away, but what else would we do with them? Everyone in the family already had copies and, apparently, the bookstores weren't interested in selling them. We'd figure it out later, I reminded myself as I lugged the packing supplies to the house, leaving the garage doors open. I could pack up Aunt Nanette's china. The furniture in the guest bedroom and the roll-top desk would have to be moved another day.

I was unlocking the front door with the keys Mitch had left me when a black Camry crunched over the gravel driveway. The door stuck and I leaned into it with my shoulder as I watched Detective Kalra step out of the car. Today she was dressed in a wool jacket over a thick blue sweater and tan corduroy pants.

"Hello," she said as she climbed the steps. "Moving things out already?"

"Not for me," I said as I picked up the flattened boxes. "Would you like to come inside?" I asked. "I think the temperature is dropping."

"Thanks." She picked up the box of newspapers and followed me inside. "A cold front's coming through. There's a possibility of frost tonight."

I hid a smile. From her tone, you would have thought that a blizzard was on the way. I still couldn't get used to the thought that a hard frost was a big deal, but here, like in middle Georgia where we lived, an overnight low of thirty-two or below was a major weather event. If the temperature was forecast to go below freezing, the local weather forecasters warned viewers as if a tornado had touched down. We're talking extensive coverage of the freeze warning with news anchors reminding people to bundle up. Did they really think we were such idiots that we couldn't figure out when we needed to wear a coat? And the plants. The forecasters would advise viewers to cover plants. It was almost a battle cry, "Hard frost possible—save the begonias!"

I glanced at the landscaping around Grandpa Franklin's house as I closed the front door. I was glad to see he had hearty bushes that could weather the cold snap. I carried the packing supplies into the kitchen and set everything on the countertop. Detective Kalra put down the box of newspapers and said, "Do you still have that business card?"

"Yes." I pulled it out of the pocket of my fleece jacket. I'd figured she'd want it. I'd already entered the phone number into my phone. I hadn't called it, but I wanted to have it—just in case.

"I'll follow up on this. I stopped by the pharmacy on the way into town and Roy was there last Monday night. The store closes at ten, but the pharmacy is open all night. A pharmacy tech confirmed that Roy was with her from nine that night until six the next morning."

I aligned the flaps on a box and ran a strip of tape over them. "And it was obvious from the pictures she showed me that she really was at that Italian restaurant. I'm sure her friends will confirm it. They went to a late movie afterward."

So Aunt Christine and Roy hadn't been anywhere near the house that night. I was relieved. I didn't want to think that she could have been involved, but with Detective Kalra's lingering suspicions, I was glad there was incontrovertible proof she'd been somewhere else.

Detective Kalra's phone rang. While she took the call, I flipped the box over and layered some newspaper in for a liner, then I moved several stacks of plates from the china cabinet to the kitchen counter. Her side of the conversation consisted of a few murmurs. I opened several pages of newspaper and set the first dinner plate in the center of it. I leaned my palms against the counter and looked up at her, not wanting to noisily crumple newspaper while she was on the phone. Her eyebrows were drawn down into a frown as she gazed at me intently. As soon as I looked at her, she pivoted away, transferring her gaze to the front door. "Right. On my way." Detective Kalra replaced her phone in her pocket and I pulled the corners of the paper over the plate. I repeated the process with a few more plates, then rolled the whole stack into a protective shell of paper.

Over the crackle of paper, Detective Kalra said, "I have to go." She was already moving to the front door. I stowed the bundle of plates in the box and followed her to the door.

"Do you think 'Anderson' talked to anyone else in Smarr?"

"I have no idea," Detective Kalra said shortly. Her carefully neutral tone surprised me. The casual, confiding tone of our conversation was gone. I realized her expression was different, too. Her face was blank, as if she'd pulled a veil of neutrality over herself. I had the distinct feeling we weren't on the same side anymore. I was off the team. "Thank you for turning over the business card, Mrs. Avery," she said in a way that reminded me of those automatic phone system menus that always sound so pleasant and accommodating, but never actually get me to the person I want to talk to. She turned and trotted down the steps.

I closed the front door and went back to the kitchen slowly. It must have been the phone call. She hadn't even wanted to look at me, which was troubling. I knew I hadn't done anything remotely out of line. I didn't even live here, so she couldn't think I was . . . involved . . . in the situation around Grandpa Franklin's death. I'd been in Georgia when he died, so I knew she couldn't think I was a suspect. I wrapped more plates in thick layers of newsprint, my movements automatic. I'd packed and unpacked so often, I didn't have to think about the rote movements. I'd finished the plates and moved on to cups and saucers when I heard the crunch of gravel again. Mitch wouldn't get back that quickly. Maybe Detective Kalra forgot something?

The back of the house was lined with windows, but the front of the house only had two windows and the curtains were still closed. I wasn't planning on being inside the house very long, so I'd left them closed. I stood on my tiptoes to peer through the small paned window set in the door and saw Detective Rickets's shaved head reflecting the bright sunlight as he climbed the porch steps. I instantly recoiled from the window, but I wasn't fast enough. The detective had raised his head as he cleared the last step and I knew he'd seen me. I opened the door reluctantly.

"Ah, Mrs. Avery, just the person I wanted to talk to," he said, stepping through the narrow opening.

"That's a change, then," I said.

He swaggered over to the kitchen and looked over the array of boxes, newspaper, and china, then with his hands on his hips, he swiveled back to me and said, "Packing up already?" Before I could answer, he walked with a cocky little spring in his step to the hallway. He leaned into the door frame. "Haven't got to the bedrooms yet, I see. What are you going to do? Estate sale? You could list some of the smaller items on eBay," he said, and picked up a silver-framed picture of Mitch's parents from a pie crust table. "That's a nice piece, too, that table," he said, pointing at it with the frame. He tossed the picture frame onto the couch and ambled back toward me, hands on hips again. "Yep," he said, his gaze traveling around the room, "this is quite a jackpot. Not like hitting the lottery or anything, but still, a pretty penny once you've cleaned it all out."

He came to a stop in front of me, just close enough that the distance was uncomfortable. "When are you moving in?" he asked.

I wanted to step back and create a little space, but I knew I couldn't. "We're not moving." I forced myself to keep my feet planted as I said, "Those dishes are for Aunt Nanette. It was a bequest in Grandpa Franklin's will."

"Oh, a bequest," he said, drawing out the last word to show his disbelief.

A white hot surge of anger raced through me. "Yes, a bequest," I said. I was so furious my hands were trembling. "Now, I think it's time you left."

"Can't do that," he said. "I've got a few questions for you."

I crossed my arms over my chest. "Why? According to you, everything is all sorted out—Grandpa Franklin died of natural causes and Stanley Anderson was just a clumsy wanna-be thief who missed a step on the stairs."

"The status of any particular case is not something I can discuss with you, Mrs. Avery. I can tell you that certain events, say, the reading of a will, or the discovery of new evidence, can cause us to reexamine a case and consider the possibility of reopening it."

"So you're saying you're reopening the case? Stan Anderson's case?"

"We are following up new leads that have come to light. The facts we find might or might not cause us to reexamine that case—or other cases."

"Grandpa Franklin's case, too?"

Detective Rickets nodded. He was going to investigate Grandpa Franklin's death, but without officially reopening the case, which would keep him in the clear with Uncle Bud, who'd wanted that investigation closed quickly. I hated his sneaky, calculated approach. It reminded me of the office politics Mitch had to deal with. I was so glad I worked alone. Juggling being a mom and a professional organizer was tough, but at least I didn't have to deal with sly, manipulative crap like this every day.

"Okay, so ask your questions. Fire away." Anything to get rid of him. Who did he think he was, barging in here and strutting around like he owned the place?

"Seems Franklin Avery's will surprised just about everyone."

"News travels fast in Smarr," I said.

"Well, the will combined with the information you so thoughtfully passed on to Detective Kalra," he said her name with a faint inflection, a flicker of derision, then he shrugged and continued, "raises questions . . . unexpected inheritance and all."

"We certainly weren't expecting it."

"That so?"

"Yes," I said, then decided to ask a question of my own. Who knew—he might answer it. "The man who died here . . . Stanley or Anderson or whoever he was, have you found anything new about him?"

"Kalra's handling that," he said dismissively. "Probably won't come to anything."

"How can you say that?"

"He was a stranger—didn't know Mr. Avery. Probably a coincidence."

"A coincidence?" I said, my voice raising.

"Yeah. See, when something bad happens, people like to blame it on a stranger." He took a step closer. "That way, their little world is safe," he said, his breath heavy with the smell of old coffee. "No one they know could do something horrible. But most of the time, the bad guy isn't some stranger, someone who was passing through town. No, most of the time, the bad guy is right there in the middle of things." He'd been speaking softly, but now he shifted back to his normal tone of voice. "I hear that your husband and Felicity Avery have a history," he said, releasing another wave of bitter coffee breath.

I was speechless for a moment, which isn't unusual when I'm in a heated discussion. When my adrenaline starts pumping, it seriously messes up my thought process and I never seem to be able to think of snappy comebacks until later—much later. Hours, even days sometimes. But this time, I was tongue-tied because Felicity was the last thing I expected him to talk about.

"Mrs. Avery," he prodded, leaning forward slightly.

"That was a statement, not a question," I said flatly.

"Oh, so you want to play it that way, do you?" He wheeled away from me and walked to the kitchen where he leaned one hip against the counter. "So were you aware of their past?"

"I don't think one date in high school qualifies as a 'past.'" I took a deep breath of fresh air.

"You did know. Interesting," he said. His close-set eyes narrowed. "What is the nature of their relationship now?"

"Now? Felicity is his cousin-in-law," I said, impatiently. "Unless you have something important to discuss, I have things I need to do." I walked briskly into the kitchen and began noisily wrapping cups and saucers.

He raised his voice. "When were they last in contact?"

I paused, my hands full of a half-wrapped stack of saucers. "Felicity and Mitch? At the attorney's today."

"No, before Mr. Avery died."

"I don't know . . . Christmas, probably. I think we talked to them then."

I went back to folding and he watched me for a moment, then said, "I can subpoena his phone records, you know."

"Fine. Do that," I said as I felt my pulse rising. "Waste your time."

"Oh, I think your husband's phone records might prove to be very interesting."

I stuffed a bundle of paper into a corner of the box and slapped more newspapers down on the counter. "Why?"

"Because he gained the most from Mr. Avery's death. I understand you and your husband don't own a home. Well, you didn't own a home until this morning. Is that correct?"

A jolt of anger fired through me, setting my heart to thumping. "Are you seriously suggesting that Mitch had something to do with—," I broke off. I was so angry I couldn't get the words out.

"It's just mighty interesting to me. With Mitch inheriting this house . . . makes me wonder. Where was Mitch last Monday night?"

"Home," I snapped. "We were in Georgia. There's no way we could possibly be involved in this . . . this . . . scenario you've pulled out of thin air."

"So he was home, was he? And *you're* his alibi? Convenient."

"It's not convenient. It's the truth!" I sputtered.

He went on as if he hadn't heard me. "Things aren't going so good for Dan and Felicity. Anyone can see that. And the word around town was that she expected to inherit this house, along with a good chunk of change, I imagine. With Mr. Avery seeming to be going strong health-wise, maybe Felicity decided to do something to help things along." Detective Rickets shoved his hands in his pockets and strolled over to the windows that lined the back of the room. "Course, she probably wouldn't want to do it herself and Dan seems too timid to be involved . . . but she might think of an old boyfriend, someone like Mitch."

"That is the most absurd thing I've ever heard." My hands were shaking so badly I braced them on the countertop. I pressed my palms down hard on the coolness of the Formica. "Mitch would never do anything like that."

"Oh, you'd be surprised what people will do. Especially what people—men, to be exact—will do for a pretty lady. Not that you're not attractive, but Felicity . . . she's kept herself in shape nicely and that can't be discounted."

"That is outrageous," I sputtered. I was so furious I could barely talk. "And baseless. I think you should go."

"I'll leave," he said, and sauntered across the room.

As he passed me, he pulled a brown envelope out of his back pocket and tossed in on the newspaper. "You might want to take a look at that." He opened the front door and said, "Don't worry about getting those back to me. I've got another set. I'll be in touch." He pulled the door closed with a thump.

I stood there staring at the envelope, my hands bearing down on the cabinet, then I snatched it up and fumbled with the flap. A small stack of pictures fell out on the newspaper. They were all of Mitch and Felicity.

Chapter
Fifteen

I don't know how long I stood there staring at the jumbled photos. The one on top was a snapshot of Mitch and Felicity standing in a parking lot beside a red car on a blindingly sunny day. They were the only people in the picture. The sun was behind them and their expressions were shadowy and indistinct. Mitch's arm was extended, almost touching Felicity's tan shoulder. I could tell she was smiling as she leaned toward him. I ran through my memories of the times we'd been with Dan and Felicity. Surely this was a picture from one of our visits to Alabama or maybe the family reunion? Felicity was wearing a light blue tank top that revealed every toned muscle and shapely curve. Mitch was in a white collared polo shirt and tan shorts. I scanned the blurry background, but didn't see anything familiar that would help me place the photo in a recognizable context.

Finally, I reached out and touched it with the tip of my index finger, as if I might get a severe burn or shock from touching it. Carefully, I pushed it aside and revealed the next photo. Mitch and Felicity embracing. I closed my eyes and swallowed. This could not be happening. Mitch and Felicity? It was impossible. Mitch would never do something like that. Never. I opened my eyes and looked at the picture again. It's happened to other wives, a little voice whispered. I grabbed the rest of the photos and quickly flipped through them. They seemed to have been taken only a few seconds apart. In the next photo, Mitch and Felicity were standing apart, then he handed her a small cardboard box. I was flipping quickly. It was almost like watching a stop action movie. There was another embrace, this time Felicity closed the distance between them and kissed Mitch on the cheek. That picture was the last one.

I pressed the stack to my chest. I felt weird. Light-headed. I turned around and slid down to sit on the floor. I tipped my head over and rested my forehead on my knees. For a while I sat there with my eyes closed, breathing deeply. Finally, when my head felt normal again, I leaned back against the cabinets and looked at the photos again. Okay, I lectured myself, calm down. You've always trusted Mitch. Don't leap to conclusions.

Why didn't I recognize the photos or remember this happening? Because you weren't there, the small voice whispered again. And Mitch had been so quiet and reserved lately. I bit my lip and forced myself to focus only on the pictures. I rubbed the corner of the paper between my thumb and finger. It wasn't photo paper with a glossy finish. It was plain typing paper. I frowned. The paper meant these pictures had probably been downloaded and printed from a computer. Had someone e-mailed them to Detective Rickets? I shook my head. Why would someone do that? Was this some sort of tip that the sheriff's department received?

I went back through the photos, scrutinizing each one, but I didn't see anything that would help me place where or when they were taken. The last one had a faint line down it that seemed to follow the outline of Mitch's body. I squinted, pulling the paper closer. Was the line from the printer—too much ink? Or were these photos not even real? I'd only dabbled with photo editing software, but I knew some of the programs were pretty advanced. Could someone have photoshopped Mitch into those pictures? It might be hard to fake an embrace, though. I drummed the photos against my leg.

And why had Detective Rickets given me a set? The police didn't usually go around handing out evidence, even copies, to people involved in an investigation.

He wanted to know what I would do with the photos, I realized. I scrambled to my feet and went to the front windows. No sign of his car, but I was willing to bet he was tucked away into some hidden driveway or curve of the road, waiting to see what I did, where I went after he'd dropped these photos on me.

My phone rang, startling me. I checked the caller ID. It was Mitch. I blew out a breath that sent my bangs flying. "Hello," I said, my voice sounding strained and oddly formal.

"You okay?"

I cleared my throat. "Ah—give me a minute," I said and swallowed, then cleared my throat again. "There. Mitch, did you . . ." I paused, not sure if this was a conversation I wanted to have on the phone. Did I want to see his face when I asked him? "Ah . . . today I saw some—," I broke off. Should I even mention the pictures? Maybe it would be better to ask him point-blank about Felicity. Save the pictures, in case he denied it. My stomach roiled. "Never mind," I said.

"You sure you're all right? You sound . . . odd."

"I just swallowed wrong. I'm fine now," I said brightly.

"Now you sound really weird." He paused for a second. I didn't say anything. "Okay," he said, concern in his voice. "I'm at Mom and Dad's house. I called Aunt Nanette and asked her to drive over and pick you up. Everyone is fine, but there's been a fire."

"This doesn't look too bad," Aunt Nanette said as she put the car in park in front of Mitch's parents' house.

"It looks exactly the same," I said as I climbed out of the car. Mitch had assured me everyone was fine, that he had both kids with him. They hadn't even smelled a whiff of smoke, much less been anywhere near the fire, but I ran around the side of the house to the backyard. Everyone was in a group at the far end of the pool. Nathan saw me and ran. "Mom! Mom, the fire truck came. A *real* one. It had its sirens on and everything. It was the coolest thing ever."

I swept him up in a hug. "Where's the fire truck now?" I asked.

His lower lip popped out in a pout. "It had to leave and the fireman said we can't go back inside. Not for my Legos or for clothes or *anything*."

Livvy ran up to me. "*The Spiral Secrets* is inside and I have to have it. And my blue purse. I have to have my purse. It's got my reading list." Tears sparkled in the corners of her eyes. Nathan wiggled out of my arms and sprinted off to Mitch, who was making his way toward us across the lawn. I squatted down to Livvy's level. Losing her reading list would be a huge calamity for her. And she'd been so proud of her signed book from Maggie Key, too. Losing either—or worse, both—would probably be a tragedy. "Do you remember where you left them?"

"By the front door. Dad told me to leave them inside, so I did," she said, and shot a dark look at Mitch.

"I'm sure your book and purse are fine. The front of the house looked okay, so they're probably sitting right where you left them. We'll get them as soon as we can. And if something happened to them, we can re-create your list. You've got your books at home that you've read and we can ask the library for a list of all the books you've checked out. It probably won't be long before we can go back inside," I said, and gave her a quick hug.

She swung away from me to follow Nathan sluggishly to a plastic playhouse set up at the far end of the backyard, as Mitch reached my side.

"How long have—" My words halted as I turned to look at the back of the house. Until that moment, I'd been facing the backyard, concentrating on the kids, but now the house had my full attention. "Oh, my," I said, reaching for Mitch's hand. The back corner of the house, the guest bedroom, and part of the sunroom looked like something from the local news. Charred window frames surrounded broken out windows. I could see at least three holes in the roof. Black smears radiated up from the windows, marring the white-painted brick. Water pooled in a few shallow spots on the patio and in the grass. The sunlight glittering off the surface of the water was an odd contrast with the dry, yellow grass. "No one was hurt? What happened?"

"No one was inside. Mom was out showing a house. I was in the garage with Dad, unloading the tools. The kids were playing in the front yard when we saw dark smoke drifting over the roof. We called nine-one-one and Dad used the water hose to wet down what he could until the fire truck got here, but there wasn't much we could do."

"I'm so glad you're okay," I said, leaning against him.

He squeezed me closer. "Of course, I'm okay."

"And the kids . . . ," I said, and my legs suddenly felt like I'd run a mile or two. "If they'd been inside . . . alone . . ." I turned and looked across the lawn. Livvy was inside the plastic playhouse. Nathan was rhythmically opening and closing the shutters on the house as fast as he could.

"They weren't," Mitch said firmly, but I heard the slight quiver in his voice.

"How bad is it inside?" The sunroom and adjacent guest room formed the back wall of the house.

"I haven't been inside, but the fireman who talked to Dad earlier said the rooms at the back of the house are the worst. Sounds like they'll have to be gutted and rebuilt. I don't know if the fire reached the family room or kitchen. Someone from the fire department is in there now."

"Then that means everything we brought is probably gone," I said, trying to remember what we'd had in our suitcases and what we'd left at home. I gestured at our clothes. "This is it—all we have are the clothes on our backs."

Mitch nodded. "Everything else is probably ruined, either from the fire, or if it didn't spread back that far, then from the smoke and the water."

Mitch's parents were a few feet away. Caroline was sitting motionless on the edge of a chaise longue near the pool, her hands tucked between her knees, staring at the decorative blue tiles that surrounded the patio. Bill had his hand on her shoulder, his gaze riveted to the house as he spoke on his cell phone. Caroline was still in her Realtor clothes, a taupe sweater and black skirt, and heels. I remembered she'd had a home to show after the reading of the will. She'd probably come straight here when she got word about the fire. "Your parents must be devastated."

"I think they're in shock," Mitch spoke quietly, but I didn't think he needed to worry about his parents overhearing his words. They looked so lost and withdrawn that I doubted they'd even noticed he was speaking.

"Someone should get them a blanket," I said, making a move to break away from Mitch's embrace. But at that moment, Aunt Nanette came into the backyard, carrying a lilac Windbreaker and a brown blanket. She draped the blanket over Bill's shoulders and put the Windbreaker over Caroline, who reached up mechanically to hold it in place.

A man in full firefighting gear emerged from what had been the door frame on the back of the sunroom. He crossed the patio and walked around the end of the pool to Bill and Caroline. We were close enough that I could hear him as he said, "Well, we were able to contain the fire to the two rooms at the back of the house. The fire damage is minimal. The smoke and water damage are more severe. You're fortunate that the French doors to the sunroom were closed. That helped keep the fire from spreading into the main portion of the house."

I breathed a sigh of relief, since it sounded like Livvy's most precious belongings were probably safe.

Bill asked, "Can we go back in?"

"Yes, you can go in now, but I wouldn't recommend staying there. You're going to need to get someone in here who specializes in fire cleanup—water and smoke removal. Contact your insurance company. They'll have some names for you."

"Can you tell us what happened? Where it started?" Bill asked. Caroline continued to sit on the chaise longue staring at the water lapping at the edge of the pool.

"Looks like a candle was the source of ignition."

Bill's forehead wrinkled and he looked toward Caroline. For the first time, she pulled her gaze away from the pool and looked at the fireman. "We don't usually burn candles. They make me sneeze."

"A candle fell onto a rug—a light brown rug. Woven. Natural fiber."

"The sisal, yes," Caroline said quickly, looking more animated.

"The burn pattern indicates that the fire moved pretty quickly. It spread to a sofa that was on the rug, then up the wall that separates the sunroom from the room next to it, the back bedroom. Not as much damage in the bedroom," he added. "So why do you have candles in the house, ma'am, if you're allergic?"

Caroline shrugged. "Gifts. I keep them because they're a nice decorative touch, but we don't burn them."

I looked at Mitch and said softly, "Why didn't you tell me? I sure hope the candle that caused all this trouble wasn't the peaches-and-cream one I gave her for Christmas."

"I didn't realize. She never said anything," Mitch said.

"She probably didn't want to hurt our feelings," I said. How many candles had I given her over the years?

The fireman asked, "You're sure you didn't light that candle? It could have been yesterday, even. We see that a lot—someone lights a candle and forgets to blow it out. These candles that are three, four, five inches in diameter can burn for a long time and people forget to blow them out."

Caroline shaded her eyes as she looked up at Bill. "We've had quite a few visitors lately. I suppose someone could have lit a candle either today or yesterday . . . ," her voice trailed off uncertainly.

Bill ran his hand down over the scruffy stubble of his beard, then glanced in our direction. "No," I said quickly. "It wasn't us. I didn't light it. Mitch never lights candles—doesn't even notice them, actually," I said, cutting a look at him, "and our kids know candles and matches are strictly off limits."

"It could have been someone who came by yesterday," Caroline said. "Maybe Julia? We'll have to ask her or Wes. Of course, the whole family has been in and out of the house for days and we've had so many visitors."

"It's a fairly common occurrence. I wouldn't worry about it, ma'am," the fireman said.

Through the open gate at the side of the yard, I saw a police car roll to a stop at the curb. Detective Rickets's insinuations came flooding back. I pulled Mitch a few steps away. "Did you meet with Felicity recently?"

I knew it was abrupt and there might be a better way to handle the question. Maybe I shouldn't ask it at all . . . just wait and see what happened, but there was something about seeing the burnt rooms and the smoke scars above the windows that made everything very basic. I'd never liked manipulation and innuendo and strategy. I'd much rather be straightforward. Either Mitch was sneaking around or he wasn't. Either he'd tell me the truth or he'd lie. Better to get everything out there and find out what he had to say.

"What?" Mitch said, frowning. I knew him well enough to know he wasn't playing for time. He was puzzled at the unexpected turn our conversation had taken. "Did you see Felicity? Give her a package?" I asked.

"Oh, yeah," he said, his face clearing. Then he lowered his voice. "The birthday stuff."

"What?" I scanned his face. All I saw was his normal open expression.

"Remember, Felicity threw that surprise birthday party for Dan about a month ago?"

"No."

"She called and wanted to know if I had any pictures of him . . . baby pictures, T-ball, stuff like that."

"Why would she call you?"

"You know Aunt Jenny. How she's always on the cutting edge—ready to try anything new. She's into recycling and, what did she call it? Living light, I think."

"Yes," I said, thinking that was a phrase I'd have to remember. I could identify with trying not to accumulate clutter.

"Well, she scanned all her photos, everything from when Dan was born right up until a few months ago and saved it on her computer. Then she got a virus and lost all her data."

"What does this have to do with you?"

"Felicity was throwing Dan a surprise party and wanted to do a slide show. Dan and I did almost everything together when we were growing up. I had tons of pictures of him in all those photos that Mom sent me last year after she cleaned out the garage."

"So you gave those photos to Felicity. Why don't I remember this?"

"Well, she called the day after Nathan got sick with that croupy cough. You were pretty tired."

"Oh, yeah," I said. "I vaguely remember you digging through photo albums and boxes one afternoon after work." I'd been so tired, I'd gone to bed right after dinner and Mitch had taken care of the kids that night. The next morning, he'd left on a short trip.

"Why didn't you just mail them to her? Or scan them?"

"Man, you really were out of it that night. You don't remember that I had a RON in Montgomery that night before we went on to Oregon?"

"Your trips always blend together for me," I said. The big ones, the long trips, stood out, and the exotic locations were easy to remember, but Mitch was always coming and going and it was hard to remember every destination.

I knew RON was military-speak for Remain Over Night, so that meant Mitch had landed in Montgomery one day and departed the next day for Oregon. "So you met with her in a parking lot somewhere?" I asked.

"At the gym. She didn't want Dan to know, so I met her after work. Now, why the third degree?" Mitch's normal relaxed and good-natured attitude had slipped into something more serious.

I blew out a breath, a sigh of relief, because I knew Mitch. I knew he was telling me the truth. This wasn't some clever lie or elaborate scheme he'd engineered to cover up something. I remembered the next night with Nathan had been another rough one—I'd spent most of it holding him on my lap as we sat on the edge of the tub, the shower blasting hot water so the steam would help his croupy cough. I'd been dead on my feet the next day and I was pretty sure I'd slept every spare moment I could. Mitch probably had mentioned his meeting with Felicity and I'd been so tired and worried about Nathan that it hadn't really registered. And now that I thought about it, I did remember pictures of Dan's birthday party. Felicity had posted them on Facebook.

"And after you gave her the photos, you went back to your hotel?"

"Yes," Mitch said slowly. "I went to dinner with the crew at—it was Applebee's, I think."

"So you were with someone? The crew can confirm you were with them at dinner and went back to the hotel?"

"Yes," Mitch said evenly. "They can even confirm that I gave the package to Felicity. They drove me there on the way to dinner and watched me hand it off to her in the parking lot. Now, I've answered all your questions. Suppose you tell me why you want confirmation of my movements that night."

"Oh, it's not for me. It's for the police."

Ellie Avery's Tips for Preserving Family Treasures

Digital Memories

- Transferring documents and pictures to digital files can be time consuming, but it does have advantages. Besides having a backup copy, you'll also be able to copy, crop, and print at will.

- Be sure to create an organizing system in your computer. Most camera software programs download photos by date, but you can rename the file before you download if you'd rather organize by event or other category.

- Take the time to rename your photos with specific labels that will help you find them.

- To make sure your photos are looked at and enjoyed, download them to digital photo frames or create a slide show of your favorites and set it as your screen saver.

- You can even create digital scrapbooks.

Chapter
Sixteen

I took the stack of photos out of my jacket pocket. "They're going to want to talk to you about it. Detective Rickets blindsided me with these." I handed them to Mitch. "These are copies. I think they're from an anonymous tip. He thinks you and Felicity were . . . involved . . . and that she convinced you to . . . do something about Grandpa Franklin."

Mitch stared at me for a moment, then said, "That's ridiculous!" Bill turned to look at us and I pulled Mitch a few steps farther away from the group around the pool. "I would never—he was my grandfather!" Mitch's words were as disjointed as mine usually were when I got upset. The difference was Mitch rarely got into the flabbergasted state he was in now, but I knew exactly what he was trying to say.

I tightened my grip on his arm. "I know that. I know you'd never do anything like that. And that's what I told Detective Rickets, but I'm sure he'll have some questions for you."

"But you weren't sure about the other part," Mitch said, his dark gaze holding mine. I could hear the astonishment and hurt in his voice as he said, "About me and Felicity?"

Dang it. I'd been trying to gloss over that part, but he knew me too well. I threw my head back to look at the sky, which was now a translucent blue as the sun dipped behind the trees. "Mitch, you've been so weird lately—quiet and withdrawn. You don't talk to me. I don't know what's going on in your head. Next thing I know, everything's fine and it feels like we're back to normal. Then, you recede again and I don't know why. What's going on?"

Mitch shook his head and sighed. "We've got to get away, by ourselves, and talk. I'm trying to work something out. It's complicated and I know how much you worry. I was trying not to stress you out. You see . . . ," he broke off as Detective Rickets arrived at his side.

"I see you've shown him the pictures," he said.

I had a very base urge to put both hands on his chest and shove him away. Mitch was finally opening up to me, talking to me, and then Detective Rickets butted in. I balled my hands into fists and kept my arms clamped to my sides. "Could we possibly discuss this later? As you can see, Mitch's family is in the middle of dealing with a house fire."

Detective Rickets raised his eyebrows at my tone, then looked back at the house. "Not a lot you can actually do right at this moment. Seems as good a time to have a talk with Mitch as any. I'm sure you understand that we have to follow all leads and can't be distracted with unrelated issues. You certainly were insistent that we investigate Mr. Avery's death earlier. What's changed that makes you want us to back off?"

I smiled tightly. "I'm so glad to see you're taking your duty so seriously . . . now." I rotated my shoulders and unclenched my fists. "Go ahead, talk with Mitch. I'm sure you'll find what he has to say is fascinating. I'll check with Caroline. See if I can do anything." Mitch caught my hand before I turned away and said, "It'll be fine." I nodded and walked briskly to the pool and sat down beside Caroline.

Her shoulders were hunched as she held the Windbreaker closed with one hand. Nathan and Livvy had moved to another corner of the backyard. They were sitting in the yellow grass building something with sticks.

"How are you doing?" I asked Caroline.

She shrugged. "Honestly, I don't know. To have this happen on the heels of the funeral . . . it's almost too much to take in. Thank goodness no one was in the house. I'm sure there's something I should do, but I really have no idea what it is." Her hand dropped limply into her lap as she gazed at the back of the house. "Everything will have to go—carpet, drywall, everything. We just finished enclosing that patio last summer."

"I know," I said, thinking it would be disheartening to see all your hard work destroyed. I knew that sunroom was her favorite place in the house. "It's amazing that it takes so long to build something and that it can be ruined in minutes," I said as I twisted around to look for Mitch. He was talking to Detective Rickets, who seemed to be doing more listening than questioning, which I figured was a good thing.

The light was dimming and I shivered in the cool air. I was glad the kids had been wearing their jackets when the fire was discovered. At least I knew they were warm and I didn't have to try and get inside the house to get more clothes for them. Caroline let out a tiny sigh. "That's true of everything in life, don't you think? It's always easier to tear down than to build up." The jacket had slipped again and now hung on only one of her shoulders. She didn't seem to notice the dropping temperature. I'd never seen her like this, reflective and still. She was always in action. And she focused her energy with laserlike precision. This catatonic state wasn't like her at all. Maybe it was just the blow of the fire after the funeral, but it did worry me a bit.

"I'm sure Uncle Bud will help. He can probably have a crew out here in a day or two, right?"

Caroline murmured an absentminded agreement. I wasn't sure if she'd even taken in what I said. "Listen," I said, switching gears. "Mitch and I wanted to talk to you about the house, Grandpa Franklin's house." Maybe the topic of real estate might distract her from the fire damage.

"Okay."

"Well, Mitch and I were talking about it in the car today after we left Gus's office. You know that we would only be able to use it a few times a year and we wouldn't want it to sit empty. We wanted to ask you about the real estate market."

"The real estate market here in Smarr?" she asked as she looked over at me. I felt like I finally had her full attention. "You're thinking of selling it?"

"Not necessarily. We wanted to talk to you about selling versus renting."

"Things are better, but it's still a buyer's market," she said as she reached back and repositioned the Windbreaker over her shoulder. She gathered the fabric into her hand again and shifted toward me. "The rental market is pretty tight right now. People are skittish about buying with the economy the way it is, so I think that's what's driving the demand for rentals. And Grandpa Franklin's house is in the Harvey Elementary School district, which is one of the more sought-after schools. You wouldn't have any trouble renting it."

"Well, that's good. You'll list it for us, if we decide to rent it out?"

"Of course. Whenever you're ready."

"That may be awhile. Whatever we do, we'll have to do something with all Grandpa Franklin's things first."

"Oh, that probably won't take as long as you think. Will you keep the living room furniture?"

"I don't know. We haven't even thought about individual pieces yet."

"Well, if you decide you don't want it, Aunt Nanette says she'll take it. She's always liked that couch. And remember, I've got contacts—consignment shops, antique stores, used bookstores, junk haulers. You name it, I know someone who'll take it away."

"What about all those copies of a single book?" I asked. "I don't think any consignment store or used bookstore will want those. At least, not all of them." Those books were weighing on me. They were heavy, bulky, and took up so much space. "This afternoon, I kept thinking about how many trips it would take to get them to a dump. And they're so heavy, it would cost a fortune just to throw them away. And then there's the fact that they're *books*—it feels almost immoral to throw them away."

Caroline patted my hand. "I know, dear, but we all have a copy and you can keep a few boxes with extra copies. There are companies that recycle books."

"Book recycling?"

"Yes. They haul books away and shred them. Sad, but sometimes there's nothing else to do. I had a client a few years ago who was downsizing—moving from a four-bedroom to a one-bedroom patio home. She was an avid reader and had one bedroom chock-full of paperbacks. She donated what she could to the library and then sent the rest off to be recycled."

"Hmm . . . interesting," I said, filing that bit of information away with a mental note to do some research on book recycling later. As a professional organizer, I might need to use a company like that in the future. Of course, it looked like I would probably have the opportunity to check into book recycling sooner rather than later.

Bill, who'd been pacing around the backyard as he talked on his cell phone, ended his call and joined us by the pool. "Okay. I've got us booked into a hotel for tonight. The insurance adjustor will be out tomorrow morning and I've got a call into a cleaning crew for tomorrow afternoon."

"Do you really think we need to spend the night at a hotel?" Caroline asked. "I hate to go off and leave the house like this."

"Our homeowner's policy covers the hotel stay. The smell of smoke is going to be pretty strong in there and the fire department shut off the gas and electricity. Those won't be on until tomorrow. Mitch and I will board up the doors and windows, so everything will be secure."

"All right," Caroline said.

Bill looked at me and said, "We've got rooms for you and Mitch, too."

I was about to say that Mitch and I could stay at Grandpa Franklin's house, but then I paused. Call me superstitious, but I wasn't sure I wanted to sleep in a house where a man had died. Mitch and Detective Rickets were still talking. No one seemed to be paying any attention to them. They probably assumed the detective was here because of the fire. Detective Rickets's back was to me and Mitch made eye contact with me over the detective's shoulder.

Uncle Bud came through the gate into the backyard. He was carrying several white paper bags from Chick-fil-A. "Anyone hungry?"

he asked as he set down the bags on the patio table. He dropped a hand on Caroline's shoulder. "Bill called me. You doin' okay?"

"I'm all right."

"There's a lie, if I ever heard one," Uncle Bud barked, then opened the bags. "I didn't know what the kids would want, so I got chicken nuggets."

"That's great. They love those," I said as I went over to help him get the food out, touched that he'd thought of the kids. I called them to the table. The aroma of fried chicken enveloped me. I inhaled deeply, realizing just how hungry I was. Caroline stood up and began handing out drinks. Detective Rickets went to the back gate and Mitch walked toward the table. I hurried over to the edge of the patio and met him before he joined the group around the table.

"What happened?" I asked as I picked up a chair.

Mitch grabbed another chair and said, "I told him what happened. He wasn't happy about it, mostly because I think he knows it's all going to check out and I'll be off the suspect list."

"That's good," I said, relief sweeping through me. "Are you going to tell the family about it?" We were walking back across the patio, each carrying a chair as we talked in low tones.

"About what? Detective Rickets made it clear that there's not a formal investigation. He's just poking around—his words, not mine. I'm not going to bring it up, unless I have to. They have enough to deal with right now."

We positioned the extra chairs around the table. I scooped Nathan up and settled him in a chair and removed from his reach the toy that came with his meal, substituting chicken and apple slices for the toy. "You know the rules. Eat first," I said as I dipped a waffle fry into ketchup.

Uncle Bud handed me a padded envelope he'd set on the table beside the food. "And this was on the porch."

I popped the crispy, lightly salted French fry into my mouth as I reached for the envelope. My name was printed on a large white label above Caroline and Bill's address. I wiped my fingers on a napkin, then ripped the tab open.

"Who would send me something here?" I said more to myself

than to anyone else. There was a single sheet of paper inside. It was folded in half. I opened it and went still.

There were two lines printed on the page in a tiny font. It must have been ten point or less. I squinted and read,

It wasn't an accident.
Go home.

"Ellie, did you get something to drink? We've got Diet Coke over here and a root beer, which would you like?" Caroline asked.

I heard the question, but couldn't process an answer. Mitch, who'd been helping Livvy open her milk, looked at me. "Ellie, what's wrong?"

I handed him the paper. His gaze flicked over the words, then snapped back to me. "Where did this come from."

I held up the envelope. "Here. Uncle Bud said it was on the front porch."

Uncle Bud wiped his mouth with a paper napkin and nodded. "Yep, I saw it when I drove up." He was speaking in his normal hearty tones, but as his gaze bounced from Mitch to me, he spoke more slowly, "So I picked it up along with the mail from the mailbox. Something wrong?"

"It's a—," Mitch broke off, glanced at the kids, and lowered his voice, "threat." The kids were busy arguing over who had the better toy and didn't notice what he'd said.

"Or a warning," I added. I'd recovered enough from the shock that I'd flipped the envelope back over to look at the front again. "No postage at all. Someone dropped that off on the doorstep."

"Dropped what off?" Caroline asked. "What are y'all talking about?"

"I'll see if I can catch Detective Rickets." Mitch handed the paper to Bill and jogged to the gate at the side of the yard. Caroline was on one side of Bill and Uncle Bud was on the other. They both leaned to look over his shoulder.

"Does that say it *wasn't* an accident?" Caroline put her chicken sandwich on the table as she pulled Bill's arm to see the paper better. "But that's crazy. No one would intentionally set our house on fire."

Bill cleared napkins and drinks and set the paper carefully down on the table. "Anything else on the envelope?" It was the most serious I'd ever heard him sound.

"Just my name." I put it beside the paper. "And your address."

Caroline frowned at the table. "This has got to be a joke. There's absolutely no excuse for practical jokes like this."

"Maybe it wasn't a joke," Bill said, balling up his napkin and tossing it beside his empty sandwich wrapper.

"Of course it was a joke. A sick, sick joke," Caroline said stoutly. "Why would someone single out Ellie, of all people, to send this to?" Bill and Uncle Bud exchanged looks as Caroline continued, "There's no one in the world who doesn't like Ellie . . ." Her voice trailed off uncertainly as she caught the meaning behind the significant looks.

"Except Felicity," I said, voicing what everyone else was thinking.

"I hear you've got some interesting mail here," said Detective Rickets as he crossed the lawn to the patio table with Mitch beside him.

I gestured to the paper and envelope and explained I'd just opened it. "Interesting," Detective Rickets repeated. He looked at the items without touching them, then asked who'd seen it first. Uncle Bud recounted bringing it in with the mail, then said, "I'm sure this is some sort of juvenile prank."

Detective Rickets looked at him hard before saying, "Possible." His voice was completely neutral.

Nathan began wiggling out of his seat. "Mom, can I have my toy now? I ate everything. Almost." He turned his wide brown eyes, so much like his dad's, on me. He knew how to use them, just like his dad, too.

"Fine," I said. After I'd checked to see that Livvy had eaten most of her food, I removed the toys from their plastic wrappers and sent them off to play in the yard. While I'd been taking care of the kids, Detective Rickets had produced evidence bags and was carefully putting the paper and envelope into them. To Bill and Caroline, he said, "I'll pass this along to our county forensics team and inform the fire marshal."

Uncle Bud frowned and said, "Now, Joel, you know there's no need for that."

"Afraid there is," Detective Rickets said, and turned to me. "Mrs. Avery, who knows you're staying here?"

"Family. I don't know anyone else in Smarr besides family."

"And some members of the family were upset with the terms of the will," Detective Rickets said.

"Yes, Felicity was very upset."

Uncle Bud said, "Ellie, you can't—"

"She's only telling the truth," Mitch said firmly. "And I think Detective Rickets already knows about the scene at Gus's office, anyway."

Uncle Bud looked disapproving, but to my surprise, Detective Rickets ignored his thunderous expression and continued to ask questions until he'd established that the only time the envelope could have been left on the porch was sometime after the fire had been noticed and before Uncle Bud arrived, a window of about an hour.

When he finished asking questions, Detective Rickets put away a small notebook he'd been writing in and picked up the evidence bags. He gave a curt nod to Uncle Bud and left. We sat around the table for a few moments in silence, then Caroline stood up. "Well, I think we should get what we can from the house, board up the windows and door, and then go to the hotel. I'm sure everything will be . . . cleared up tomorrow," she finished lamely.

None of us believed her, but it was cold, and almost fully dark now. It had been a long day, full of unexpected news, and I felt numb and weary. The kids were starting to bicker over their new toys, so we quickly cleared the trash away, then went into the house through the front door to see what we could salvage.

Chapter
Seventeen

"What if it wasn't Felicity, who left it?" I said as I slathered butter on a waffle and waited for Mitch to put down his juice glass. Mitch and I were in the restaurant of the Hampton Inn with morning sunlight streaming over our table and the drone of the local morning news running in the background on the requisite television. Why was it that we had to have televisions in every public space now? The house fire hadn't made the news, thank goodness—reporters and camera crews were the last thing we needed.

I pulled my attention away from the news and checked on Livvy and Nathan. Our table for four had two plates with half-eaten waffles, eggs, and muffin crumbs. Livvy was curled up on a couch in the corner of the dining room, a book in her hand and her blue purse tucked beside her leg. Last night, we'd found her purse and reading list along with her signed book, all unharmed. I had a feeling she was going to keep those things close to her from now on. We'd also brought all the kids' clothes with us, but she hadn't been nearly as interested in saving her clothes.

Most of the damage had been contained to the back of the house. I'd been relieved to see that the guest room was still intact. The furniture and bed were drenched with water, but the closet had been on the far side of the room, so we at least had clothes to wear. They were smoky, but we'd used the hotel laundry to wash some of our clothes last night. My T-shirt and hooded sweatshirt only had the scent of laundry detergent on them now. From the floor beside the couch where Livvy was sitting, I could just see the top of Nathan's head. I could certainly hear him as he made screeching and braking noises. I knew he'd stuffed five toy cars in his pockets before we left the room for breakfast and I was sure those cars were now making incredible, gravity-defying jumps.

Mitch speared a chunk of watermelon. "Who else is there?"

"Uncle Bud."

"You really think he'd type up a note and a mailing label to get his point across?"

I chewed thoughtfully on a bite of bacon, then said, "Okay, so you're right. That doesn't sound like him at all. He does seem like the type of person who'd threaten you to your face, not in an anonymous letter, but if he really wanted to throw someone off, wouldn't he do something totally unexpected—like print a letter and a label?"

Mitch shook his head as he picked up a piece of buttered toast. "No. I can promise you Uncle Bud didn't put that envelope on the porch. It's just not something he'd do. And why would he care if we left town? He actually wants us here to help sort out Grandpa Franklin's estate."

Theoretically, I agreed with Mitch, but I couldn't quite let go of the idea that Uncle Bud might be involved. "He's the one who pressured the sheriff's office not to look too closely at Grandpa Franklin's death."

Mitch cut a bite of sausage. "Ellie, we've been over this before. Uncle Bud isn't doing anything suspicious."

I sighed, opened my mouth to argue, then thought better of it. I wasn't going to change his mind about Uncle Bud. I swallowed some orange juice and mentally moved on. I was tired of the roller-coaster ride that our relationship had become during the last few days. Felicity might thrive in a stormy, contentious atmosphere, but I wanted to avoid any more fights if I could help it. Mitch could think what he wanted, but I knew there was a real possibility that Uncle Bud was involved in the weird circumstances of Grandpa Franklin's and Stan Anderson's deaths.

I thumped my glass down on the table and said, "Well, then that only leaves Felicity. Do you think *she's* got the personality to do something like that?"

"Write a threatening note? Oh, yeah," Mitch said instantly. "I've told you about how she can hold a grudge. I'm sure she's still upset about the will. She probably won't talk to us until, oh, probably Thanksgiving would be a good bet."

"So you think Felicity set the fire?"

Mitch angled his silverware across his empty plate. "I didn't say that. I said she wouldn't be above writing a nasty note and slipping it onto the porch anonymously. "That fire was probably an accident and she saw a way to take advantage of the situation to hurt us."

"Not us. Me. The letter was only addressed to me," I said as I placed my napkin beside my plate.

"True, but, I don't think that means any—," Mitch broke off as his cell phone rang. He pulled it out of his belt clip. "It's the squadron. I have to take this." He answered, spoke a few words with his hand over his other ear, then said, "Hold on. I can't hear you. Let me go outside."

Mitch walked through the lobby and paused for the double doors to slide open, then stepped outside. I went to get a refill on my orange juice and had to wait as a hotel employee, a woman with generous curves that stretched her uniform of a cotton polo shirt and polyester pants to the limit, removed an empty pitcher. "Hold on, hon," she said to me. "Here's a full one." She replaced it with a pitcher filled to the brim with orange juice. "So anyway," she said, turning to another woman, an employee who was wiping tables near her, "they say that Franklin Avery was a miser and didn't trust the banks." She hugged the empty pitcher to her chest. "He hid his fortune." Lowering her voice, she leaned closer to the woman and I inched back slightly to hear her. "It's somewhere around Smarr," she hissed.

"Get out," the other woman said in a normal tone of voice. She tucked the cloth into her waistband, then picked up a stack of plates and silverware. She had spindly arms and black hair pulled back from her head in a long braid.

The woman with the pitcher leaned a hip against a chair, settling in for a good gossip. "I'm serious. I heard it at the gym from one of his relatives."

I groaned softly and went back to pouring juice. So Felicity was spreading rumors about hidden loot. As if we didn't already have enough to deal with.

I turned around to head back to the table and smashed into someone in my path. Juice shot out of my glass, spattering my sweatshirt and the floor.

"Excuse me." The woman who'd nearly taken me down stared at me as if I was the one who'd barreled into her. She was a stout woman of about forty and had small, dark eyes and short pale hair that looked as stiff and dry as the yellow grass outside. She flicked her hand to remove a drop of juice, which sent the black caftanlike sleeves of her coat flapping. She transferred her haughty look to the two hotel employees, who were moving a table so they could clean up the juice. "Well? Don't you have any towels? Napkins? Something to clean up this mess?"

The employee who'd been clearing tables slammed down a SLIP-PERY WHEN WET sign at the woman's feet and handed her a few paper napkins, then gave a bigger stack to me. "Thank you," I said as I daubed at sticky droplets on my throat, then pressed the napkins to the stain on my sweatshirt.

The other hotel employee sized up the situation. "I'll get a mop," she said before grabbing the empty pitcher and escaping.

"Now—," the stout woman peered at the name tag pinned to the woman who'd been clearing the tables and said, "Opal, the front desk is unmanned. It's inexcusable that I should have to track down an employee. I'm already behind schedule. Where are Stan Anderson's belongings?"

"Umm, let me get a manager," Opal said.

"That won't be necessary. Simply give me his suitcase—you must have it stored somewhere around here. It's a black rolling bag with a brown stripe. He was in Room three-twenty-three."

"I'm sorry, ma'am. I can't do that. I'll get the manager."

"Of course you can. I'm his sister. I've just spent hours with the police. They told me his belongings were here. I don't have time to wait. I have a plane to catch."

"I'm sure the manager won't mind if you help yourself to breakfast," Opal said, placatingly. "I'll be right back."

The woman sighed elaborately. "I should have known this wouldn't be simple."

I finished wiping my hands and tossed the napkins in the trash as the woman looked over the breakfast bar. She wrinkled her nose. Two petulant voices carried across the room.

"Stop it."

"I'm not *doing* anything."

"Yes you are. Stop it!"

I strode across the room so that I could prevent all-out fighting in the hotel dining room.

"You're throwing away his clothes?"

I backed out of Grandpa Franklin's closet, my arms full of men's shirts, pants, and a few suits, and rammed my elbow into the dresser. Aunt Christine was standing in the doorway with her fingers pressed to her mouth. She looked like someone had just punched her in the stomach.

"No, we're donating them to charity," I said as I dropped the load onto the bed and rubbed my elbow. Who'd moved that dresser? It hadn't been so close to the closet the last time I'd been here.

I shook out my arm, then pushed up the sleeves of my sweatshirt. No cut, but I would have a bruise later. After I'd stopped Livvy and Nathan's escalating fight at the hotel, I'd returned to the room to change into clothes that didn't have juice on them. By the time I'd returned to the lobby, Stan Anderson's sister was gone. Once Mitch was finished with his phone call, we'd loaded everyone up in the van and driven to Grandpa Franklin's house—I still couldn't think of it as *our* house—because we had so much to do. We'd spent an hour walking through the rooms, jotting notes, then I'd tackled the clothes removal. Mitch was in the garage. I wasn't sure what he was doing out there—getting rid of things, I hoped.

"Oh, are you sure you have to do that?"

"Well, do you know anyone who would wear these?" I asked as I removed the clothes from the hangers.

She rubbed the faded fabric of a plaid shirt between her fingers. "I suppose you're right. They're too small for any of the men in the family and even Roy would never wear these. They're not his style." She picked up a shirt and folded it into thirds. "It's just such a shame, clearing out everything of his."

I opened a trunk at the foot of the bed. It contained a jumble of lightweight summer clothing. I closed the lid. I didn't want to pull out any more clothes while she was here since she was already distressed. I could clean out the trunk later. I walked over and put a hand on her arm. "We have to. I know it's painful, but if we're going to rent the house . . ."

"Rent it!" she exclaimed.

"Well, we can't live here. Mitch's job is in Georgia. And we won't be stationed there forever." Mitch and I had talked about it on the drive over and decided renting was the best solution for now. I steered her out the door and into the living room. "And that way the house will be lived in. We don't want it sitting empty."

Mitch had just come inside. "Mitch, can you help Aunt Christine load the landscape print into her car?"

"Already done it."

Aunt Christine was looking around the living room as if she was checking to make sure nothing had changed. "Well, why don't you walk her out," I said, giving him a significant look.

He raised his eyebrows, but took Aunt Christine's arm and walked her to her car. I stepped onto the porch to check on the kids. The late afternoon sun cut through the tranquil air and warmed the boards of the porch. It was so quiet I could hear the faint swish of the occasional car on the road.

After running around the house and yard for a couple of hours, the kids had discovered several board games in the hall closet. "Look, Mom, *wooden* checkers," Nathan had said, fascinated because his games only had plastic pieces. Livvy was sitting sideways in the porch swing with her legs extended across the seat and a book in her hand. I tilted my head to get a better look at the cover and realized she was reading Grandpa Franklin's memoirs. I'd read it a few years ago when we got our copy and was surprised the stories about fishing and exploring the woods held her attention.

"How's the book, Livvy?" I asked, and it took her a few seconds to drag her focus away from the book.

"What?"

"Good book?" I asked again.

"Yeah. I like it," she said, already refocused on the pages. Her blue purse was on the porch beside Nathan. He'd taken the game pieces from the checkers and chess set and spread them onto every available space. I saw a rook, a bishop, and two queens propped on the railing as well as several checkers stacked into a small wall placed in front of a row of pawns. "Don't lose any of those pieces," I told Nathan.

"Okay," he said as he made an exploding sound and used the king to knock down the stack of checkers.

Mitch trotted back up the steps and said, "Those chess pieces are as good as Legos." We walked into the house together.

"Thanks," I said. "Aunt Christine was so sentimental about Grandpa Franklin's clothes. She didn't want me to give them away. I can't imagine how she'll feel when we start to clear out the furniture."

Mitch eyed the couch. "Ah, Aunt Gwen called this morning and asked what we're doing with the furniture. If we aren't keeping the couch, they want it for their waiting room at the office."

"Aunt Nanette wants it, too," I said. "Your mom told me last night, but I'd forgotten about it until now." I rubbed my forehead. "What are we going to do? We're not going to be able to give everyone what they want."

"We could draw numbers and then let the person with the lowest number have their pick."

"Like that present swapping game we play at Christmas? I don't think that would go over very well."

Mitch's phone beeped and he pulled it out to check a text message. "Great. Dan wants to know if we're keeping the ladder in the garage. He needs one." Mitch's mouth quirked down. "Estate sale?"

"I don't know—someone will be upset if we sell everything. And what would we do if there are things that don't sell? We'd be right back in the same boat." I ran my hand over the back of Grandpa Franklin's chair. "Do your parents want anything?"

"They haven't mentioned anything in particular to me. They're too busy with the fire." Mitch's parents had left the hotel early that morning to meet the insurance people, the fire marshal, and the cleaning crews at their house. Mitch dropped onto the couch and let his head fall onto the back cushion. I rubbed the back of my neck and sat down in the chair beside him. My shoulders and legs ached from a long day of packing and carrying boxes. I eyed the stack of boxes and trash bags lined up near the front door. So far, I'd only removed things that were either specific bequests in the will or things that I didn't think anyone would care about. No one was going to want his toiletries, clothes, or stacks of magazines and newspapers. "That reminds me," Mitch said. "The fire marshal's finished and says the fire isn't suspicious."

"Even considering the note and the fact that your mom doesn't burn candles?"

"I don't know about those things, but, apparently, there's no evidence of anyone setting the fire. I guess candles get knocked over pretty often."

"Great, another one," I said.

"What?" Mitch tilted his head so he could see me better.

"Another coincidence. Another thing that looks like foul play, but isn't."

"Ellie . . ." Mitch closed his eyes. "We're not going there. There's no foul play." I opened my mouth to protest, but he continued, "Anyway, Uncle Bud's got a demolition crew coming tomorrow. There was water damage to the carpet and the ceiling in the living room, so they're going to have to completely redo that, and the roof, too."

Okay, I wasn't going to press my point about the suspicious things that had been happening. No matter how he tried to ignore them, they were still happening and it looked like I was the only one in the Avery family willing to try and figure out what was going on. I stared at the shaft of sunlight streaming in the front window and watched Livvy's head bowed over her book. Let the other stuff go, for now, I told myself, and tried to focus on what Mitch had been saying as he purposefully steered the conversation in another direction.

I rotated my shoulders. I had to at least make an effort. "How long will that take?"

"Quite awhile. Mom said since they have to rip out the drywall in the living room, they should go ahead and redo the kitchen, too."

"That's a long time for them to stay in a hotel." I sat up straight as a thought occurred to me. "Mitch, why don't they stay here?"

Mitch raised his eyebrows. "What?"

"It's perfect—they can stay here while the repairs are done at their house. You know how that goes. It always takes longer than you think it will. They could stay here and we could leave everything in the house—all the furniture—and we won't hurt anyone's feelings."

"That could work, but we'll have to clear the place out eventually."

I slumped back against the cushion. "True, but we could come back and do it this summer when we have more time. And by then, well, maybe we'll have figured out a way to divide all the stuff. We can even keep working on it—in fact, I need to call that number that your mom gave me this morning for the book recycling. If we can get that taken care of, think of all the space it will free up in the garage."

Mitch nodded. "It could work. The house wouldn't be empty. Mom and Dad are going to need a place to stay and this isn't that far from their house."

I jumped up and went to get my purse and phone. "It's perfect. We'll do as much as we can. We'll start with the garage because your parents will need all the stuff in the house—the furniture, dishes, and linens. After the repairs are finished on their house, we can come back and clear out the house this summer. It'll be easier to rent during the summer, too, I bet, since that's when most people want to move anyway."

I called the recycling company and set up an appointment for them to remove the boxes. Their first opening was over a month away, but I made the appointment and asked them to call me if they had a cancellation. I'd have to make sure someone could meet the truck since we'd be back home by then. I clicked the phone closed and turned back to Mitch. "Well, that's a relief. One less thing to worry about."

I heard a car crunching over the gravel, then the slam of a car door. "I hope that's not someone coming to claim a lamp or the TV," I said.

Mitch laughed. "That TV is so old we're going to be lucky if Goodwill takes it. No, I think that's the babysitter."

"Hello . . . anyone home?" a female voice called as footsteps came up the porch steps.

"We are!" Nathan said, and Queen trotted through the open door, tail swishing.

"What? Do we need a sitter?" What was I saying? We could always use a sitter.

"Remember how I said we needed to get away on our own? How does dinner at Quincy House sound?"

"Ah–nice, but will they let me in the door, looking like this?" I asked, pointing to my dusty jeans and sweatshirt.

"I had the rest of our clothes sent out to be cleaned this morning. They should be back by now. So, dinner? Just you and me."

I smiled. "You have to ask?"

Ellie Avery's Tips for Preserving Family Treasures

Genealogy
Discovering your family history generates a lot of information. To organize family data:
• Create a filing system for each family name you're research-

ing. You'll want paper files for hard copies as well as an organized filing system on your computer.

- Create subcategories for legal documents (marriage, birth, and death certificates), family charts, interviews, correspondence, etc. As your research grows, you can expand your filing system. For instance, begin with a file for correspondence. As it expands you can separate it into Correspondence "A–M" and "N–Z."
- Copy and/or scan important documents, then work with the copies, to preserve the original documents.
- Store original documents in archival-safe storage boxes or albums.

Chapter
Eighteen

Mitch looked up from the menu. "Wings? Mozzarella sticks?" We were in Jody's, a hip bar a couple of blocks from the community college. "Mozzarella sticks sound good," I said, nearly shouting so Mitch could hear me over the din. I'd actually been ready to leave for our date early and we had thirty minutes to kill before our dinner reservation. Amazing how much easier it was to decide what to wear when I only had about four choices. My little black dress would have been perfect, but the thought of wearing it made me feel sad since I'd just worn it to Grandpa Franklin's funeral. And I didn't want to be melancholy tonight. I was already feeling nervous and edgy at the thought that Mitch was going to tell me what had been weighing on him for so long. Since my choices weren't that extensive, I'd dressed up my long-sleeved white T-shirt, jeans, and quilted red jacket with a floral scarf. The scarf, in rich red, blue, and gold tones, had been a Christmas gift from my friend Abby. After I'd unwrapped it, she'd dragged me to my closet and pulled out several things, including the red jacket, and held the scarf up to show me how many outfits I could wear it with. I tended to be a bit of a remedial dresser. Abby was much better at coordinating clothes than I was. Accessorizing, especially with purses, was my forte. I was carrying my black Kate Spade Quinn, one of my favorites.

As Mitch placed our order for drinks and an appetizer, I crossed my arms and leaned on the wooden table, which had several initials carved in it. We were in a small booth at the side of the crowded restaurant. The steady beat of the Eagles singing "Heartache Tonight" thumped through the room. I hoped the song wasn't an omen. "Crowded in here," I shouted.

"Yeah. It's always been popular, but I've never seen it like this. Dan told me they have better food than they did when I lived here."

I nodded and decided it was too noisy to attempt a serious conversation here. Mitch must have come to the same conclusion because we spent most of the time eating our mozzarella sticks, people watching, and talking a little about the kids and how they were handling everything that had happened over the last week.

As I munched on the mozzarella sticks, which were good—crispy golden brown on the outside and gooey, cheesy inside—I caught sight of a familiar face moving through the crowd. Well, actually, it wasn't his face I noticed, but his curly hair. "Look, isn't that one of the brothers from the funeral home?" I asked Mitch.

When he reached a table filled with other guys in their twenties lounging back in their chairs, legs and arms splayed all over the place, one of them said, "There's the Grim Reaper."

The guy with the curly hair said, "They're already dead by the time they get to me."

Mitch nodded. "Yeah, that's Jake. The youngest."

I watched him give the guys fist-bump greetings and sit down. "Do you think he told the truth that day about Grandpa Franklin's casket?"

Mitch shrugged. "It could have happened."

"You really think some college-age kid took a funeral home van for a joyride? A joyride that only went around the funeral home parking lot?"

"Hey, I didn't say I believed it—only that it's possible. Sometimes truth is stranger than fiction."

"Somehow I don't think that's the case here." I plucked the last mozzarella stick from the plate. I broke it in half, the warm cheese sagging between the two halves as I pulled them apart.

Mitch took his half and said, "I know that look."

"What?" I asked around my last mouthful.

"You've got to leave it alone," Mitch said, and popped the cheese stick in his mouth.

"The police never really questioned him. Detective Rickets decided the whole thing was a prank practically as soon as he got there," I said, thinking of Detective Kalra. I would love to try and convince her to talk to Jake, but she'd dropped all communication with me since Mitch's brief stint as a suspect. She hadn't returned the one phone message I'd left for her after the fire, and it didn't look like I should hope for more information. She'd gotten what she wanted: the case was being unofficially investigated and I supposed she couldn't be in contact with me since I was so closely associated with the Avery family. Although that fact had been a plus with her before, I thought sourly.

"What's that face for? Are you still brooding about Jake?" Mitch asked as he signaled for the bill. "We've got to get going."

"Okay," I said, feeling resigned. Jake would never tell me what really happened and short of walking up to his table and asking point-blank—a situation guaranteed to get zero results—there was no way to find out. I stifled a sigh and told myself to let it go. There was nothing to do about it and I had other things to worry about tonight. I put my napkin on the table and grabbed my purse. "I'm going to the restroom before we leave."

A few minutes later, I was shaking as much water off my hands as I could. The automatic-air hand dryer was broken and there wasn't a paper towel in sight. I wiped my wet hands on my jeans to dry them, then shouldered open the restroom door. I stopped short on the threshold. Jake was standing at the end of the short dead-end hallway. His back was turned to me and he was talking on his cell phone. His other hand was pressed to his ear to block out the laughter, conversation, and music that filtered down the hallway.

"I told you, I'm not going to do it." Even this far away from the source of the music, he had to raise his voice to be heard and I could clearly understand each word. "Didn't you hear me? No. I don't care how much. Look, I helped you take the casket, but I'm not doing anything else—"

He broke off as he glanced over his shoulder. As soon as he spotted me, he flushed and jammed a button on the phone to disconnect the call. "Bad connection," he said as he turned to face me. He tried to follow his words up with a chuckle, but it came out more like a choke. "Can't hear a thing in here."

"Oh, I can. I heard something about a casket."

"Don't know what you're talking about." He made a move to step by me. I shifted. Since things had worked out this way, I wasn't about to let him leave without at least trying to find out more about the casket now that I had the opportunity.

"Do I know you?" Jake asked, pressing closer to the wall and trying to slide by me.

"Yes. We met the day before a funeral."

"We arrange so many funerals . . ."

"Well, I'm sure you'll remember this one. It was Franklin Avery's funeral. The one where he disappeared the day before? Ring any bells?"

Jake stopped trying to slink past me and squared his shoulders. "Look, ma'am, I'm not sure what you're talking about. If you have an issue with Grisholm's Funeral Home, then you'd need to call our office directly."

"Jake," I said in a pitying tone of voice, "I heard you say that you helped someone take the casket. Since I doubt that any other body or casket has gone missing lately, I'm sure my friend Detective Kalra will want to talk to you about that statement." Okay, that was a fib. A whopper of a lie actually, but he looked scared and he didn't know that Detective Kalra had disappeared like a kid does when bedtime is closing in. He shook his head and I said, "Or, she can just get your phone records to see who you were speaking to."

Jake ran his fingers through his curly hair. "It's your word against mine." He didn't sound at all convinced with his warning.

"Yes, but who do you think the detective will believe—you or me? I think you've had a few scrapes . . . a few escapades?" If he knew about the things that had happened to *me*, he'd laugh in my face and walk away. What had happened to him was nothing compared to being involved in a few murder investigations. My palms were sweating and I was starting to feel guilty about the way I was badgering him and the lies I was telling. A thought occurred to me. Whoever he'd been talking to was going to pay him for more help. Well, I could pay, too. I reached inside my purse and found my wallet. I had three twenties.

"Let's look at it this way. We trade." I held up the twenties, which were folded in half. "I give you this. You tell me what happened." What was the going rate for information? I hoped it wasn't more than I had in my hand.

Jake pursed his lips to one side, then gave a quick nod. "But no names."

I jerked the bills back as he reached for them. "There has to be names."

"Sorry, then. Call the police on me if you want. I've got more to worry about from . . . them."

I could see a resolve in his expression that hadn't been there before. There was something else in his face, too. Was it fear? He'd been on the verge of telling me what happened, so I said, "Fine. No names, but it has to be the truth."

He nodded. "The truth."

"Okay. What happened? Because I don't believe for a minute that some stranger took a van from the funeral home for a joyride."

"Yeah. Well, it was the best I could come up with on the spur of the moment."

"So what really happened?" I asked.

"I met . . . this person who knew where I worked. 'They' said if I'd help them get Mr. Avery's casket, they'd pay me."

"So how did you get this person access?"

He shrugged. "It was easy. I gave them a map of the funeral home and told them when the casket would be in the hallway on the rolling cart, waiting to be moved to the viewing room. We'd never had to worry about locking up."

"So you didn't physically help them move the casket?"

"Are you kidding? No way. I just told them how to get it and where everything is. Helping—," he almost slipped up and said a name, but caught himself in time, "the person would be wrong."

"But looking the other way is okay?" I asked, sarcastically.

"They were going to get to that casket one way or another. If I didn't help them, there would have been a break-in."

"So why steal the casket . . . why not just come to the viewing?"

"Well, you can't really check out a casket and the body while the whole family is hanging around, can you?"

I'd thought it was just the casket, but his words meant . . . "They wanted to search the casket *and* the body?"

He reached for the wad of bills in my hand.

I stepped back. "I don't think I've gotten my money's worth. All you've told me is what I already thought happened. You helped someone steal a body. Did you see this person that day?" He shook his head and I asked, "So how did they pay you?"

"There was an envelope on the dashboard of my car." No wonder he'd been in such a hurry to get to his car after the casket had gone missing.

"How much?"

"A thousand dollars."

I was struck speechless for a moment. A thousand dollars? Someone *really* wanted to know what was in that casket. And my sixty bucks seemed paltry in comparison. I handed over the money and he brushed by me.

I turned. "Wait. What did they want you to do now? I heard you say you wouldn't help them."

He fanned the bills out, saw it was only sixty bucks, and a look of dissatisfaction crossed his face. "I think I got ripped off. I've already told you too much." He shoved the money in the pocket of his cargo pants and walked away.

It was something that he didn't want to do. And he was scared of this mystery person, someone who had offered him money. Jake had turned it down. He didn't seem like the type of person who'd turn down money that quickly. He must either really be afraid of the person . . . or was he holding out for another offer and more money? Hard to say with him, but there had been something in his face when he said he was more worried about "them" than the police. And was it one person or a group of people? He'd referred to "this person" as well as to "them."

The steady murmur of conversation from across the table stopped and I tuned back into my surroundings. Mitch had been talking and I'd been so lost in my own thoughts I'd completely missed what he'd said. I looked up from the sweet potato tart we were sharing for dessert. He paused as he took a bite, then continued, "Anyway, I'd heard a couple from Florida bought the place a couple of years ago."

We were in the restaurant at Quincy House. When I'd returned to the table at Jody's after talking to Jake, Mitch had been holding my coat for me. We'd hurried to the car and made the short drive to Quincy House, which was only a few blocks away.

We'd toured the house before, years ago when we were first married and Mitch brought me here on the familiarization tour of Smarr. The exterior of the house with its twin curving staircases and wrought-iron balconies set in a large park with huge live oaks hadn't changed, but the inside was completely different.

The new owners had turned Quincy House into a boutique hotel with a trendy restaurant. Mitch had picked sushi for his dinner. I'd opted for the haute cuisine version of pulled pork and a salad with a bunch of different types of lettuce that I couldn't pronounce, much less identify. I'd expected the house to be full of dark wood antiques, but they were going against type with their decorating. Pale wood floors and walls painted in shades of lilac, baby blue, and pale yellow accented the modern silver light fixtures and curved chrome chairs. Splashes of color, modern abstract paintings, dotted the walls. It wasn't at all what I'd expected and I wasn't sure if I liked it or not. The contrast of modern elements with the traditional architecture was interesting.

I angled my fork into the crust of the tart and said, "I bet some people weren't happy about the remodel."

"Mom said the planning and zoning meetings were pretty lively there for a while. Something about paint colors and historical accuracy."

"I'll bet," I said, thinking of the fuchsia accent wall in the entryway.

We finished off the tart and talked about Smarr and how it had changed, until our waiter brought the bill. Once that was taken care of, we stared at each other over the flame in the small lamp on our table. Mitch had seemed reluctant to bring up whatever had been bothering him—I'd begun to think of it as "the issue"—during dinner and I hadn't forced the topic. Our conversation had wandered from topic to topic. What to do with Grandpa Franklin's house, the upcoming book fair, Nathan's sudden announcement that he wanted to play the guitar, and a smattering of other things. Deep down, I was a little worried. Whatever the issue was, it was something he didn't want to share with me. Or he couldn't. We'd never been in a place like this in our marriage and it scared me. I swallowed and forced my thoughts away from speculating on what he might want to talk about. Of course, that was how I got lost in thought earlier and missed part of the conversation.

I threaded my fingers through his and leaned a bit closer. "I thought we were going to talk."

"We were," Mitch said, and squeezed my fingers. "But I didn't want to ruin a nice evening."

I felt all the fancy food I'd just eaten churn in my stomach. Whatever he had to say could ruin our dinner?

Mitch let go of my hand and put the black padded check folder on the table. "Let's go for a walk."

"A walk? Isn't it a little cold for that?"

"Nah, it's not that bad," Mitch said as we retrieved our coats and stepped onto the porch.

"Well, it's not as cold as it has been. I'll give you that," I said, noting that my breath wasn't coming out in frosty white puffs. "Where are we going to walk?"

As we strolled down the curve of the steps, Mitch took my hand and guided me to a gravel path that wrapped around the house.

"The grounds," he said with a sweep of his free hand, indicating the wide expanse of grass interspersed with fountains, shallow pools, and low hedges in geometric patterns. The fountains and pools were empty now and looked a little forlorn in the chilly air, but there were enough strategically placed lights that the garden didn't feel forbidding or scary.

We strolled along the gravel path in silence for a while, our linked hands swinging companionably. "I've been doing a lot of thinking lately," Mitch said. I turned my head to look at him while we walked. His gaze was focused on the gravel path, his thoughts concentrated inward. "The last few years . . . well . . . things have changed. We're not the same couple we used to be."

I felt a frisson of fear spike through me. I'd worried about what had been bothering Mitch, but I'd pushed away the thought that something was seriously wrong, but now . . . those words, the "we've changed" speech. I'd been on the receiving end of the "we've grown apart, we want different things" talk before. Of course, that had been years ago when I was dating, but to hear those words now . . . I stumbled on an uneven section of the path and Mitch gripped my elbow to steady me. I looked into his face. It was darker here and I couldn't see his expression. I'd always thought our marriage had a solid underpinning that couldn't collapse, but . . . those words worried me.

We'd reached the end of the formal gardens, which were marked with another hedge, this one higher, towering over Mitch's head. This area wasn't as well maintained as the grounds closer to the house. The hedge hadn't been trimmed recently. It was shaggy with new growth and there were gaps where the bushes had died and hadn't been replaced.

"Here, I want to show you something," he said, and stepped through one of the gaps in the hedge. I followed him, wanting to ask what he was thinking, but as I stepped through the hedge, I paused to let my eyes adjust to the blackness. It was even darker on this side. As my eyes adjusted, I could make out the dim forms of huge, gnarled oak trunks, their high, spreading branches blocking out the faint starlight. I couldn't see any Spanish moss, but I knew if it were daylight, I would have been able to see it dripping from the tree limbs above. "What's this place? Another park or something?"

"No, it's still part of Quincy House. They just don't do anything with it. Their property goes all the way to the road over there. See down there?" Mitch said.

"No. I can't see anything."

Mitch's arm materialized beside my face, his hand pointing off in the distance. "Down there."

"Oh." I saw several pinpricks of white light, a chain of them in the distance. "Those lights that are so far away? Yes, I see them," I said, thinking that Mitch suddenly seemed relaxed. Had I been wrong? Maybe he wasn't winding up to tell me he wanted something different than I did? But his words . . .

Mitch interrupted my thoughts as he wrapped his arm around my waist and turned me to the right. "Those lights over there? That's Holloway Park. Dan and I used to ride down there when we were kids. We'd climb trees back there, too. No one cared."

"It's too bad he's so busy with his new job. You haven't seen much of Dan," I said.

"Yeah," Mitch agreed as we walked along.

There was a smaller, rougher path that curved to the left and we walked along it at a slower pace because of the darkness and the uneven ground. "And if we were feeling really daring, we'd race over here to this side and climb over the fence into the cemetery," Mitch said. My eyes had adjusted to the darkness and I was able to see a low brick fence set with wrought-iron bars that extended up to at least six feet high. The trees ended at the fence and on the other side of the bars I could see the wide, flat grounds of a cemetery, the headstones heavy slabs of darkness.

"We used to dare each other to climb the fence and steal a flower from one of the graves."

"Mitch, that's awful," I said, "stealing flowers from graves."

"Hey, it could have been something worse."

We walked along the edge of the fence, the dark trees looming on one side and the open plain of the cemetery on the other. The large headstones gave way to a more modern area with smaller markers set flat into the ground. I stopped and looked at a large stone fountain glowing dimly in the starlight in the cemetery. "That looks familiar," I said. "Mitch, this isn't the cemetery where Grandpa Franklin's buried, is it?" I didn't know the layout of Smarr all that well and was disoriented from our walk, but I hadn't thought we were near the cemetery we'd visited last week.

Mitch's voice was quiet. "Yes, it is. It's the biggest cemetery in Smarr. For a few minutes there, I forgot. I was just thinking about Dan and me when we were kids."

"It's okay," I said. "Come on, let's go back and—" I stopped to listen. "Did you hear that?"

"Why are you whispering?" Mitch asked, but he'd lowered his voice, too.

"It sounded like a cry, a yelp—something in pain," I said, looking past the iron bars. "A cat, maybe?"

A metallic clank rang out through the blackness. On the far side of the fountain, a round light bounced as a very human voice cursed. The light went out. Mitch and I looked at each other as muted footfalls pounded away from us.

"Mitch, we should get out of here," I whispered.

Mitch shook his head and hopped onto the brick part of the fence. "No, they're gone now. Probably teenagers. I hope they weren't tagging."

If gangs were spray-painting their symbols on gravestones, that was about as low as you could get. "I guess that metallic sound we heard could have been paint cans. Are there gangs in Smarr?"

"There are gangs everywhere," Mitch said as he gripped the iron bars above his head, placed one foot on the brick and boosted himself up into the air. "I'll check and see. If they were tagging . . . then we need to call the police. Looks like they left something over there on the other side of the fountain."

"Careful!" I said as Mitch swung himself over the iron points that topped the fence. He landed on the other side with a thud. He paused a moment, then said, "Been awhile since I've done that."

He walked by the fountain and stopped.

I climbed up on the brick part of the fence. "Mitch, what is it?"

He muttered, "No way," and continued to stare at the ground.

"Is it graffiti?"

"No." He strode back over to the fence, pulled his phone out of his belt clip, and punched in three numbers, his face set and angry. "Someone was digging up a grave—Grandpa Franklin's grave."

Chapter Nineteen

While Mitch was explaining the situation to the 911 dispatcher, I walked along the fence, looking for a gate or a break. Unlike the hedge, there were no gaps here. I gave up looking for another way into the cemetery and shoved my purse through the iron bars. Good thing I was wearing jeans and not my little black dress. I climbed up on the brick portion, grabbed the iron bars, and tried to imitate Mitch's vault over the sharp points at the top. He pulled the phone away from his face. "Ellie, what are you—no, wait—"

I didn't come close to his graceful maneuver, but I made it over. I landed hard on my feet and felt the impact jar my legs. "I'm sure I'll feel that in the morning," I said as I stood up cautiously from the crouched position I'd landed in.

Mitch ended the call and came over. "Are you okay? Why didn't you wait?"

I dusted off my hands and picked up my purse. "I wasn't going to stay on the other side of the fence by myself. Classic horror movie stuff—creepy cemetery, two people separated. Then—*bam!*—before you know it, one of them disappears." My tone was light, but I was only half joking. I had no desire to stand around on my own in the almost total blackness. "How long until someone gets here?"

"A few minutes." Mitch put his phone away and we walked back around the fountain to where we'd seen the bobbing circle of light. "There isn't a caretaker on site, so we'll have to wait for the police."

We both stopped a few feet from the disturbed grave. I squatted down to see better. "Look, they left a knife," I said, pointing to— but not touching—a Swiss army knife.

Mitch pushed a large rectangle of fresh sod with his shoe. The edges were smooth. "They used it to slice through the grass," he said, "and forgot to pick it up when they ran."

I stood up and stepped around a long pile of dirt. "How long do you think they'd been here?"

"Maybe an hour. Looks like they only made it about a foot down."

I looked over the mound of dirt and back to the shallow indentation in the ground. "To dig all the way down . . . to the casket . . . that would have to take hours, but what else could they have been doing?"

"Nothing. They had to be trying to get to Grandpa Franklin's casket."

"Are you sure it's his?" I asked. The plaque had been ordered, but it wasn't complete and hadn't been installed yet. There was only a small numbered marker set in the ground.

"I'm sure," Mitch said. "His grave was on this row, third from the fountain."

I looked over and counted the rest of the headstones. This was definitely the third slot away from the fountain, and all the other graves had markers with names. The first police car arrived at the cemetery entrance, flashing bright pulses of light over the graves.

"You folks make a habit of walking in graveyards at night?" Detective Rickets asked.

"We weren't walking in the cemetery," I said sharply. Mitch pressed his hand into the small of my back and gave me a warning look.

Lights had been set up on stands, exposing the dark scar of fresh earth, which contrasted with the dry grass that covered the rest of the cemetery grounds. Flashlight beams bounced around the cemetery, sporadically illuminating the darkness, then skipping on to another patch of dead grass as officers moved about. It was one of these beams of light that hit Detective Rickets's face and I thought I caught a glimmer of humor in his eyes.

"Get that light out of my eyes," he barked. The light skimmed to the ground as someone said, "Sorry, sir."

Was he teasing us? I peered through the darkness, trying to see his expression, but even with the ambient light glowing and flickering, I couldn't clearly see his face. The extremely polite sheriff's deputy who'd first responded to the 911 call was gone. As soon as Detective Rickets arrived, he'd sent the deputy packing and begun asking questions himself. I had my elbows tucked into my waist and my feet pressed close together in an effort to conserve all the body heat that I could. We were going on an hour being outside and the temperature had dropped. We were sitting a few feet away from the exposed grave on a chilly, backless marble bench.

"We've already told you that we were walking on the grounds behind Quincy House and only came over here when we heard noises and saw the flashlight," I said.

Mitch moved his hand to my upper arm and squeezed, rather tightly. I swiveled my head toward him, trying to give him a significant look that I hoped the detective wouldn't pick up on.

Mitch said, "Do you have any more questions, Detective? Anything else you need to clarify?"

"No, I think I've got the picture now."

Mitch and I stood up. Detective Rickets pressed his hands deeper into his pockets, causing the fabric of his jacket to pull tighter over his shoulders. "I'll have a deputy drive you back to your car," he said as he escorted us away from the grave.

As we walked along the path behind the detective, Mitch asked, "Why do you think someone would dig up his grave?"

Detective Rickets stopped walking and turned to face us. "Well, as I see it, there are three possibilities. One, it could be a random thing. But since we haven't had any problems with desecration of graves here lately—or ever—and, considering all the unusual events happening in the Avery family, I doubt this incident is coincidence. Two, someone believed that rumor that he had his money buried with him."

Mitch said, "Grandpa Franklin wasn't wealthy and he didn't have anything put in his casket. You can check with Uncle Bud about the estate. What money Grandpa Franklin had was used to pay for the funeral and the rest was given to the family."

"I know that. I've checked his bank accounts and the will. But what I'm saying is that the rumor mill in Smarr is running overtime and someone out there may *think* it's true. Or, third, someone's getting nervous."

"Nervous?" I said.

"Nervous, as in someone's afraid there's something—evidence— that could incriminate them in his death and they were trying to get it."

"But to try and dig up a grave in one night with a shovel . . . ," I said.

"I didn't say this person was smart. Obviously, it was someone without a lot of experience in working outdoors. You'd need a backhoe to get down to the casket quickly."

Mitch was still fixed on Detective Rickets's earlier statement. "So you think there's something in the casket . . . will you . . . are you going to try to . . . exhume . . ." Mitch was having a hard time putting his thoughts into words and if he was imagining the Avery family reaction to having the casket unearthed, I could see why he was stumbling around. Exhumation was not a scenario that would go over well.

"I know that's not something your family would look favorably on. We'd only do that if there was no other way." I was surprised at his kind tone. He turned and walked briskly to the gates of the cemetery where several sheriffs' cars were parked.

"Detective Rickets," Mitch said, "My grandfather . . . if he . . ."

The detective placed a hand on his shoulder and said, "Son, your grandfather was a fine man and if someone . . . well . . . if someone gave him a shove into the hereafter before his time, I want to catch that bastard." Detective Rickets glanced at me and said, "I may not have been so enthusiastic in the beginning, but I am now. If there's anything that doesn't add up, I'll keep at it until I find out what really happened."

He handed us off to a deputy and we were climbing into the car when Detective Kalra walked up. "Thanks, Peterson. I'll take them," she said to the deputy who was holding the back door open for us. She slid into the driver's seat.

Normally, I would be half fascinated and half frightened to ride in the back of a sheriff's car, but I was so surprised at Detective Kalra's move that I was distracted from my surroundings.

"Sorry to leave you in the lurch like that at Mr. Avery's house," she said through the grill that separated the front seat from the back. "I got the call that Rickets was on his way out there and since Mitch was a suspect, I had to get out of there. Good thing you were in the clear," she said to Mitch, "otherwise my life would be a lot more complicated." She looked at me. "Does he know about it?"

"Ah—that Grandpa Franklin might have been . . ." I trailed off and Mitch ran his hand through his hair.

"Yes, she filled me in," Mitch said. As Detective Kalra drove along the undulating road, the street lights flicked over us, a steady rhythm of light and shadow. I studied his face in the alternating light for a few beats. His expression was a mixture of resignation and determination. "Can you tell us anything about the investigation?"

"This stays between you two, okay?" I nodded quickly and she said, "Obviously, you're not a suspect," Detective Kalra said, making eye contact with Mitch in the rearview mirror for a second before focusing on the road again. "You already know that your aunt and the pharmacist are in the clear. Ditto Felicity and Dan. Both have alibis—not each other—for the night he died."

"Really? That's interesting," I said, looking at Mitch. His eyebrows had shot up to his mussed hairline.

I leaned forward and said quietly, "What about Uncle Bud and the fire?"

"Nothing yet on that," she said as she pulled into the parking lot of Quincy House.

"And Detective Rickets? He's onboard now?" I asked, still surprised at his quick change.

"He's onboard," she said grimly and threw open her car door, muttering, "overboard, more like it."

"I hope the kids didn't wear out Aunt Nanette," I said as we walked into the hotel lobby.

It was only nine o'clock, even though it felt like it was hours later. We'd had a fairly quiet ride back in the car and when Mitch put the keycard in the lock and pushed down on the handle, the burst of noise that hit us was a bit of a shock. Aunt Nanette was sitting in the middle of one of the double beds with a book in her hand, Livvy on one side and Nathan on the other. The kids were in their pajamas and their attention focused on the television, which was tuned to a kid's game show that involved high-pitched screaming, slime, and lots of splashy graphics. The kids each had a bowl of ice cream on their laps and a ring of chocolate around their mouths. Queen had been curled up at the foot of the bed, but she sprang up and bounded over to us.

"They said they were allowed to watch this show," Aunt Nanette said as she shifted around and crawled out of the bed. She pulled off her reading glasses and put them in her purse along with the book.

"Oh, they are." Once you got past the slime and the graphics, the questions were actually educational.

Aunt Nanette said good night to the kids and hugged them, not in the least worried about getting ice cream or chocolate syrup smeared on her clothes. "Hope you don't mind about the ice cream, but I promised them ice cream after we finished setting up at Book Daze."

"How did that go?" I asked, wondering if the kids had behaved themselves. I knew Livvy could plop down somewhere and get lost in a book for hours, but Nathan, well, his attention span was shorter and it was hard to get anything else done when someone was demanding to be read to.

"They were brilliant. Nathan was happy to mark on boxes and Livvy found some books."

"Sixteen, Mom," Livvy piped up. "Can we go back and get them?"

"We'll see," I said.

Aunt Nanette called Queen to her side and said, "They're on hold at the checkout if you want to come by and pick them up—or *some* of them," she said with a wink. "You'll want to be there early. Doors open at eight. So how was your dinner? Have a nice time?"

"Er—dinner was great, but afterwards . . ."

Mitch, who'd been rubbing Queen's ears, straightened up and motioned for Aunt Nanette and me to follow him out into the hall. "There was an incident in the cemetery . . . ," he said, and explained what had happened. "It looks like there will be a full-blown investigation of Grandpa Franklin's death. The case will be reopened."

Aunt Nanette buttoned her coat and said, "About time." She saw Mitch's surprised expression. "Well, there's been all sorts of hinky things going on. About time someone got to the bottom of it. You're both probably exhausted. I'll let the rest of the family know and I'm sure that bald detective will be in touch with us tomorrow." She clipped on Queen's leash. "You have agreeable children, Mitch, dear. I'll babysit them for you anytime." She patted me on the shoulder. "Good night, Ellie."

As we returned to the room, I said, "She took that better than I thought she would. Do you think the rest of the family will react the same way?"

Mitch frowned. "I wouldn't count on it."

Livvy's spoon clinking into her empty bowl brought our attention back to the more urgent matter at hand, bedtime. While Mitch was supervising teeth-brushing, I set the empty ice cream bowls on the room service tray. My stomach rumbled as I placed the tray in the hall. Room service sounded pretty good. Between the microscopic servings at dinner and our rambling walk, not to mention the fence climb, I'd burned off all my dinner and was starving. Sadly, room service wasn't an option. It was hard enough to get the kids to sleep in the cramped hotel room, and a room service delivery thirty minutes from now would keep them awake even longer. But the gift shop never closed.

I snatched a keycard from the dresser. "Mitch, I'm starved. Want anything from the gift shop?"

"Ice cream!" Nathan responded, and Livvy nodded her head in agreement around her toothbrush.

I shook my head. "You've already had ice cream. This is for me and Dad."

Mitch looked up from wiping Nathan's face and said, "Dinner was kind of light. Dove bar?"

"I'll do my best," I said, and dropped a quick good-night kiss on Nathan's and Livvy's heads, then swept out the door before they could beg to stay up until I got back. I knew Mitch would have them tucked in bed before I returned.

The lobby was empty except for a woman standing at the high counter of the front desk. I went in the empty gift shop and perused all the chocolate offerings. They didn't have Hershey's kisses, my snack of choice, but they did have Hershey bars. And Twix bars. I picked up one of each. I'd exhausted my chocolate kiss supply days ago and needed to stock up on chocolate, any kind of chocolate. It was an essential daily ingredient for me. I picked up a double chocolate Dove bar studded with nuts—might as well go all out—and emerged from the tiny gift shop. I deposited my loot across the counter of the front desk.

The woman was still there. She was gripping the edge of the counter so tightly that her knuckles were standing out in white relief on her already pale hands. "But it *has* to be here. They told me to come here, that you had it," she said, and her voice was thick with frustration.

"I'm so sorry, ma'am, but we don't have it. His sister picked it up earlier. You'll have to get in touch with her—"

The woman released her grip and slapped her palm on the counter. "Weren't you listening? *I'm* his sister. His suitcase couldn't have been picked up earlier because I didn't get into town until two hours ago."

The desk clerk, a teenager with longish brown hair and a bit of acne on his chin, looked at the woman uncertainly. "You don't have another sister? Because that's who picked up his stuff this morning—his sister."

"No. I'm his only sister. Are you saying that you handed off his personal belongings to some stranger?"

The desk clerk blinked, then began tapping keys on the computer monitor. "I wasn't on duty this morning . . ."

"Did you ask for ID?" the woman asked as she ripped open her purse and pulled out a wallet. Her fingers were trembling so much that she had trouble with the snap, but she managed to open it and work her driver's license out of the plastic cover. She smacked it down on the counter. "Because I'm Rochelle Anderson." She jabbed the card. "Now, who picked up his suitcase? It certainly wasn't me."

I heard the name "Anderson" and looked at her more closely. She had the same heavy, rounded features of her brother. The desk clerk tapped more frantically on the keyboard, then flipped a few pages in a binder. He stopped, opened his mouth, then closed it again. Clearly, the manual didn't detail how to deal with this situation. "I wasn't on duty this morning . . ." he repeated, uncertainly.

"Who was? Let me talk to them."

"That person's shift is over."

The woman took a shuddering breath and said very slowly. "Get me your manager."

"I'm sure I can help you—"

"Get. Me. Your. Manager."

The kid gulped, nodded, and disappeared into a door behind the desk.

I stood there with my melting ice cream, debating if I should say anything or not. Reticence had never been one of my strong points. "Excuse me," I said. "I think I saw the woman who picked up the suitcase."

Ellie Avery's Tips for Preserving Family Treasures

Other Memorabilia
Some items don't lend themselves to photo albums or they are

so special that you'd like to have them on display. One option for these items is to group similar objects together and create a shadow box. This works well for military memorabilia—a shadow box is a great way to display military coins, patches, medals, and dog tags. Any item from arrowheads to seashells to buttons will have more impact if displayed together.

Chapter
Twenty

Pink, puffy eyelids rimmed the woman's pale blue eyes and her lipstick was gone, except for a trace of pink lip liner that ringed her mouth. A pair of gold-rimmed glasses was shoved up on her head, holding back strands of her brown hair, which was graying at the roots and hung limply against her collar. She looked close to sixty and had dark circles under her eyes and deep grooves of wrinkles running from her nose to her chin. "What? You saw what happened?"

"Yes. I was in the restaurant this morning," I said, gesturing to the empty room near us.

The woman gripped my wrist. "You have to tell me what happened. It's my brother. He—," she stopped abruptly, swallowed, then said, "he just died and I want to get his things. I know they're not much, but I want them. They were his and some stranger shouldn't have them."

"Of course," I said, and twisted my wrist, hoping she'd let go because her hand was like a vise. She didn't let go, so I said, "A woman came in. I was waiting and I noticed her because she was . . . well, she was pushy and loud. She said she'd just come from the police and they told her the suitcase was here."

She released her grip on my arm and sagged against the counter. "But that's where I've been, the police and the county coroner. I had to identify his body."

"Do you need to sit down?" I asked, afraid that she'd faint. Her skin had gone an ashy gray color.

She didn't respond, so I took her arm and guided her to a club chair next to a table. What had she said her name was? I spotted her drivers license, still on the counter, and went to pick it up. Rochelle Anderson. "Rochelle," I said, handing her the license, "do you feel light-headed?"

She took the license and shook her head. "No. No, I'm all right. So many shocks." She closed her eyes and rubbed her forehead with one hand. I thought about telling her to put her head between her knees, but then she opened her eyes and seemed to gather herself. Her skin didn't look so washed out. She gripped the license. "Sorry. Today has been . . . awful."

"I can't imagine what you've been through," I said. How awful it would be to have to identify a body, especially a sibling. I thought of my brother, who'd been such a pain teasing me when we were growing up. But he'd also threatened that horrible Joey Matson when he was making my fifth-grade life miserable. I swallowed hard and I felt a wave of compassion for Rochelle. How would you cope, knowing that someone so close to you was gone? "I think you're holding up really well, considering. Would you like me to get you a glass of water?"

"No. I'm better, now that I'm off my feet." She ran a quivering hand over her forehead, wiping her fringe of bangs to the side. "The morgue. I'm still shaky from that."

I nodded. Even if he'd been carrying identification, Stan Anderson had used another name in Smarr, so the authorities would have to positively identify him to make sure he really was who he said he was. "I should tell you that your brother died in my husband's grandfather's house, so I know a little about what happened."

I thought she was working out the convoluted explanation of kinship, but she dropped her hand away from her forehead and asked, "Why was he at that house?"

I said, "I just know he was found in the house. Did you know he was here?"

"No," she said, sitting up straighter. "I live in Huntsville, which isn't that far, and I can't imagine why he'd come this far and not come to see me. That's why I want to see his luggage. There might be something in it that would show if he was coming to see me. Maybe he was going to call me and come over after he finished . . . whatever he was doing here."

"You don't know why he was here or why he was in Franklin Avery's house when he died?"

"I have no idea why he was at that particular house or even why he came here in the first place. He lived in New York. Why Smarr, of all places? Not that it's not a charming town," she added, looking anxiously at me to see if she'd hurt my feelings.

"Oh, I'm not from here, either. We're in town for a funeral, the grandfather I mentioned earlier. Did the police tell you that it looks like your brother had visited the house before?"

Rochelle's forehead wrinkled as she said, "Yes, they asked me about that . . . and that he used a different name, but I've never known him to do anything like that. He worked for an insurance company."

"Really? What did he do?"

"He was in their public relations department. He wrote brochures, newsletters, press releases, that sort of thing."

"So he didn't want to open a restaurant here, a pizzeria?"

Rochelle looked helplessly at me. "No, not that I know of. He never mentioned anything like that at all. He seemed fine, happy with where he was. The only thing I ever heard him talk about was writing a novel someday."

"Oh, what about his car? Anything in there? Have the police found it?"

"Yes, it was parked pretty far up the road from the house where he died. He parked near some bushes that almost covered the car, then walked to the house. It was a rental. Nothing but maps and some fast-food containers."

"He came to the viewing before the funeral. I met him." I tried to think of something nice to say about the man, but all I could remember was that he didn't have a good grasp of personal space boundaries. "He was pleasant," I said lamely, and wished I hadn't said anything. Damning with faint praise and all that. "Was your father a friend of Franklin Avery's in the war?"

She stared at me. "The war? No, our father was never in the military. Did he say . . . ?"

"Yes," I said, and she winced. "He said your father knew Franklin Avery, that they'd served in the war together and that your father wanted him to pay his respects."

She shook her head sharply. "Our father passed ten years ago." She looked at me, her eyes glassy. "Why would he lie? Why would he come down here and not tell me?" She pulled a tissue out of her pocket and daubed at her eyes. "I just don't know." She sniffed, then pushed back her shoulders. Her voice was harder, more businesslike as she asked. "Did they give that woman his suitcase this morning?"

"I don't know. An employee went to get the manager."

"Seems to be a common occurrence around here," she said tartly as she stood up. "Tell me again what happened."

I repeated what I'd seen and told her what the woman looked like. "Do you know who it was?"

She shook her head. "No, I can't think of anyone who looks like that."

"Was he married?" I ventured. "The woman looked like she was close to his age."

"No. Divorced, a long time ago. But his ex-wife . . . no, never in a million years would anyone describe her as heavy." She shook her head briskly as if clearing it. "Thank you for talking to me. I don't know why Stan did all these things. He's always been a . . . well, rather boring person, I guess. Not someone who goes around with false names, made-up stories, and breaks into people's houses. Not like him at all."

"Could it have been something to do with his work?" I asked. Corporate espionage seemed pretty far-fetched, but we didn't have any other explanation at the moment.

"I don't think so," she said slowly. "It was insurance, after all, nothing high-tech. He just wrote their brochures and pamphlets and ad copy."

That certainly didn't sound like anything that would give anyone motivation to steal his things . . . or give him a reason to break into Grandpa Franklin's house either. Grandpa Franklin had nothing to do with public relations or insurance. "No big ad campaigns?" I asked, grasping at straws. "Something national?" I knew from my own background in public relations that companies invested big money in advertising. Product positioning and marketing strategies were guarded closely.

"No. Pendleton Life doesn't advertise nationally," she said as we turned and walked back to the front desk. "I really must speak to someone here and find out what happened. Where can the manager be?" She looked around the desk for a bell. Even though her words weren't that different from the woman who'd made such a scene this morning, it was Rochelle's tone that made all the difference. She wasn't imperiously demanding service, she was anxious and worried. She pressed the crumpled tissue into her pocket and said, "I still have to get in touch with the funeral home about having Stan's body sent back home. Since the coroner has released it. I guess I'll have to do that tomorrow."

"You're not using Grisholm's, are you?"

"No."

"That's good."

"Why?"

I shook my head. "Never mind. Long story."

I heard voices in the room behind the front desk. I hoped it was the manager, with the suitcase. Rochelle propped her elbows on the high counter and was rubbing her forehead again. "I still don't understand any of this," she said. "Why would someone want my brother's suitcase?"

I didn't have an answer for her.

"So did they have the suitcase?" Mitch asked before he took a bite of the ice cream bar.

We were sitting side by side on the bathroom floor of the hotel room. When I'd returned from the front desk, Mitch had met me at the door. The room was dark, except for a tiny night-light burning on the far side of the room. I always left a night-light in the suitcase because it came in handy when we traveled. "Listen," Mitch had whispered, and I heard the steady rhythm of deep breathing.

"They're asleep?" I asked, amazed. "That fast?"

"It wasn't all book browsing tonight with Aunt Nanette. She made them work for their ice cream and had them hauling books and boxes. They were pretty tired and it is late, for them," Mitch said as he moved to the bathroom. With the door securely shut to block out any light that could wake the kids, we'd layered several dry towels on the floor and settled down to eat our snack. There was no way we were going to risk waking them by turning on lights in the room.

The candy wrapper crinkled as I tore it open. "No. That's what took them so long. Apparently, the morning shift gave the suitcase to the rude woman, but they didn't make a note of it in the computer, so the night manager looked everywhere—all the storage rooms and closets—to make sure the suitcase wasn't here before they broke the news to Rochelle."

Mitch shook his head as he tilted the ice cream bar and caught a piece of chocolate that had broken off and was sluicing down the side.

I broke off a piece of the Hershey bar. "What?"

"It's just that you're calling her Rochelle, like you've known her for years, when you've talked to her for what, about ten minutes? You have quite a talent for connecting with people, you know. They trust you."

"I couldn't walk away and leave her there at the counter. She almost fainted." I shifted and shoved a towel behind my shoulder blades, which were pressed against the bathtub.

Before I'd come upstairs to the room, the manager had finally reappeared at the front desk, apologizing even before she crossed the threshold. The teenager had followed the manager, switched out my melting ice cream bar for a frozen one, put all the food on our room account, and drifted back through the doorway. By that time, the manager had admitted the suitcase had been given to the woman who'd asked for it that morning.

I sighed. "I know you think I should leave things alone, but I can't walk away from someone who needs help. She looked so shell-shocked and forlorn."

"Yep, that's your downfall right there, you care."

I twisted so I could see his face. "Is that a criticism?"

He licked the last of the ice cream and chocolate from the wooden stick. "No, it's a compliment. You should be in politics. With your caring face and the way people trust you right off the bat, you'd be unbeatable."

"Thanks," I said guardedly. "That's not usually your position."

"No," Mitch conceded. He tossed the stick and ice cream wrapper in the trash and said, "The only reason I object to your tendency to gather up every stray you run across is that it usually gets you in more trouble, but—"

I punched him in the shoulder. "You're the one who brought home Rex," I said, referring to our dog that we'd adopted by default after one of our neighbors had moved.

"That's technically true, but you know you wanted to keep him just as much as I did. And if you'd let me finish my sentence, I was going to say that Stan's sister probably told you more than she told the police. If there's ever going to be an answer to why he was in Grandpa Franklin's house, we need to know everything we can."

I stared at Mitch for a moment. "So you're okay with me trying to figure out what happened?"

"Yes. I want to know. Like Aunt Nanette said, *about time.*"

"Even if it was someone close to you or the family?"

Mitch nodded. "Even if."

That was the last thing I'd expected him to say. His expression was a mixture of serious resolve and resignation. "Okay . . . well, I'm glad you feel that way. It's too bad that Rochelle didn't really know anything about why he was here." I popped another rectangle of chocolate in my mouth and chewed thoughtfully. "And despite the autopsy, we still don't know for sure if Grandpa Franklin's death was from natural causes or . . ."

"Murder," Mitch finished for me. "It's okay. You can say it. All this activity does indicate that something isn't right."

I folded the candy wrapper into a tiny square. "You know what I still can't figure out? Why would someone want to hurt Grandpa Franklin? Did he have any enemies?"

"Not that I know of," Mitch said with a shake of his head.

"What did you mean about secrets?" Mitch frowned at me, and I said, "You know, when we first got here, you said Grandpa Franklin had a lot of secrets."

"Oh, that. I didn't mean he had something to hide. He *knew* a lot of secrets—other people's secrets." Mitch squinted at me and said, "Kind of like you. People confided in him, probably because he could keep things to himself. He always had the inside story on everyone in the family."

I'd been folding creases into the candy wrapper, but I stopped and looked up at him. "If he never told, how do you know about the secrets?"

"I spent a lot of time there with him when I was a kid, playing in the woods and just hanging around. People would come by and visit. A lot of time, they'd sit on the porch swing and talk." Mitch shrugged. "They'd forget I was there and I heard lots of interesting stuff, like about Uncle Bud sponsoring the Little League team."

I concentrated on flattening a fold in the wrapper as I said, "Uncle Bud, now there's someone who keeps popping up every time something happens." I gave up on my candy wrapper origami and tossed it down. "But he doesn't make sense, either. As far as I can tell, he didn't have any reason to hurry Grandpa Franklin's death along. Uncle Bud makes plenty of money, so he doesn't need the inheritance and even though he's the executor of the will, he doesn't get a large chunk of the estate. And even if his secret generosity came to light, well, that's not so terrible that you'd kill to keep it quiet. But why did he get the investigation into Grandpa Franklin's death shut down?"

"Maybe it's exactly what it seems. He didn't want the Avery family to be the focus of news reports and a criminal investigation."

I shifted my position, pulling my legs in and sitting up straight. "There's got to be something we're missing."

"Let's shift everything around, take Grandpa Franklin out of the equation."

"We can't take him out. Stan visited his house under a false name and Stan died there," I protested.

"I know, but think of it this way. If Grandpa Franklin was the issue, why would Stan go back to his house after he died?"

I opened my mouth, then stopped. I twisted sideways and ran my arm along the cold porcelain of the tub. "He'd only go back there if . . . there was something there he wanted. But what could it be? There's nothing valuable there. We've looked at everything."

"I think we need to go back to the house tomorrow and make a very careful search," Mitch said.

I nodded, but was thinking about something else. "Remember the slit cushions on the recliner? Did Aunt Christine ever ask Felicity about that?"

"Yes. She denied doing it, but Aunt Christine thought she was lying."

"What if she wasn't?" I asked. "What if someone else is searching Grandpa Franklin's house? We assumed Felicity slit the cushions because she took the Depression glass, but what if that's all she took? And why would she damage the furniture if she thought she and Dan were going to inherit everything?"

"Because she was looking for his fictional stash of money," Mitch said.

"But the cushions were slit before the will was read. At that time, she still thought he was wealthy and the money would be distributed through the will. The rumors about the hidden money hadn't started then. I think someone's been searching Grandpa Franklin's house and it's not Felicity. Maybe Stan was in on it somehow, I'm not sure, but I think that someone's still looking around the house. The dresser in the bedroom has been moved—I hit my elbow on it today. It wasn't that close to the closet and, now that I think about it, the clothes in the trunk were messed up. Aunt Christine said Grandpa Franklin was very exact in the way he kept his things. He wouldn't have left the clothes like that. And the fire and the note— it makes sense. Whoever is doing the searching wants us to leave town. If we're not at the house packing and cleaning, the person—the searcher—is free to look all they want."

"Why wouldn't they just search at night? We're not in the house now."

"I bet they are!" I practically bobbed up and down. "That dresser has been moved since yesterday, so it had to have happened during the night, after we left. We were back there pretty early this morning. I suppose whoever is doing the searching has a life, too. A job to go to, a family—something that prevents them from being there all the time. And we've been coming and going at pretty irregular times, so that could make them cautious, too. They can't search all night and then stay up all day. They're probably only able to spend a few hours there." I gripped Mitch's hand. "And his grave! Maybe the plan wasn't to dig up Grandpa Franklin's grave to cover up evidence, but to search his casket. What are they looking for?" I sagged back against the tub, frustrated. "Ugh, this is like algebra. Find x. I hated those equations. We don't even know what they're looking for. We don't know what x is."

Mitch nodded, but pulled out his cell phone and a business card. "What are you doing?" I asked.

Mitch consulted the card, then dialed. "Calling Detective Ricketts."

"Why?"

"Because since we disturbed the person at the cemetery, they may have headed back to Grandpa Franklin's house."

"Well, why don't we just go check ourselves?"

"Because we're not going to intentionally put ourselves in a bad position."

"Right," I said, realizing just how carried away I'd been with my theory. "You're right. That would be stupid."

Mitch apologized for calling so late, then asked the detective if he could have someone check Grandpa Franklin's house tonight. "Oh, I see. Well, thank you." Mitch hung up and said, "Detective Ricketts says he sent an officer out there after the incident at the cemetery. There hasn't been any activity. He said he'll contact us if anything changes."

"Oh," I said. "Well, you're right. We should still check the house tomorrow."

"Yes, after we go to Book Daze. We promised Aunt Nanette and Livvy."

"We'll be lucky to get out of there after a couple of hours."

Three hours later, I was staring at the chink of light coming in from under the door frame. I'd done a pretty good imitation of Nathan that night, falling into a deep sleep almost instantly as soon as Mitch and I went to bed. But something had woken me and now I was on the other end of the spectrum, as wide awake as if it was the middle of the day. I rolled onto my back and watched the smoke detector light blink while I listened to the sounds of my family's breathing—Nathan's slightly raspy deep breaths, Livvy's shallower more nasal tones, and Mitch's rumble of breath that was almost a snore. It was kind of comforting to listen to the symphony of breathing and know we were all here, safe and warm. I tried to relax myself into a sleepy state, but I couldn't do it. My thoughts kept bouncing all over the place.

I rolled over on my side and watched the rise and fall of Mitch's chest. My thoughts kept bouncing back to what Mitch had said during our walk after dinner, but I skittered away from contemplating what he was leading up to. Much better to think about other things. Much better. I shifted up on one elbow and carefully leaned across Mitch to pat the bedside table on his side of the bed. My fingertips connected with his phone and I gently pulled it over the surface until I could touch the button that made the display light up. Nothing. No calls. Mitch's breathing changed and I retracted my arm. "So you're awake now, are you? No more Sleeping Beauty?" he said, his voice gruff and sleepy.

"Yeah. I was checking to see if Detective Rickets had called. He hasn't."

Mitch made a noise between a snore and a grunt and his breathing evened out again.

I snuggled down on my side and tucked my hand under my

cheek as I watched him sleep. He'd said we weren't the same couple we used to be. Those words seemed to echo around in my head.

"Mitch, are you still awake?" I whispered.

"Um-hmm," he said faintly.

"Because I know this probably isn't the best time, but I can't stop
thinking about what you said. It's driving me a little crazy, because I
don't think we've grown apart."

He didn't move for a long moment.

I flipped onto my back and let out a sigh. Great time for a heart-
to-heart. Was I a coward or what? I'd picked the one time when I
was guaranteed to get no response.

"I never said that," Mitch said quietly.

I rolled back to my side and saw Mitch was blinking at the ceiling. "I said we'd changed."

"That we're not the same people we were before," I said. My
heart was beating quickly and I didn't want to think about why I was
suddenly so nervous.

Mitch rolled onto his side to face me. "We're not. We want different things than we did ten years ago. Ten years ago, we wanted ad-
venture and excitement, to see new places and do new things.
We've got two kids now," he said, his voice barely above a whisper.

"Yes," I said. "I don't see where you're going with this. Are you
talking about us? You and me?"

"I'm talking about us, as a family. Where we want to go from
here." He propped himself up on one elbow and raked his fingers
through his hair. "I'm really mushing this up, aren't I?" he said,
using one of Livvy's favorite expressions for when she messed up.

"I'm completely confused," I said.

"Okay. In a year and a half, my commitment is up."

I rolled onto my back. "Oh! I see. I hadn't thought about that in a
while. Nine years," I said quietly. "That's what you've been stress-
ing about?"

"Yeah. Stay in or get out," Mitch said.

"Oh, Mitch. Why didn't you just come out and tell me?" I asked
as I rolled onto my elbow, mirroring his posture.

"Well, I've done some checking. The airlines aren't hiring. I can put in applications, if they open their windows, but right now everything's closed. The economy, you know. And I've only found a couple of openings at reserve units, but they'll probably be gone before I get out."

I was a more here-and-now kind of girl. I was concerned with today, tomorrow, and next week. I rarely had time to think long-range. Mitch's commitment date was so far away that I hadn't even thought about it. "So you're saying, either we get out and hope the airlines pick you up or you find a reserve job." The airlines were the natural follow-on job for a military pilot. Mitch had tons of flight time on his resume.

"Or we stay in. Guaranteed paycheck."

I blew out a deep breath. "That's not something you want to give away, especially now with so many people out of work."

"But it would mean more moves," Mitch said, and I was very aware of the soft cadence of the kids' breathing. "And we both know how hard the last move was on your work."

I wrinkled my nose. "It almost killed it. Another move would probably finish it off," I said. Did I want to keep starting over, trying to drum up clients and reestablish myself every three or four years? "Not to mention the deployments," I added. Those long separations were hard to endure and, right now, the deployment locations were legitimately dangerous places. Usually air force guys deployed and returned home, but no base was immune to attack. I swallowed. "I don't know. I see why you've been so distracted, but surely we've got time. A year and a half is a long time."

"If I'm going to separate, I have to turn in paperwork several months ahead of time."

"Oh."

"Not right away. But we do need to start looking at all the options."

"Well, I . . . I don't know what we should do. . . . I haven't thought about it at all."

"I know." Mitch shifted and wrapped his arm around me, pulling me close. "Take some time, think about it from all different angles," he said, his breath right above my ear.

"Okay." I relaxed into the warmth of his body. "Well, that went so much better than I thought it would."

"Mmm? Why?"

"I thought you were trying to tell me you wanted out."

"Of what?"

"Our marriage."

A low-pitched laugh sounded in Mitch's throat. "Like you'd get rid of me that easily," he said. "I must be out of it, if you have any question about my commitment. I'll have to show you . . . ," he said as he trailed kisses down my neck. "We are going to search that house tomorrow from the attic to the last kitchen drawer and figure out what is going on. And we definitely need to change these sleeping arrangements."

I couldn't have agreed with him more.

Chapter
Twenty-one

Maggie Key leaned closer to the microphone and lowered her voice. "I'll let you in on a secret," she said, addressing the boy in the second row who'd asked if she ever got stuck and couldn't figure out what to write in the Infinity mysteries. "Everyone gets stuck. I don't care who you are—if you're writing a paper in fifth grade or if you're writing a book. There's a point when you don't know what to say or what's going to happen. The great thing about writing fiction is," she paused dramatically to scan the audience of elementary-age kids and their parents before she smiled widely and said, "I make up stuff! Now, I know you can't do that in your writing assignments at school, but I can and I love it. For instance, when I was writing *The Hexagon Riddle*, I needed Zoe and Hunter to be able to see what had happened three years before and I couldn't figure out how to do that until I hit on the idea of having Mrs. Kettering's little red car become a time machine." Maggie Key smiled. "See? I made it up! It's a wonderful system!"

Livvy tugged at my sleeve. "That doesn't sound right," she whispered when I leaned down.

"I know," I said, thoughtfully. Something in those words bothered me, but I couldn't figure out exactly why.

Livvy squirmed closer and said, "The red car didn't belong to Mrs. Kettering. It was Karen's car. Their neighbor. Remember?"

Livvy was a stickler for accuracy. She remembered practically every word of every story she'd ever read. She used to correct us if we missed a word in her bedtime story. I figured she had a bright future if she went into something like accounting or science where each tiny variable had to be exactly right.

"She probably just mixed up her words," I assured Livvy, but I was still trying to figure out why those words didn't sound quite right to me, either.

Nathan leaned around Livvy and handed me several pieces of notebook paper. "Here, Mom. Save these. Don't throw them away," he instructed me in a loud whisper.

I put my finger to my lips. Besides Nathan's scribbles, there were several games of tic-tac-toe on the paper. Mitch had let Nathan win most of them. I folded the papers and put them in my pocket as I smiled over Nathan's head at Mitch.

"Look, there's Aunt Nanette," Livvy said.

Aunt Nanette had been standing off to the side of the crowded room, but as she walked to the podium, she said, "That's all the time we have for questions. A big round of applause for Margaret Key."

As the applause died down, Aunt Nanette said, "Margaret will be signing books in Room two-o-one. You can buy Margaret's books in the New Books area. That's near the snack bar. And don't forget to stop by the Friends of the Library Used Book Sale in Auditorium B. Our next speaker is Donna Hoover, who will talk about her new cookbook, *Southern Fried Synthesis: Haute Cuisine Meets the Old South.*"

Book Daze had taken over Smarr's Civic Center, converting the meeting rooms and auditoriums to a book lover's paradise. I'd found several new authors who looked promising and Mitch had a thriller tucked under his arm along with a book about fire engines for Nathan.

Livvy jumped to her feet. "Can we go get my books, now?"

"Sure," I said, thinking that the sooner we got to the house and began searching, the better.

"All sixteen?" Livvy asked, hopefully.

"We'll see," I said.

"Aunt Nanette said they're at the checkout."

The checkout line stretched the length of the building. Mitch took one look at the line and said, "I'll see if I can find Aunt Nanette. She might be able to expedite this process."

"What's *expedite?*" Nathan asked immediately.

"It means speed things up," I said.

"Good," Livvy declared, "because I don't have anything to read."

"Nothing?" This did not sound like my book-crazy child. "What about Grandpa Franklin's book? Did you finish it?"

Livvy became fascinated with the hem of her sleeve. "Yeah, sort of," she mumbled.

We shuffled forward a step. "That's usually a yes or no type question," I said.

Resigned, she stopped picking at her cuff. "No, but the good part—the letters from Sal—are over," Livvy said. "Now, there's just a long story about camping in the woods."

"Well, if you want to read, then I guess it will have to be that book."

"I can't. I put it away where I found it, like you always say to do after I'm finished with stuff." She smiled at me, hoping for bonus points for following my often-repeated directions.

"I'm proud of you for putting it back. A few more minutes and we'll have the books you picked out," I said.

Her shoulders drooped. "I'd rather read about a stupid camping trip than be bored."

"Sometimes it's okay to be bored," I said sharply in an effort to cut off a whiney outburst. "You don't have to be entertained every second of the day. Look around. People watching can be fascinating."

Her mouth turned down. She didn't agree.

"Livvy, it's so good to see you here!" exclaimed a voice behind me. Livvy's face lit up and I turned to see Maggie Key. She continued to address Livvy. "Have you found some good books?"

Livvy nodded and said, "Yes, but they're all at the checkout. I don't have them yet."

Ah, the honesty of children. If something is bothering them, they don't hide it. I edged into the conversation. "I'm sure they'll be worth the wait. Your talk was great. We enjoyed it."

"So glad you liked it." She glanced at her watch and said, "I have to scoot. I'm supposed to be in the signing room right now. Enjoy the festival."

"Thanks," I said as she scurried away. We moved up another millimeter. Livvy plopped down on the floor with her back against the wall with an exaggerated sigh.

My phone rang and I answered it. An unfamiliar voice, a teenage girl, asked for Ellie Avery. I identified myself.

"This is Recyclables Unlimited," she said, boredom dripping from each syllable. "We've had a cancellation and could make the pickup at 929 Mimosa Drive today. Are you interested in moving up your appointment?"

"What time?"

"They'll be in your area in about . . . oh, thirty minutes," she said.

Moving out all those stacks of boxes would free up quite a bit of room in the garage and I hated to turn down an opportunity to speed up the cleaning-out process, but the line was so long. "I'm not sure I can make it out there in time," I said.

"Okay. You were on the cancellation list, so I had to call you. No problem."

I saw Mitch moving through the crowd and said, "Wait. I may be able to work it out." I tilted the phone away from my ear as he said, "I couldn't find Aunt Nanette, but I did run into Chris Evan. I haven't seen him since the state basketball finals my senior year. He's heading this way."

I quickly filled him in on my phone call. "I'll run out there, let them in the garage, and then swing back by here to pick you and the kids up."

"Oh, I see how this is going to work out," Mitch said, nodding to the wobbly line that stretched out into the distance. "I get to wait it out."

"And catch up with your friend. No box moving," I coaxed, and when he nodded, I tilted the phone back to my mouth. "Yes. I can be there."

With the warm sun beating down on my back, I removed the padlock, then shoved hard on the garage door to move it over the slight rise of ground where it usually stuck. The hinges groaned as the door folded back on itself, revealing the dim interior. I dusted off my hands and checked the time. I had about fifteen minutes before the recycling truck arrived, so I made a quick circuit of the garage. Inside, it was chilly. I zipped up my jacket and hurriedly paced to the back of the garage, amazed at what a difference a few trips to the Salvation Army and the dump had made. I crossed my arms as the nippy air brushed against my face. The garage was by no means empty, but it looked better. After the boxes of books were gone, there would be room to park a car.

Mitch had borrowed Uncle Bud's truck and made several trips to the Salvation Army drop-off point loaded with stuff that we knew we didn't want and that no one else had asked for. The stockpile of backup appliances was gone. I thought of all the toasters, Crock-Pots, electric can openers, and mixers. I hoped they made some thrift store shoppers happy. At least they were out there where someone could use them, instead of stored away in here collecting dust. Mitch had also made at least a few runs to the dump, clearing out trash and anything that was broken or too decrepit to donate.

I thought I heard the revving of a large engine and hurried to the door, glad to be back in the sunlight, but it was just a large pickup rumbling down the street. I stood in the sunshine for a few moments, soaking up the warmth. It was a clear, cloudless day with sunshine so bright it hurt my eyes. Tiny specks of green spotted the branches on the trees outside the garage. Spring wasn't far away. Reluctant to go back into the cold garage, I went up the steps to the house to retrieve a box of books. Grandpa Franklin was an avid reader. Besides the books in his bookcases under the back windows, I'd found books scattered throughout the house. I had collected all those extra books and put them in a box. I hefted it outside and settled on the porch steps in the sun's glare, since inside the house it was about the same temperature as the garage.

I pulled out books and began stacking them around me. Biography, history, and political thrillers were his favorite types of books and those stacks reached my knees, but there were also some westerns, mysteries, and an occasional self-help book sprinkled into the mix. I pulled out a book that was stacked facedown in the box. I flipped it over and saw that it was a biography of Jefferson Davis. I put it in the biography stack, then paused. There was something . . . I frowned and reached for the book again. It was a soft-cover book with a photo of Jefferson Davis on the front cover. I flipped to the back cover again. A black-and-white photo showed the two authors, a man and a woman, each seated at desks, which had been shoved together so that they faced each other. The authors were turned sideways, smiling at the camera. The photo had been taken fifteen, maybe twenty years ago, but I still recognized them. Her hair was darker and styled in a puffy, feathered hairstyle that brushed the boxy shoulder pads of her dress. The goatee was missing, but he actually *had* hair, quite a bit of it. I shook my head, amazed that I was looking at a twenty-year-old picture of Stan Anderson and Maggie Key.

Ellie Avery's Tips for Preserving Family Treasures

Preserving Memorabilia
- Use archival paper and special plastic sleeves.
- Use archival spray to preserve newsprint. Be sure to spray both sides of the newspaper to prevent acid transfer.
- Transfer photos, video, and home movies to digital storage. There are professional services that will transfer older video and home movies, if you don't have the equipment to do it yourself.

le channels about Jackson, maybe ten years ago. It had won a ton
wards. Had it been based on their book? I shook my head. That
n't important here. What was important was that Stan Anderson
Maggie Key had been married once. Could they have still been
rried when he came to town? I didn't think so. Rochelle had said
n was divorced and worked at an insurance company in New
k. And Maggie wrote middle grade mysteries and lived in Smarr.
at would bring Stan here to Smarr? And Maggie, too, come to
nk of it. Out of all the places to live, why here? What did they all
ve in common here in Smarr?

My gaze focused on the list of books they'd written. What if they
ere writing another book together? But why keep it quiet? And if
ey were writing a book, why would Stan arrive in town and say he
anted to open a pizzeria and make a documentary? And why was
e in Grandpa Franklin's house when he died?

I gripped the page, wrinkling it. What if they were working on a
ook, but not together? I stood up and walked to the end of the
orch, the book tucked in my elbow. What if they were both work-
ng on a new biography of another famous Southerner, like Addi-
on McClure? Grandpa Franklin knew her and both Maggie and
Stan had contacted him. Grandpa Franklin even had letters from
the author. That had to be it—the letters. I rubbed my forehead.
Oh my goodness. Letters from Addison McClure would be something a biographer would want. A primary source that had never
been published before. And the letters were from Addison Mc-
Clure, so reclusive and so loved by readers. Oh, this was big. Sally
Addison McClure! Sally, Sal for short. Or, Sal as in *letters from Sal*.
Oh my god.

I pressed my hand over my mouth. Livvy had been reading those
letters. Grandpa Franklin must have put them in one of his memoir
books and Livvy thought they were a story. My second-grader was
carrying around original—*original!*—letters from one of America's
most beloved authors? Probably shoving them in her purse or
putting smeary peanut butter fingerprints on them. Where had she
put them? She'd said she put the book away where she found it.
They had to be with the rest of the books in the garage.

Chapter
Twenty-two

I read the first paragraph under the photo, then read it ag
"Sandy Keenor is the pen name for a husband and w
team. They have collaborated on over ten biographies of
figures, including the critically acclaimed *Jackson's Legacy*
currently under development at a major motion picture
The rest of the paragraphs lauded the current book, calling
perspective on a turbulent time in U.S. history."

Husband and wife? Sandy Keenor? Was I wrong? Th
wasn't anything close to Stan Anderson or Maggie Key. I s
the picture again. No, that was definitely Stan and Maggie.
acted like they didn't even know each other at the viewin
would they do that? Did the police know about this connec
patted my pocket, looking for my cell phone, but it was em
was locked in the car with my purse. I'd get it in a minute. I s
think about what I was going to say before I called one of th
tectives.

I flipped back to the front of the book to the page that liste
books they'd written. All of them were biographies of South
ers—Robert E. Lee, Jefferson Davis, Harriet Tubman, "Shoel
Joe Jackson, Andrew Jackson, and Margaret Mitchell. I recognize
few of the titles. And there had been a miniseries on one of the

I stepped over the stacks of books, watching my feet as I trotted down the steps so that I didn't knock anything over. I stopped short. A person blocked my path.

"Maggie. You scared me." I gripped the handrail to steady myself as I came down the last step. My heart skipped into high gear. "I didn't hear your car." Logically, I knew she couldn't appear out of thin air at the foot of the steps, but it certainly seemed as if she had. I looked behind her and saw only my minivan.

"That's because I didn't drive. I know all the trails through the woods from my morning jogs." I'd forgotten she lived a short distance away. I glanced up at the houses on the rise, then back to her.

She was still dressed in the floral print denim jacket, white shirt, and black pants she'd worn at the book festival. She'd changed her shoes from black flats to sturdy running shoes and I could see an uneven edging of fresh mud around the soles.

"What a shame," she said as she plucked the book I was still carrying out of my hand. "Well, I can see there's no need to beat around the bush now. I'd hoped I could talk you into letting me borrow the letters with the promise of returning them, but now it will have to be the other way." She pulled a gun out of her jacket pocket and I suddenly found it hard to breathe. It felt like a steel band had been clamped around my chest. Little black dots pricked the edges of my vision. I made myself take a deep breath.

"Letters?" My vision cleared and I focused on the gun. It was small and that's about all I could say about it. Mitch was into hunting. He'd know what kind of gun it was. I couldn't look away from the dark circle at the end of the barrel. She held it casually, comfortably, as if it were a pen or some other innocuous, everyday item.

The dark circle bounced back and forth as she waved the gun. "Ellie," she said sharply, and my gaze skittered from the gun to her face. "There. That's better. Where are McClure's letters?"

Her back was to the sun, casting her face into shadow. I squinted to see her better. She looked perfectly calm. Her hands weren't trembling—mine were—she wasn't licking her lips, or nervously looking around. She raised her eyebrows impatiently. "You're going to have to focus here, Ellie, if we're going to get this done."

I cleared my throat and kept looking at her face. No need to look at the gun. Odd that such a small thing could be so lethal. I was suddenly aware of the brush of the breeze through the bushes below the porch, the call of a bird in the distance, and the smell of her perfume, a light powdery fragrance.

"That's better," she said. "The letters? I heard Livvy say she'd read the letters from Sal. Where are they?"

"Right, the letters," I said, licking my lips. I forced myself not to look up the driveway behind her. It couldn't be that long before the recycling truck arrived. If I could string her along until then . . . well, I wasn't sure what I could do, but at least there would be someone else here besides me—a witness, maybe two. Surely that could keep her in check. There was only one problem. "I don't know where the letters are, exactly." A look of distrust shadowed her face and her dainty fingers tightened on the gun. I pressed my damp palms against my jeans. I didn't need to actually find the letters, just delay. The letters were in the memoir. Livvy had said she put it away when she finished reading it. "They're in a book. One of Grandpa Franklin's memoirs," I said.

"Spare me the details. Where?"

"The garage," I said, fighting to keep the note of triumph out of my voice. That would keep her busy. "Livvy put the book away, so it's in the garage. I don't know which box, but it will—"

"Okay. That's enough," she barked. I realized she wasn't as cool and collected as she'd seemed. She backed up a step and waved me toward the garage with the gun. "You first."

The crunch of gravel under my feet sounded loud. I felt jittery, like I'd just touched an electric wire. I stopped at the garage's threshold and pointed to the boxes. "Somewhere in there," I said, my voice coming out in a croak. I cleared my throat and watched her.

She looked at the boxes, then back at me. "You're not serious." She stepped closer to me and I backed up until the rough wood of the garage door snagged at the fabric over my shoulder blades.

"I promise. It's in one of the boxes. Livvy told me she put it back." I was relieved to see that the tape had been cut on many of the boxes, so theoretically it could be in any one of those.

The tip of the gun bit into my ribs, setting off another asthmatic breathing pattern in me. "You better not be lying to me. Because if you are . . . I know where your kids are." She stared at me with a level gaze, her brown eyes the same color as the dead leaves scattered on the ground. She didn't blink and my heart seemed to contract.

My kids. She was threatening Livvy and Nathan. My brain disconnected for a moment because what she was suggesting was too terrible. I forced myself to swallow the bile surging up my throat. Not my kids. I couldn't let my thoughts go there. "I'm not lying," I said, fighting to get my words out without them sounding choppy.

"Then get to it," she said impatiently, and pulled the gun away from my side.

I met her cold stare even though inwardly I was alternating between icy fear and flaming anger. I tried to push all that emotion down so I could think clearly. I crossed to the boxes and she walked in a sweeping circle behind me, so she could see me and the driveway.

The flaps on the first box were folded together so that they interlocked. I tugged and a puff of dust sprayed into the air. The box was about half full. I picked up a book and flicked through the pages, praying that the letters wouldn't be in the first one I came to, which would be the most likely location for Livvy to have returned the book to. But I couldn't quite see her mastering the tricky folds of the box flaps, so maybe the letters wouldn't be in this box. That would be good . . . as long as Maggie didn't get too impatient. I took a steadying breath and focused on the task at hand.

"Higher. Let me see what you're doing," Maggie barked, and I raised the book so she could see it.

"Nothing." I flicked through the rest of the books in that box, then moved the box to the floor. The next box was the same. The dark blue cover of the memoir repeated over and over again, filling about half the box. All the edges of the books looked pristine, as if they hadn't been opened but I pulled out copy after copy, fanning the pages so that Maggie could see there was nothing between the pages.

I thought I heard a heavy engine outside. Please be the recycling truck, I prayed. Trying to cover the possible noise it would make in the driveway, I said, "You had me completely fooled that first day. Quite a performance."

Instead of downshifting to turn into the driveway, the engine accelerated, continuing down the street. I fought down a surge of disappointment. "With your distraught act. 'Poor Mr. Avery. Is he okay?' "

"Oh that. That wasn't an act. I was distraught. I needed to know where the letters were."

My hands were dusty and dry as I pulled open the next box. "So you really didn't know what had happened to him?" I said, in an effort to keep the conversation going. Surely the truck wouldn't be much longer.

"Oh, I knew he was unconscious, she said flatly. "Endless trouble that caused me, too."

I turned to look at her hard face. "You did that to him?" The words slipped out before I could check them. Not good. Not a good thing to say, I thought.

But she waved the gun, unruffled. "No, he was already like that when I got there that night," she sighed, a deep, irritated sigh as if someone hadn't refilled the paper tray in the copier. "I'd hoped to search his house while he was sleeping, but when the storm rolled in and he didn't come out of his room, I knew something was wrong. He'd told me he wasn't able to sleep through thunderstorms. He'd watch their progress on television until they'd passed through. Since there was no noise from his room, I thought maybe I'd messed up— that I'd somehow missed him leaving the house and that he wasn't home. I looked in his room and saw him, lying there in bed, not moving, as those tremendous claps of thunder sounded, and I knew. Christine showed up so quickly that I barely had time to get out of there before she came in." Maggie waved the gun. "Keep working. Stay at it."

I swiveled back to the books as she said, "No, it would have saved me so much time, if he'd just lasted a few more days. I almost had him convinced. Then he had to go and slip into unconsciousness. Do you know how inconvenient this has been for me?" she asked, and I could hear the agitation in her voice.

"I can't imagine," I said mildly.

"My editor's breathing down my neck. I had to tell him my computer crashed to buy more time. And my agent! Calling and calling. E-mailing practically every hour. I barely had time to search this place with all the damage control I was doing."

I flipped through book after book. I kept my gaze on the books, my tone conversational, but I was completely zeroed in on what was going on behind me—her words and listening for any noise from the driveway. "But, somehow, you found time. You pulled the plywood off the window and got in the house again."

She didn't answer. I'd been racing through the books and there were only three unsealed boxes left. Maybe the letters weren't in the boxes after all. What would I do if I got to that last unsealed box and hadn't found the letters? Despite the coolness in the garage, I'd worked up a sweat as I plowed through the books and shoved the boxes around. I consciously slowed down the movements of my hands. Where was that recycling truck? I removed a book, the last one in the current box, and flipped through it. I set it aside and picked up the empty box. As I turned to put it on the stack of empty boxes, I said, "And Stan's arrival in town must have made things worse for you. He wanted the letters, too, right?"

Her face tightened and her eyes narrowed as she said, "Those letters were mine. I'd done the research and tracked them down. I'd spent a year in this backwater and he thought he could waltz in here and take them out from under my nose. He was wrong about that."

My palms were gritty with a layer of dust. I used the back of my hand to push my bangs out of my eyes. "He got pretty close, pretty fast. That must have put you on the defensive."

She bristled. "He wouldn't have gotten the letters. He was too impulsive. He didn't even have a plan when he searched the house—just wandered from room to room, randomly opening drawers and looking under tables. It was laughable."

"So you were both in the house at the same time? The night Stan died?"

She blinked, refocusing on me. "Back to work," she snapped.

I opened the next box. I could hear her moving around behind me. "Such an idiot," she muttered under her breath and I hoped she was talking about Stan. I was amazed that this was the same woman who'd been so nice to Livvy. It was all an act, even from the first moment I met her at the tape line when she'd asked about Grandpa Franklin, oozing concern and caring. My hands went still and I looked back at her. Now I knew why her story about the red car during the author talk had bothered me. "You made up the red car, didn't you?"

She'd paced to the end of the garage, but she turned sharply. "What?"

"The day Grandpa Franklin died—you said you'd seen a red car parked in his driveway. You made it all up, just like in your books. You were scattering clues: the red car, the gym flyer in the funeral home van. You wanted the police to suspect Felicity."

She raised one shoulder as if it was not a big deal. "I'd done my homework. It was easy to watch his house. My desk has a wonderful view. I can see everyone arriving and leaving. So interesting to watch the dynamics play out from above. Almost like writing a book. I began to get a feel for the characters. I had no idea manipulating real people could be so entertaining." Her expression turned darker as she said, "Of course when I saw him carted off to the hospital I knew that if he died, there would be an investigation. I made sure it focused on someone besides me, that's all," she said. "Haven't you found it yet?" She fixed her gaze on me and closed the distance between us, tension and anger radiating from her very pores. "I'm beginning to think you're playing games with me and you don't know where the letters are, after all. If you're fooling around with me . . . I have no problem getting on with this myself." She spoke very softly, almost a whisper as she said, "Killing someone is very simple. It's all in the way you do it. A shove at the top of the stairs and it's all over." As I looked into her very blank and empty eyes, I knew that was exactly what had happened with Stan.

There was a small sound, a tiny intake of breath, from the other side of the garage.

Chapter
Twenty-three

We both swiveled toward the source of the sound. "Come out here," Maggie shouted. In the deep shadow by the corner near the door, a figure slowly rose from a crouched position. All I could see was the rough outline of a tall female figure with light-colored hair. It wasn't until she inched forward with hands raised that I recognized the rude woman from the hotel.

"Harriet." Maggie spit out the word. "I should have known you'd turn up. There's money involved, so you couldn't be far away."

"Now, Maggie," the woman said, her tone miles away from the imperiously commanding one I'd heard from her at the hotel, "I want to help you—give you a little advice."

"Advice? Really, Harriet? Is it going to be like that advice you gave me the last time we talked—*Children's books are a dead end*?"

Harriet cleared her throat. "I'll admit, I was off on that one. You saw that trend coming and I didn't." She grimaced as if those words had been extremely painful to say.

Maggie laughed sharply. "How many times have you regretted that? All those commissions . . . they could have been yours." I remained motionless, doing my best to imitate the stacks of boxes behind me. If only they weren't at my back, I would have been able to ease away, since Maggie was so focused on Harriet. "I should have known you were involved. You clued Stan in on the letters and he dashed down here, didn't he?"

"No, it wasn't like that at all," Harriet said.

Maggie spoke over Harriet's protests. "How did you know about them?"

Harriet shrugged her wide shoulders and circled her hands, giving up on her denial. "There were rumors," she said vaguely.

Maggie's hand had sagged a bit when Harriet had stepped out of the shadows, but as she waved her hands around, Maggie yanked the gun back to a level position. Maggie's gaze flicked to me and she edged sideways so she could see both of us. "So when he died, you scurried down here."

To claim his suitcase, I silently added. She must have thought he'd found the letters. But they hadn't been in his suitcase.

"No, it's not like that at all. When I got word that Stan . . . about Stan, I knew I had to come and talk to you."

"Have you been following me? I thought I saw you earlier at the festival. But then I thought, No, that can't be Harriet, she'd never attend a lowly regional book festival."

"I did want to talk to you," Harriet admitted, "but I was waiting for the right moment."

"I don't think so. I think you realized the letters were still out there and you were waiting for me to find them, so you could take them from me. You'd probably hand them off to some hack who'd churn out a book in a couple of weeks."

"No," Harriet said, moving forward, her gaze intensifying. "No. I don't want them for a book. That's why I wanted to talk to you. Do you realize how much those letters are worth?"

"Worth? They're worth a new reputation. They're my ticket back into legitimacy. Kids' books make me a lot of money, but they don't get much respect, let me tell you. Those letters will cause an earthquake in academia and the literary world. They're mine, Harriet. I'm going to rock the literary world *and* the commercial one, too. Morning show interviews, chat shows, television book clubs. I'm going to be a household name and I'm not sending one penny of it to you as a commission."

"I don't want to sell the book for you. Do you know how much the letters *themselves* are worth?"

Maggie squinted at her. "What do you mean?"

Harriet tilted her head slightly and raised one shoulder in a coy movement. "Just that there are certain parties involved who would pay to own the letters. I was approached because, well, because someone was under the impression that I was still your agent, but that's neither here nor there, now. I know there is money to be made on those letters and I know the person who will pay top dollar for them."

Maggie stared at her for a long moment. "How much?"

Harriet glanced at me for the first time as if she didn't want to talk in front of me, but then she said, "Millions."

Maggie laughed, a full-bodied sound from deep in her throat. "Sure, Harriet. That's a great story. You know what? You could write a book."

"It's true," Harriet said, some of the haughtiness creeping back into her voice. "Did you know that a letter from Beatrix Potter sold several years ago at auction for hundreds of thousands of dollars?"

Maggie breathed in sharply and Harriet pressed on. "How many letters are there, Maggie? Ten? Twenty? Think about it. It adds up. You have provenance, too, so that will keep the price high. They've gone from McClure to this Avery person, who gave them to you before he died because of your love of literature." I wasn't sure, but there seemed to be a sneering undertone on the last few words directed at Maggie, but she didn't catch it.

"Who is this person?" Maggie demanded, leaning forward slightly.

"Anonymous," Harriet said quickly, and I had to wonder if she was lying to make sure she'd get in on the deal. My heart was fluttering in my chest. This could go very badly for me. If they agreed to work together, then it would be two against one. I licked my lips and tried to think what to do. The recycling truck should have been here by now. Something must have happened and they weren't going to show. Mitch would be wondering where I was, but he'd probably just catch a ride out here with someone. My insides seemed to flip-flop at the thought of Mitch and the kids walking into this scene.

I had to do something. I looked around the garage for some-thing—anything—that I could use to get out of this mess, but the boxes hemmed me in. I was marooned on a patch of concrete. The closest things I could reach were cobwebs. An old push broom and a Weed Eater leaned against the workbench, but since they were on the other side of Maggie, they wouldn't do me any good. I didn't have anything on me, not even my phone, I thought, as I inched one of my hands up into my pocket. Nothing there but a peppermint and Nathan's papers with his tic-tac-toe games.

"So do we have a deal?" Harriet asked. "I'll help you sell them. We split the money fifty-fifty."

, I watched Maggie's face as she debated fame and esteem from her colleagues or cold hard cash. I worked the paper around so that most of it fit into my palm, but didn't pull it out.

Maggie nodded sharply and Harriet's shoulders relaxed. She smiled brightly. "Perfect."

"Not quite," Maggie said, turning her hard gaze full on me. "We still don't have the letters. I think you haven't been honest with me, Ellie," she said, stepping closer. "I think you don't know where they are." Maggie raised the gun higher, pointing it at my head.

"I do. I know they're here." I turned back to the boxes and picked up a book. "Mitch moved these around the other day, so they're mixed up, is all. They have to either be in this box or the next one."

"Or the next one, or the next," Maggie said. "I know what you're doing and—"

"Wait! Here they are." I kept one hand on the rim of the box and held up the papers with the other. Harriet surged closer. Maggie snatched the papers from my hand, her attention fixed solely on them. They were still folded in half and as she struggled to open them with one hand, I gripped the edges of the open box, swiveled, and heaved it at her chest. A hot pain shot through my back.

The weight of the box toppled her over. There was a sickening thud as she hit the floor and went still. The gun, which had fallen from her limp hand, spun away and lodged under the lawn mower by the workbench. I stared at her for a second as she lay there. I wasn't sure if she'd just had the wind knocked out of her or . . . something else. She didn't move, but I could see the books that had tumbled out and landed on her chest were moving up and down slightly as she breathed.

Harriet rushed forward and I scrambled to pick up another box, but instead of charging at me, she skidded to a stop beside Maggie. She dug around in the books and I thought she was trying to move them off of Maggie so she could check her pulse or do CPR or something, but she gave a small victorious cry and scrambled to her feet, clutching the still-folded papers. She didn't even look at them, but ran at full speed out of the garage. I could hear her heavy tread as she pounded over the gravel and down the driveway toward the road. Once she cleared the curve, I couldn't see her, but I faintly heard a car engine start and accelerate away. She must have parked along the road—I didn't notice her car when I arrived.

I stared at the driveway for a moment, but the scene was quiet except for the faint call of a bird and a tree branch scraping against the window in the slight breeze. I carefully edged closer to Maggie. Her eyes were closed, but she was definitely still breathing. I let out a shaky breath. I felt like collapsing onto the dusty floor myself, but first I had to get my cell phone. I'd gone a few steps on legs trembling so badly that I probably looked like a toddler learning to walk, when I stopped. First order of business, I decided, was find that gun, *then* call 911.

I tiptoed around Maggie and fished the gun out from under the lawn mower. I hurried out of the garage with the gun in my pocket, the heavy weight banging against my side. I tugged the doors to the garage closed and snapped the padlock into place.

I never thought I'd be glad to see Detective Rickets, but when his official car crunched over the gravel and pulled to a stop at the foot of the porch steps, I definitely felt relieved. I stood up and carefully moved around the piles of books still dotting the steps. I knew it was only a short while ago that I'd been sitting in the sun sorting the books, but it felt like several days had passed since then. I pointed to the padlocked garage and told him what happened.

"Maggie Key's in there? Unconscious? You left her there?" he asked as he took the key to the garage padlock I held out.

"I certainly didn't want to stay in there with her since she'd threatened to shoot me. Oh, the gun," I said, and drew it out of my pocket.

Detective Rickets started at the sight of the gun, then relaxed when I put it in my flattened hand and held it out to him. He took it carefully as an ambulance pulled in behind him. He waved them to the garage and told me to wait where I was. I was happy to sit back down on the steps since my legs weren't much sturdier than they had been earlier.

I put my elbows on my knees and rested my forehead on the heels of my hands. A pair of brown Sketcher shoes appeared in my line of vision. I knew those shoes. My gaze traveled from the shoes, up the rather nice fitting jeans, to the lightweight gray sweater, and finally to Mitch's brown eyes. Unlike Maggie's eyes, his were warm and sympathetic. He'd been my second phone call and had said he'd get there as soon as he could. "Hey," he said. He sat down beside me on the step and wrapped an arm around me.

I leaned my head against his shoulder and felt the rest of the worry drain away. It really was going to be okay. I'd given him a jumbled and not too coherent explanation on the phone of what had happened. I had to give him points for not quizzing me, he just sat there with his arm around me. "Where are the kids?" I finally asked.

"With Aunt Nanette. Uncle Bud let me borrow his truck," Mitch said, nodding to the heavy-duty pickup parked beyond the ambulance. "So it was Maggie," Mitch said with a hint of disbelief in his voice.

"Yes it was," I said firmly, and sat up. "How am I ever going to explain this to Livvy?"

"I think we'll have to say Maggie made a bad choice," Mitch said. "Good choice" and "bad choice" were the current mantra at her school for encouraging kids to do the right thing.

"Killing someone is an awfully bad choice," I said. "Do you think it will upset Livvy?"

"I'm sure she'll be upset and disillusioned, too. But kids are resilient and if anyone understands good and evil, it's kids."

"Well, that's true, I guess," I said, thinking of some of the ugly things that I'd seen and overheard at the playground, which could be a pretty cruel place at times.

I heard the doors of the ambulance close and looked up to see it lumbering slowly out of the driveway. Detective Rickets strode up to us. "She's regained consciousness and wants a lawyer. It was all a big misunderstanding, according to her. Says Mr. Avery told her where to find the letters and she came to pick them up, when you turned violent and attacked her."

"That's not true," I sputtered.

He held up his hand. "Don't worry, Mrs. Avery. It won't take us long to pick her story apart. We've already been up to her house and found a muddy shovel in the trunk of her car. If I was a betting man, I'd feel pretty confident about placing money on the odds that it will match the dirt from the cemetery. We'll get her cell phone records and find out if she'd contacted this woman who met her here."

"They acted like they hadn't seen each other in years."

"We'll find out. Why don't you folks head on home. We'll wrap everything up and get in touch with you later today."

He walked away to confer with another officer and I reached down to pick up the scattered stacks of books. "What happened with the recycling truck? Why didn't they show up?"

"Flat tire," Mitch said. "They called my cell phone when you didn't answer."

There were a few books in the box that I hadn't pulled out. I moved those into a corner of the box and uncovered a copy of the memoirs. It was with the stacks of books I'd picked up from the end table beside Grandpa Franklin's recliner. This copy of the memoirs was worn around the edges. Slowly, I pulled it out and opened the front cover. Several pages of stationery were tucked into the book. They were almost the same size as the book pages and fit seamlessly into the groove between the cover and the first page of the book. "Mitch, look," I said as I gently opened the pages.

"Do you think . . . ," he said, leaning over my shoulder.

The ink was faded, but still readable. The first letter was addressed to Frank. "It could be from anyone," I said. "I'm sure Grandpa Franklin received tons of letters," I said, trying not to get my hopes up as I carefully turned the page over. The signature was a quick scrawl, but I could make out the word. It was signed, "Sal."

Ellie Avery's Tips for Preserving Family Treasures

Organizing Books
Don't overlook old books as you organize your family memorabilia. Family Bibles, journals, signature books, memoirs, cookbooks, and household account books can provide a wealth of information as well as firsthand accounts of everyday life.
- Store in cool, dry place.
- Copy pages to preserve information.
- Use a book stand when reading old books to prevent damage to the spine.

Chapter
Twenty-four

"You didn't have to do this," I said.

Aunt Christine pushed a plate into my hands. "Of course I did. I couldn't let y'all leave town without breakfast. Help yourself. Breakfast casserole is on the stove."

"Don't forget the grits," Bill said with a wicked gleam in his eye. "Ellie loves grits."

Aunt Christine flapped her hand at him. "Go on, get out of here and stop bothering her. There're no grits today. Nanette's brought a fruit salad and there's some ham, biscuits, and hash browns, too. I made plates for the kids and sent them out back."

Bill ignored Aunt Christine and stayed right where he was, carefully splitting open biscuits and layering butter and jelly on them.

"How did everything go last night?" I asked. Bill and Caroline had moved into Grandpa Franklin's house yesterday. The cleaning and repairs had begun on their house and it was a mess of drywall dust and torn-up carpet at the moment.

"Fine. Fine," he said, his teasing manner dropping away. "We sure do appreciate it."

"So much nicer than the hotel," Caroline chimed in.

"We're just glad it will help you out."

There was enough food spread around Aunt Christine's small kitchen to feed thirty people. If the whole Avery family showed up to tell Mitch and me good-bye, she might need that much food. Conversation interspersed with the squawks and whistles from Einstein's bird cage filled the house with a noisy energy.

"So what was the verdict on the fire?" I took a generous helping of the famous breakfast casserole—a mixture of eggs, sausage, bacon, and cheese—then reached across the counter for a biscuit and felt a twinge in my back as I stretched. It had been three days since I threw the box at Maggie and my back was almost recovered. As long as I didn't pick Nathan up, I seemed to do all right.

"It was ruled an accident," Bill said.

"Just because they couldn't find any proof she did it." Caroline leaned close to me and said, "I think it was Maggie Key. The police didn't find a thing to link her to the fire, but she was involved in all those other strange things that were going on, so why wouldn't she have had her hand in the fire, too?" She paused with the salt shaker poised over her plate. "Breaking the window at Grandpa Franklin's house, paying Jake to let her have access to Grandpa Franklin's casket, and then digging in the graveyard, those things have been proved. Anyone who'd do those things wouldn't think twice about knocking over a candle to set a fire. We only lock the back door at night, so it would have been easy for her to slip in, set the fire, and get out, especially since Bill, Mitch, and the kids were in the garage and the front yard. Once the fire was discovered, she could have dropped the note onto the front porch while everyone's attention was drawn to the back of the house. She wanted you and Mitch to leave so she'd have unlimited access to the house to search for the letters. It all fits together."

I had to agree with her. "It does make sense," I said.

My phone rang and when I saw Detective Kalra was the caller, I excused myself to answer it. We'd talked the day Maggie was arrested, but I hadn't heard from her since then.

"Ellie, I thought you'd want to know we found Jake's phone number in Maggie's outgoing call log. She taught a night class at the community college and Jake was one of her students."

"So that's how she knew him. I'd wondered about that. What will happen to him?" I asked.

"He's getting a deal. He'll testify that he helped Maggie get access to the casket and that she tried to pay him to help her dig up Mr. Avery's grave."

"And Maggie?"

"No deal for her," Detective Kalra said, and I could hear a tinge of satisfaction in her voice. "The crime scene technicians found carpet fibers from the rug in Mr. Avery's upstairs hallway on Maggie's shoes along with some traces of blood, Stan's blood. Even though she'd tried to clean it off her shoes, there was still enough in the crevices of the soles for a match. And I thought you'd find this interesting: she had a folder on her computer dedicated to the Avery family. It was similar to her writing files, but instead of fictional characters, the Avery files had descriptions of every visitor to Mr. Avery's house, photos, and any tidbit of information she could get out of Mr. Avery. It became quite an obsession with her."

"Were there photos of Mitch and Felicity?" I had to ask, even though I knew Detective Kalra probably hadn't looked through every single file.

"The ones Rickets dropped on you? Yes, those were there. At that point, she was following Felicity closely, since she was one of the most frequent visitors. I guess she was hoping to get some information on Felicity that would help her get the letters. I think she was going a little overboard there, but from looking at her files, I can see she wasn't thinking too clearly on a lot of things."

"So she sent the photos to Detective Rickets?"

"From a library computer, so even though we'd traced the IP address, it didn't do us much good. The computers are open to the public and patrons can get a day pass without a library card."

"She went to quite a bit of trouble to turn your attention to Mitch," I said.

"At that point, her goal was to keep us focused on anyone but her."

There was something that was bothering me. "If she was keeping such a close watch on the house, why didn't she know about Stan? I could have sworn that she was surprised to see him at the visitation."

Detective Kalra said, "We think he visited Mr. Avery when she was giving a library talk in Huntsville." I could hear a voice shouting at Detective Kalra in the background. "I have to go. Rickets and I have a press conference with the DA to announce the charges in ten minutes. I wanted you to hear the details from us before they were broadcast."

"Thanks, I appreciate that." I hung up and shared the news about Maggie with Bill and Caroline. "Ironic that she'll be infamous now," I said. The story had been the top of the local news for twenty-four hours and a few of the national news channels were starting to report on it as well.

"I call that poetic justice," Bill declared.

"Oh, I forgot to ask the detective one of my questions," I said. "I was wondering about the pen name Stan and Maggie used for their books, Sandy Keenor. I wonder why they used that name?"

Bill laughed. "It's an anagram made from their last names, Key and Anderson."

I thought about it for a few seconds, but couldn't work out the letters in my head. "I'll take your word for it," I said.

Bill and Caroline carried their plates to the dining table as Felicity's strident voice carried clearly across the room and caught my attention. "So I told her we have to be open twenty-four–seven. That's the only way to do it." She pointed her fork at Mitch to emphasize her point. As soon as Felicity walked in the door this morning, she'd announced that she had a new job for a soon-to-be-open fitness center. "We'll have the best equipment in town. State of the art. And I've got big plans for the childcare area. It's going to be so awesome—inflatables and video games. Nothing else in town will be able to touch Elite Fitness."

"Sounds great," Mitch said, managing to wedge a few words into the conversation before she began expounding on the benefits of having a spa associated with the fitness center.

Dan appeared beside me. "Juice or coffee?" he asked.

"Juice, thanks," I said, taking a glass from him.

"So how long should I wait before I rescue him?" Dan asked, nodding toward Mitch and Felicity.

"He's had all that interrogation training, so he should be able to hold up for a couple more minutes," I said. "Seriously, though, I am happy for her. She sounds so excited."

Dan sipped the coffee and said, "Yeah. It's a new project for her. She needs that, an outlet." I dug into the savory breakfast casserole and wondered if the people who had hired her realized what a whirl-wind she was. She'd focus every ounce of her forceful personality on her job. I felt a little sorry for her new boss, but I was relieved that she'd switched her focus off of Grandpa Franklin's house.

She still wasn't happy about the way things had worked out with the will, but she'd accepted that things weren't going to change and she and Dan weren't going to get the house. I took her chatting with Mitch and the bright smile and good morning that she'd said to me as her way of moving on. Apparently, she was going to throw herself into this new job with the same enthusiasm and single-minded de-termination that she'd applied to getting the house. "So everything is okay for you guys?" I asked, tentatively, not sure if that was a topic that I should broach or not, but Dan didn't seem to mind.

"We're fine. She always comes around. Sometimes it takes longer than others, but it always happens." Dan concentrated on the coffee cup. "Sorry about . . . everything."

He would have said more, but I cut him off. "Don't worry about it. It all worked out."

Dan smiled at me with his lopsided grin. "Thanks, Ellie. I'd bet-ter get over there. I don't know how much more Mitch can take."

"His eyes are starting to glaze over."

"Watch this," Dan said.

He loped across the room and flung his arm around Felicity. "Enough about the gym."

"Dan, I told you, it's not a *gym*," Felicity said. "He never listens. It's a fitness center. There's a huge difference . . ."

As Felicity went on, Dan winked at me. "Works every time," he mouthed.

Mitch slipped away from them and joined me in the kitchen as I was polishing off a flaky biscuit. "I saw you and Dan holed up in here."

"Hey, I wasn't sure how Felicity would react to seeing us. I was giving her a wide berth. I'm sure she throws a mean punch."

"All that kickboxing," Mitch agreed as he picked up a plate.

"I knew you'd be okay," I said. "And it does sound like she and Dan are doing better."

Mitch nodded and transferred ham slices to his plate. "I think so, too."

I added another biscuit to my plate, refilled my juice, and leaned back against the counter beside Mitch. We had a view out the kitchen window to the backyard and I could see Livvy, Nathan, and their cousins. Their almost empty plates were scattered over the picnic table and they were engaged in some elaborate game that used a beat-up Frisbee and an old tennis ball.

My phone beeped, signaling I had a text message. I ate my last bite of biscuit, licked a smidge of apricot jelly from my finger, and checked the message, then tapped out a reply. I hit send and said, "It'll be good to get back home. My organizing clients are getting restless." I'd rescheduled one consultation and two organizing sessions while we'd been gone. It was fairly quiet in the kitchen at the moment, so I tucked my phone back in my pocket. I took a deep breath. "Mitch, I've been thinking about what we should do in the next few years. The whole stay in or get out thing."

He'd been plowing through breakfast and had his mouth full. He nodded and looked at me out of the corner of his eye as he chewed more slowly.

"If we get out, the chances of you getting a flying job are pretty slim, right?"

Mitch wiped his mouth with a napkin and nodded. "Looks that way now. Things could change, but . . ."

"But we can't plan for possibilities. We have to plan with what we know now. I'm trying to think about this like one of my organizing jobs. What makes the most sense? How should we arrange things? And the thing that makes the most sense right now is to stay in."

He put his plate down very carefully on the counter behind him and turned back to me. "I don't have to fly."

"I know, but what else would you do?"

"I could find something, go back to school . . . ," he said.

"I know, but you're trained as a pilot and I know you like it."

"Yeah, I do, but my life isn't going to end if I don't fly," he said.

"I know, but is there anything else you *want* to do?" I asked.

Mitch searched my face, then shook his head. "No, not really."

"Then why would we invest all that time and energy when you have a good, secure job that you like?" I asked.

"Because it means more moves. That's hard on you and the kids and there's your organizing, too."

I took a sip of my orange juice, then said, "I've been thinking it might be time to take Everything In Its Place in a new direction—consulting."

"Consulting?"

"Yes," I swiveled toward him. "I could still keep my clients in Georgia until our next move, but I could branch out and help new organizers who are starting their own businesses. Lord knows, I've made tons of mistakes, so I could tell them how to avoid those and I could share what's worked for me."

"Do you realize you're talking faster and faster? You must really be excited about this," Mitch said.

"I am," I said, surprised to realize that as I put into words what I'd been thinking about for the last few days, my enthusiasm grew. My fingers were itching to get home and type up my ideas. "It really would be ideal. It would let me do what I love and do it on the move."

"So the move thing? You're okay with that?"

"Well, I can't say I'm in love with the idea of starting over again and again, but it's a good job that will take care of us—we don't want to throw that away right now—and as far as moving, well, once we get through the initial upheaval of the actual move, I do like getting to know new areas. And I'm getting really good at unpacking."

A voice called, "If I could have everyone's attention."

Mitch and I walked to the living room. Roy cleared his throat and straightened his glasses. "Thank you," he said. "I just want to say that I know the last two weeks have been difficult for everyone, with the loss of Mr. Avery. You all miss him." His Adam's apple worked up and down as he swallowed. "So I hope you don't think this is inappropriate coming so soon, but there's something about the death of a loved one that makes life all the more precious." He'd been addressing the whole family, but his gaze zeroed in on Aunt Christine as he said, "It makes us realize how short life really is." Aunt Nanette, who'd been standing slightly in front of Aunt Christine, took a step back as Roy moved toward Aunt Christine. Roy cleared his throat again, then dropped to one knee. "Christy, will you marry me?"

Aunt Christine's face froze, then her gaze flew around the room. I looked around, too, and no one looked upset or reproachful. In fact, almost everyone was smiling. Aunt Nanette gave Aunt Christine a little shove between the shoulder blades, which caused her to move half a step toward Roy. Her gaze settled on his face and then broke into a wide smile. "Yes, of course I'll marry you, Roy."

Applause sounded along with a few whoops as Roy stood up and slipped a ring on Aunt Christine's finger.

Uncle Bud emerged from the kitchen with a champagne bottle. He popped the cork. "Mimosa, anyone?" he called as he moved around the room, adding champagne to orange juice glasses. He ended with Mitch and me, splashing a dollop into our glasses.

"You knew he was going to propose?" I asked.

"Nah. Lucky guess."

I pointed my glass at the bottle, which had a thin layer of condensation on it. "You chilled the champagne."

"I've got connections," he said easily.

"I know you do, particularly at the county offices."

He raised a shoulder. "True. I keep an eye on things, look out for family, make sure everything turns out okay." He paused a few beats, then said, "But I don't have nearly as much influence as you. Very few people get a thank-you note FedExed to them from Addison McClure."

Technically, the McClure letters belonged to Mitch, since he'd inherited the contents of the house and they'd been in the copy of Grandpa Franklin's memoir that he kept on the end table beside his chair. We could have tried to sell them, but they'd caused enough problems for the Avery family. We'd had quite a windfall with the gift of the house and didn't want to add ownership of precious literary documents. If McClure hadn't been alive, we might have felt differently and kept them, but knowing she was alive and relished her privacy, it just didn't seem right to sell them to the highest bidder. And then there were Grandpa Franklin's wishes to consider. He'd intended to return the letters to his childhood friend. I'd spent a long time on the phone the day after I'd found the letters, trying to convince McClure's lawyer that I was an honest person and really did have genuine letters written by her that I wanted to return.

Mitch and I had both read the letters. McClure was an entertaining correspondent. She'd included stories about her neighbors and little vignettes from her daily life. There were a few mentions of her then–work in progress, the book that would become *Deep Down Things*, but these were fleeting and not very descriptive. I wasn't sure what Maggie had hoped to find in the letters, but they certainly didn't contain any startling new revelations about the secretive author. If anything, they showed she was a normal person who shopped at the grocery store, went to the post office, and thought her neighbors were annoying—hardly earth-shattering stuff. I had a feeling that if Maggie had actually read the letters, she would have been very disappointed. They were about as different from the Beatrix Potter letter as you could get.

Since Harriet had mentioned the Potter letter, I'd looked it up online and found out that letter had indeed sold for over two hundred thousand dollars. Potter had written it to a friend's sick child and it was essentially a story, with her wonderful illustrations included. I wasn't surprised that it had sold for so much money. I'm sure there would have been interest in McClure's letters, but I doubt they would have brought in the amount of money Harriet was hoping for. The police had tracked Harriet down to her New York office the day after she thought she'd stolen the letters from Maggie. Detective Rickets told me that she maintained she'd come to Smarr to attend Book Daze. She said she had talked with Maggie and then returned home. I thought that after she'd grabbed the "letters" out of Maggie's hand in the garage, she'd probably driven far away before she realized they weren't the McClure letters at all. She'd either returned to Grandpa Franklin's house and found it crawling with law enforcement or she'd cut her losses and returned to New York immediately. "Either way," Detective Rickets had said, "there's not enough to prosecute her."

"A toast," Uncle Bud called, and I could have sworn I saw him wink. He quickly raised his glass and said, "To Roy and Christine!"

My glass clinked against Mitch's as we raised our arms and echoed his toast.

"So when's the wedding?" Bill called out, and Aunt Nanette groaned.

Mitch caught my hand and said, "I think it's time to head out before they draft you as a bridesmaid or wedding coordinator."

"I couldn't agree more. Let's go home."

Acknowledgments

As always, many thanks to my editor, Michaela, for her continuing support and wonderful editing. Thanks also to my agent, Faith, for her optimism, steady encouragement, and the disappearing casket idea. A big thank you to my writer friends, especially the Deadly Divas. You make touring so much fun. And to my family—close and extended—thanks for everything. I won't list you all here. Just know that I couldn't do it without you.